THE DAYDREAMER DETECTIVE FINDS HER CALLING

MISO COZY MYSTERIES
BOOK 7

STEPH GENNARO

ONIGIRI PRESS

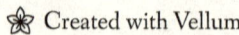

THE DAYDREAMER DETECTIVE FINDS HER CALLING

This book is dedicated to cherry blossoms.
There's nothing better than sitting under the sakura with your loved ones.

———

FOREWORD

In Japanese, the most common way of showing respect to another person's social standing is with the use of honorific suffixes that are appended on the end of either first or last names. The most common, -san, means either Mr., Ms., or Mrs.

In earlier versions of this book, and in the whole series, I did use these honorific suffixes. But for 2019 and onward, I have switched to the English way in order to make this series more accessible to English speakers. I hope you enjoy this version!

The town in this novel, Chikata, is completely fictional, though the area I put it in is not. Saitama prefecture is located to the west of Tokyo, and many of the eastern areas are considered to be suburbs of the city. Chikata is located farther out west, nearer to the prefectures of Nagano and Gunma.

CHAPTER
ONE

I rocked my body back and forth, humming and bopping gently along the sidewalk outside the Chikata Community Center while I waited for Mari to fall asleep against my chest. This was her favorite sleeping spot, nestled right between her sources of food. Who could blame her, really? So I obliged even though my mom and Kumi awaited me inside. A brisk, early spring wind whipped up the street, and I hummed a little louder to distract myself from the chills.

At least it wasn't winter anymore. In the last two years, I had grown to hate winter. First, we had our winter of starvation when I was begging for scraps from Yasahiro's restaurant, Sawayaka. My friend, Etsuko, died, and I almost got hurt trying to catch her murderer.

Then this winter, I had spent most of my time in bed. Though my first two trimesters of pregnancy went well, my third was more stressful. I bled quite a bit, and the only way to keep it under control was to rest. Thankfully, it was nothing serious, but still, the doctors agreed I should not be running errands all day and attending to my tea shop, Oshabe-cha, as well. So I'd handed off most errands to my mother, which had kept her busy, and I hired a young, recent high school graduate, Emi Asano, to work part time at the tea shop. She would leave soon for college, so I only had her for a few more weeks.

Mari's breathing steadied, and looking down at her, her arms were limp under my coat. Score! I had put my daughter to sleep again by pure magic. If I hadn't needed her asleep, I'd have buried my lips in her soft head of hair and breathed deep. Something made babies delectable on purpose. I often wanted to sleep with my arms around her and my lips on her cheeks.

The community center door swung open, and Mom poked her head out. I nodded at her indicating my success, and she waved me to her with a smile on her face.

It was nice to see Mom smile. When I thought of what she had gone through last fall, losing the house and selling the land, plus coming to grips with early glaucoma, she had a lot of things to be angry about. And she had been mad at me too for quite some time.

But recently, with Mari around, Mom had softened. She wasn't a forty-five-minute drive from her newest grandchild, but instead, only across town. She could hold Mari, push her in the stroller or rock her to sleep while I napped, feed her a bottle or just spend time with her. It wasn't perfect. Mom still guarded her private time, a little more than I thought necessary. Yasahiro and I had barely had any alone time since Mari was born.

Still, Mom had found her peace with everything that had happened.

She just needed a purpose now.

"Come on, Mei," she said, smiling at me as I slipped into the community center. "Noriko is about to get started."

"She just fell asleep," I said, in as normal volume a voice as I could. I tried to lead a semi-noisy life around Mari. I didn't want people to think they had to talk in hushed tones or not be themselves because a baby was present. Besides, we lived on a busy street, and I wanted her to sleep with trucks driving by or kids yelling to each other to and from school. But if she was in the carrier, I rarely had to worry about her waking up. The carrier put her out like nothing else.

"That was quick!" Mom smiled down at Mari. "Has she been gassy today?"

"Nope. All is well in that area."

"Teething, yet?"

"Thankfully, no." Though she was crying for three or more hours every night before bedtime. I had no idea what that was about. I walked her around the apartment as much as possible and tried not to cry with her. If Yasahiro returned home from a shift and she was still crying, I handed her off to him, inserted earplugs, and passed out. There was only so much of the crying I could take.

Mom peeked down at my chest. "Her cheeks are so pink lately. Soon. You'll see teeth soon."

I nodded, unable to muster any kind of rebuttal. Maybe I should've protested that Mom was being too pushy or nagging, but I was too tired to care. It was probably for the best.

Mom led the way to the rear conference room, and I hustled in behind her. Wow. The room was packed today! I waved to Kumi, my friend and wife of my other police officer friend, Goro. She was seated near the front, close to the front exit, in case she needed to make a quick getaway. Goro was at home tonight with Taiga, feeding them both dinner. At seven months old, Taiga was experimenting with food now, mostly chucking it at the wall or smearing it on his face. Goro loved it.

"I secured us seats near the back," Mom whispered, "close to the door, so you can exit if you need to."

I smiled at the other young mother nearby. She was around my age and had a newborn, asleep in a stroller. She lightly rolled the stroller back and forth while texting on her phone.

"How are you doing?" I whispered to her. Her blank eyes stared up at me.

"Exhausted." She sighed as she dropped her phone to her lap. "He nursed all day yesterday while I was trying to finish up a batch of soap. My husband had to learn how to pour it into molds because I could barely move."

I hissed lightly. "Ouch. I'm so sorry," I said, bowing. "I hope you get a break soon."

"I think this is it." She gestured to the sleeping baby. "Must be a growth spurt. Eat all day and night, then sleep for ages." She shrugged.

"I've been there."

And I had. I couldn't even believe Mari was already three months old. The time since her birthday in early January had flown right on by.

"Everyone, we're about to get started," Noriko's voice echoed out of the speaker from the front of the room. "Oops, let me turn that down. I know we have some sleeping babies at the back."

All the women in the class turned to smile at us. We bowed, and I tried not to be embarrassed by the attention. I tried but failed. Between the little ball of fiery hot baby strapped to my chest, my recovering hormones, and the warm room, my face blushed hard. So much for just hanging with Mom so she could learn something new.

"Okay, we're at lesson four, setting up an online store for your goods."

Everyone turned their eyes to the front of the room, and I got a reprieve from the attention. Mom rummaged around in her bag and found her notebook and pen while I stood off to the side and continued to sway and keep Mari asleep.

"Do you want to move closer? How are your eyes?" I whispered to her.

"Fine today. And no, I can get the handout at the end."

She wanted to be near me. Just in case.

I let my mind wander as Noriko Kubo, the class teacher, a former Tokyo marketing executive and entrepreneur, taught everyone how to be small business owners. I already knew a lot of this information from business school and running my own tea shop, but Noriko specialized in internet-only small businesses. Every person in the room had something they wanted to sell online. Like the young mother sitting behind me who loved to make soaps with local ingredients or the two middle-aged women across the room who designed cross-stitch patterns or the high school student at the front who made jewelry — they all were looking to supplement or replace their income with a small online business. Kumi took the class to learn how to sell all-natural bath salts and scrubs for the Kutsuro Matsu bathhouse.

What did my mom want to sell? I had no idea, and neither did she. But her best friend, Chiyo, Goro's mother, suggested she take the class. Either way, Chiyo would reap the benefits of the course either from Kumi or my mother. It was a brilliant plan, I had to admit.

"Whether you're selling one item online just to Japan, or many products to the whole world, you're going to need some kind of digital storefront and a way to process payments. Let's talk about the digital storefront first and your options there." Noriko flipped to the next slide, and everyone in the room took furious notes.

Though I hadn't talked about it with anyone, I'd been thinking about expanding and selling goods online. Bento boxes were the clear contender since I had so many of them. When my friend, Etsuko, was killed, she had her own internet business selling bento boxes. Her family didn't know what to do with the stock when she died, so I purchased most of them, and I sold them at the tea shop.

I swayed in place, letting my mind wander and daydream about this new idea. I could do it if I found a few more hours in the day when Mari was sleeping and I was awake. I imagined myself in the back room of Oshabe-cha, my painting supplies on one side, and my shipping supplies on the other, Mari asleep in the bassinet, and everything running smoothly. I held a chuckle down in my chest. There was no way it would be that easy. It was definitely a dream.

My hips ached as I swayed myself through the rest of the class. Sitting down was not an option if I wanted a quiet and sleeping baby, so I kept to my feet and did my best to stay awake. An impossible task. I had never fallen asleep on my feet, but I'd been close on a few occasions. Tonight was not the night to test my resolve.

Mom's stare was a million kilometers away as class ended for the evening.

"If you have any questions, be sure to email me, or you can use Line to text me. Oh, and I'll also have some open office hours on Monday morning at Oshabe-cha in town before the additional breakout session some of you signed up for. Thank you to Mei Suga for offering to host me."

I raised my hand in a little wave to everyone in the class, and they smiled and waved back. It was the least I could do, and this was one reason I had a tea shop, anyway. Hopefully, it brought in more business.

As everyone stood up to go, Kumi crossed the room to us.

"This is great. I've been meaning to sell my graphic design work internationally, but I wasn't sure how to do it." Kumi's gaze drifted up. "Maybe I can set up this bath salts store for Chiyo first, and then I can offer services in other places as well."

"That's a great idea. Let me know if I can help." I glanced down at Mari as she shifted and sighed. This would only be a nap. She'd wake in about ten to fifteen minutes, have a marathon eating session, and scream for a few hours before passing out until four in the morning. If I was lucky.

A small twinge of sadness swept through me as I flashed back on my previous daydreams of being a mother. Just a year ago, I had dreamt I'd be living at the home farm, the farm I grew up at, but now that place was nothing but cleared land. My mother lived in a tiny rundown apartment across town until the builders finished our new house. There were moments, like right then, where it all seemed surreal.

"Want to go out to eat?" Kumi asked us both as we slipped on our coats. "I'm sure Goro and Taiga are doing fine without me."

It was just after 19:00, so my stomach was rumbling for dinner, but Mari would wake up soon.

"You know I'd love to..." I started, and Mom looked at me, hopefully.

Just then, Mari stirred, lifted her face from my chest, and stretched her limp limbs.

"But..." I didn't get any farther. Mari's eyes cracked open, she looked up at me, and her face scrunched into a red hot mess.

I sighed, straight from my belly and out through my tired mouth. I was sure that a new gray hair was sprouting from the top of my head. Mari did not like evenings, no matter what I did. Mornings and daytime were fine, pleasant even. Anything past the afternoon nap was a nightmare. Yet at three months old, she was not ready to drop that nap.

"I think I'm going to walk home."

Kumi and Mom both frowned. I knew they weren't disappointed in me, just the circumstances, but their frowns were a punch to my gut.

Before I could tear up in frustration, I turned to take my crying baby out of the room. This was dumb. She was crying, and I wanted to cry, both for her and for my shattered life. Would the tired and worn out feeling ever go away?

Out in the hallway, students were walking out of the community center and heading on their way, but someone I didn't recognize waited outside the front doors to the classroom. She slouched against the wall, one leg thrown over the other, her boots artfully untied. She was a tiny woman, more small than petite. I envied her bulky hat and scarf, her military-style jacket, and worn-leather messenger bag. I wished I could dress like that.

Mari let out another stifled cry, nothing too loud, but she caught the woman's attention, and her face turned up to us. I thought maybe I *had* seen her before. At Midori Sankaku? The grocery store in town brought in people from all over the prefecture.

Mom and Kumi joined me just as the young woman leaned in to talk to Noriko.

"I told you I wouldn't have time to talk to you tonight," Noriko said, exiting the classroom, her arms full of books and her laptop.

The young woman peeled herself from the wall and folded her arms over her chest. "We need to talk. Now."

"There's no way I can help you," Noriko insisted.

Both of them turned towards Mom and me as Mari continued to cry.

Noriko popped on a pretty smile, and she took on the veneer of a corporate woman at that moment. Her hair was swept into a neat ponytail, and her pantsuit was pressed to perfection. She still had the business wardrobe even though she was teaching classes in the countryside now.

"Have a good night, Mrs. Yamagawa, Mrs. Suga." She lifted her hand to wave while the other young woman stewed next to her. Noriko towered over the other woman, but it didn't stop the other woman from glowering at her.

"Night," we replied, bowing and heading in the opposite direction.

But I glanced over my shoulder before we trekked into the cold night air. Noriko's shoulders were up around her ears, and the young woman was hissing at her about something. I sighed as I pulled my coat around my crying baby.

Noriko and I both had problems to deal with tonight.

CHAPTER
TWO

I was both envious of and angry with Kumi. She had no idea, of course, because it would be foolish to say it out loud. But as I listened to my baby cry and cry, I remembered Taiga's first few months of quiet, sleeping bliss and sweet smiles. Kumi had been tired, for sure, but Taiga had been an easy newborn. All he had done was nurse and sleep. She and Goro had even come over for dinner on occasion!

My jealousy soared as Mari cried in my arms, and I paced around our apartment.

Yasahiro's eyebrows drew together as I crossed from one side of the room to the other. The clock ticked over to nine-thirty, and she hadn't stopped crying for the last two hours.

"Are you sure there's nothing wrong with her?" Yasahiro asked from the couch. He could barely keep his eyes open. Only Mari was keeping us awake now.

My nerves grated an extra millimeter thinner. "Yes, I'm sure. I've already been to the pediatrician twice this week. She swears that Mari is fine. She's just going through a rough spot."

I had received the answer, "Sometimes babies just cry." An explanation I was not happy with. It was a reply I wanted to rip to pieces and stomp on. I hadn't been this irrationally angry in months. At least I wasn't angry with Mari; I was just angry with the circumstances.

Pain shot through my chest as I rearranged Mari in my arms. I was tired from holding her and from feeding her as well.

"Here," Yasahiro said, shaking his head and jumping up from the couch. "Let me hold her for a while, and you should lie down and rest."

Though the noise and the heartache of my baby crying was enough to make me run for the hills, I held her even closer for a moment. She was warm and soft, and every time I looked at her, I saw a little of Yasahiro, even a bit of my dad long gone. It was funny that I hardly ever thought of Dad until I had a baby. He had been gone since I was a kid, so my memories of him were blurry.

Yasahiro slipped his hands into my arms, and I reluctantly let go of Mari. "Eat something, and I'll take her out for a drive." The flood from the typhoon had totaled Yasahiro's car, and now we owned a small family-sized hatchback that we both loved to drive.

"You look too tired to drive." I watched him walk away with Mari cradled upon his chest. He was a natural with her and thank goodness for that because we were both fumbling our way through this.

"Me?" He scoffed. "I can run a restaurant on two hours of sleep. I'll stay in the neighborhood. I can park at the house if she falls asleep and then take a little nap myself. All the new neighbors there know who we are."

The new house. Oh, the new house! I loved this apartment, but in my head, I still always referred to it as 'Yasahiro's apartment.' And with only one bedroom and one bathroom, it was a far cry from what we needed now as a family. Mari slept in a bassinet in our room, but there were days when I craved private space. I wanted a room for her I could decorate, and I wanted our own bedroom I could retreat to. Sharing all the space of this small place was difficult.

"That's a great idea," I breathed out. "I'm going to come along."

Yasahiro's smile was wry but weak. "I'm trying to take her away so you can get a break. You've had her the past three evenings in a row, Mei."

"I know, I know," I said, grabbing our coats from the hook. "But I already ate. See? I got curry sauce on Mari's head."

I had returned home after the small business class and ate lukewarm curry over Mari's head while she screamed in the carrier. I wasn't hungry now, but I *was* tired. I also hadn't seen Yasahiro in days. I missed my husband. We slept next to each other, curled onto one another, but that was about it. He woke up to be with Mari in the morning, and I slept in an extra hour. Then I took her all day until she fell asleep at night. He would come home from the restaurant and crash into bed.

Yasahiro sniffed at Mari's head. "Huh. I wondered what that was."

"Let's drive. I want to see the house, and then you can drop me back here when she falls asleep."

"Okay. You're the boss."

Ha. Mari was the boss, and we both knew it. She was a tyrant of a boss, but at least she was adorable.

We got her into her car seat inside and rushed her down the stairs, past the entrance to Oshabe-cha, and out into the night. The car hummed as we backed out of our tiny spot and Yasahiro took to the streets. He picked the road at the outer boundary of town, knowing there were fewer stoplights to halt our progress. Until Mari would fall asleep, she would get angry every time the car came to a stop. All of her screaming must have exhausted her, though, because she fell silent after only a minute. I peeked over to look at the rearview mirror installed opposite her seat, and she was fast asleep.

"Thank goodness," I whispered, sinking back in my seat. "What is it about the car that puts her to sleep so easily?"

Yasahiro shrugged. "Don't know. Michio said sometimes babies need lots of noise to fall asleep. That the silence hurts them." Michio was Yasahiro's sous chef at Sawayaka. He was ten years older and had three kids of his own. "Maybe we should consider more white noise."

I nodded as I sunk further into my seat. "I saw a few moms talking about white noise in the online groups."

He glanced at me from the side. "You should spend more time there and see what you can dig up."

"Been too busy," I said with a yawn. "And my hand is cramping from holding Mari and using my phone at the same time."

I may not have been researching baby soothing methods, but I was ordering diapers, formula, toilet paper, and a million other things from online stores. I was also scheduling appointments for my elderly clients, or returning emails from people wanting to use the tea shop for gatherings, or handling the contractors for the house, or any other number of things I was doing. I wanted to help Mari calm down, but I had things to do too. It just broke my heart to hear her cry for so long every night.

She'll grow out of it, I repeated in my head over and over.

Yasahiro reached over and placed his hand on my knee. "Have I mentioned lately that you're a great mother?"

I smiled as I sat up straight. "I'm winging it."

I took in his red-rimmed eyes and wild hair, his crooked glasses, and two-day-old scruff. He looked every bit the tired parent as I looked, and it was super handsome. If only we had more quality time together.

"I think every parent wings it," he replied. "Every situation is different. There are no experts."

"It's a humbling job. I've had days lately when I've never felt more useless."

"I feel the same way when she's so distraught." Yasahiro's jaw tightened before he let go of his tension with a heavy breath. "I'm sure it'll get better."

"Me too. Someday."

We wound through the streets and out to our new neighborhood. The block was quiet and dark. It wasn't too late for a Thursday night, but this area of town had yet to bounce back from the great city exodus of the two decades before. Like so much of Chikata, many of the outlying neighborhoods were desolate and unoccupied. We had seen revitalization over the past five years with Midori Sankaku, the Tokyo grocery chain, coming to town, but Chikata was still slow to revive.

The place we had chosen for our new home had tons of potential. There were still a few people who lived on the block, and they were happy to have us building in the double lot. A bus stop was only two blocks away that also serviced the local elementary school and most of downtown. The rear part of our lots backed up to a wooded, undeveloped area, so it was quiet and cool during the summer. The end of construction couldn't come soon enough.

"Look," Yasahiro whispered as we approached our lot. "The second story is up."

"Wow." The last time I'd been here, only the first story had been erected.

We had chosen a futuristic, pre-fabricated house to build on the land. All the foundations and walls were made in a factory to exacting standards and assembled on site. The house would be wired with modern conveniences in mind including smart lighting and windows, solar energy, and eco-friendly heating and cooling. Plus, the house had fire-proofing and measures to help it stand up to earthquakes. The whole point of Yasahiro's brand was local, slow food that was also green and renewable. We wanted to apply that to our lifestyle as well.

Speaking of slow, the whole process of building a new house

had taught me an extended amount of patience. Permits and archaic building laws kept us on our toes during the planning stages. I had almost given up several times, especially since I'd tried to do so much of the planning from bed before Mari was born.

"Look at how the garden area is coming along." Yasahiro pointed to the side of the building where landscapers had already formed the area for our home garden. They had leveled the land, but it was all still dirt and rocks. "We should be able to plant vegetables this summer."

"And herbs, and flowers."

Yasahiro was in charge of the vegetables, and I told him I'd handle the rest. I needed a break from farming.

I let my mind wander and pictured us here in the future, our beautiful, modern home, vegetables and herbs growing everywhere, and Mari running and playing in the backyard. It would be glorious once it was built.

As my eyes took in the open parts of the house where windows would go, something moved in the back of the house. I gasped and leaned forward.

"Did you see that?" I tried not to raise my voice. Mari was still asleep.

"What?"

I tried to raise myself in the car's seat to get a better view. "Something moved inside."

"Are you sure?" Yasahiro shifted the car into gear and rolled forward a little.

"Hmmm, maybe?" I strained my tired eyes, but I saw nothing else. "Maybe not. Do you think anyone comes around here at night?"

He shrugged. "Why would they?"

I could think of a few reasons, but I didn't want to point fingers.

"There's nothing valuable in the house right now. It's still an

open structure without walls or wiring. Maybe you saw something falling over."

"Hmmm."

I stared at the house for another long moment, but nothing
moved. It was probably my imagination.

"Let's go home and get some sleep," Yasahiro said, as we
pulled away from the curb. "We can keep Mari in the car seat
until she's ready to be swaddled."

CHAPTER
THREE

The colors on the painting bled into each other as I stared at it, and I stepped away to rest my shaking hand. Shaking hands and painting did not go well together, and I didn't want to ruin a perfectly good alien landscape. Purple and yellow trees surrounded an icy lake, cracked and frosted over, while two moons hung in the sky at the horizon. I wanted to add in some flitting firefly-like points of light, but my aim was too shaky for something so precise. I took a deep breath and tried to shrug off the fatigue.

Mari burbled and cooed in her bouncy chair. She was happy to sit and stare at either me or the toy dangled in front of her. Ah, I loved Morning Mari. She was a completely different child than Evening Mari. It was too bad I was so sleep deprived that I couldn't enjoy it.

"Mei, I'm going to leave the shop to meet Mrs. Murata at her apartment and walk her over here." Emi, my part-time employee, poked her head into the back room. "The only people here are Mr. Shigimo and Mr. Hasé, playing Go."

"Mr. Hasé is playing Go?" Koshiro Hasé owned the cobbler shop next door.

Emi smirked. "They started a weekly thing about a month ago."

Huh. The things I missed while taking care of my baby.

I turned my bleary eyes to her. "Do they have tea?"

"All topped up."

What was I going to do without her when she went to school?

Emi's pink cheeks matched her pink barrettes and tights today. She pulled down the sleeves of her black-and-white striped shirt so she could pull on her black jacket. Then she took off her half apron and dusted off her jean skirt.

"Do you want me to pick up anything while I'm out? I can stop by the convenience store."

My stomach growled, right on cue. "If it isn't too much of a bother..."

"Of course not, Mei," she said, smiling at me and then Mari. Mari squealed at her.

"Okay, thank you. Coffee, please. My usual way. Tea will not cut it today. And something chocolate. Anything. I need sugar."

"Maybe some noodles at lunch today? You look like you're wasting away." Emi squatted down next to Mari and tickled her belly. "You've transferred all your calories over to this little Buddha belly." Mari squealed again with delight, and I smiled.

"Possibly. And thanks. Noodles is a great idea."

The front door to Oshabe-cha opened, and we both looked at the security monitors.

"Mei!"

It was Mom.

"Go ahead," I whispered to Emi. "She'll talk your ear off if you stay, and Mrs. Murata will never get here."

I took one more deep breath and let it out with all the shakes. I had to present a happy and content face to my mom, or I'd never hear the end of her badgering. The heavy mask I wore weighed a ton, though, and every day it slipped a little more.

Emi dipped her head at Mom as she breezed past and out the front door. Mom's head swiveled twice to watch her go.

"Where is Emi off to?" she asked, setting her bag on the table. "Shouldn't she be watching the shop?"

"I've got it, Mom," I said, setting down my paintbrush and wiping the paint from my hands. "I was just going to move Mari out to the front for snack time."

"It bothers me that you breastfeed in public." Mom's voice made my nerves crack.

"It's not 'in public.' It's in my own place of business. I'm discreet. The old men certainly don't mind." I almost laughed, but I held it in. That would've made Mom even more critical. "Emi is off to escort Mrs. Murata here and grab lunch for us. Would you like something?"

"Oh no." She waved me away. "I don't want to be a bother."

I froze for a moment as I processed this. I'd just said the exact same thing to Emi, and I was annoyed with my mother for saying it to me. Everything about the way I'd been raised, everything about the way we lived in Japan, was about not being a nuisance, not causing a confrontation. The proper ways to act were 'obvious' to elders and becoming more ambiguous to the younger generation. I glanced between my mother and my daughter. How did I want to raise Mari?

Mom crossed to the sink and washed her hands. "I have a great idea," she said, soaping up her hands, rinsing and drying them. Then she knelt beside Mari, unbuckled her from her chair, and picked her up to hold her. The two looked at each other like they were deeply in love, and my heart squeezed.

"How's my beautiful baby today?" Mom asked Mari, and Mari grabbed Mom's face.

I turned from them before tears burned my eyes. Capping all of my paint tubes, I officially ended my painting session for the day and put them away. I was too tired to paint anymore.

"What's your great idea?" I asked, sitting at the table. Mom walked Mari around the room, showing her everything on the walls, the cabinets, and the countertops.

"I know what I'm going to make and sell. Cookbooks."

"Cookbooks? That *is* a great idea!" I smiled as I settled my back against the wall. "What inspired this?"

"Well, I was going through my boxes last night, looking for my smaller clay pot, when I came across my cookbook collection."

Mom was living in a small apartment across town, a temporary solution until we built our house and she could move into Yasahiro's apartment. So most of her belongings were still boxed up or in storage.

"And I thought of all the recipes I've given to Yasahiro, and how many more I still have written down or just in my head. I should really share them, get them out there." She spoke all of this to Mari, keeping Mari looking straight at her. Mari reached out and grabbed Mom's bottom lip. Mom gently removed her fingers.

"I'm going to start typing them into the computer later today. I found my notebooks too last night."

Though I had never enjoyed my mom's home cooking as a kid, her traditional recipes were growing on me as an adult. Yasahiro tried to encourage me to eat something new every other week, and many of the recipes he cooked were ones he had learned from my mother, back before we had started dating.

"I love this idea, Mom. I don't know why I didn't think of it myself."

"I think you've been a little distracted." She hummed as she bounced Mari around. "Anyway, once I type the recipes into the computer, I'll need to figure out the rest. There's only so much I can do with my eyes. They get so tired after looking at the screen for too long."

A few months ago, Mom had laser eye surgery to halt the progress of glaucoma. And while her eyes would never get any better, at least now, they wouldn't get worse as quickly as they had before the surgery.

"I was wondering..." Her voice trailed off, and my shoulder tensed up. I felt a favor coming on. "If maybe you'd help me. You're so much better with computers and all that than I am. You take such lovely photos too."

Panic took over my brain as I imagined myself hunched over a computer late into the night, losing even more sleep. I couldn't do it. No.

But I couldn't say no to my mom.

I flashed back to Mom kicking me out of the house and trying to sell the family land to my older brother instead of me, and I swallowed. *Forgive and forget, Mei.* But somehow I doubted I would ever forget what had happened even if I'd already forgiven her. She'd come a long way in the last few months. She was kinder and more open to change even if she was still stuck in her ways. I had to give her credit for adjusting.

"Oh, wow. I'm flattered you think so." Kill her with kindness. I pressed my hand to my chest. "But I only take photos with my phone. You know, for social media and all those other online places. I don't take professional photos, like for a cookbook."

Mom frowned. This was not the answer she wanted to hear.

"But..." I held up my hand, feeling a plan come together. "You know, Yasahiro has a photographer he uses. He takes photos of the restaurant and his food. Maybe I should see if he could take your photos too?"

"Hmmm. I don't know. I bet he's expensive."

I shrugged, not willing to add another expense to our bill right now. "Let's talk to him and see what he can do. Okay?"

Mom scowled. In the last few months, watching us build a new house, support the restaurant and the tea shop, plus buy a new car and do several other projects, she had come to believe we were wealthy. I knew the truth though. We were getting by. Sawayaka was *just* profitable especially after we cleaned up the typhoon damages. And Yasahiro sold property elsewhere to pay for the building costs of the new house. Still, we had a mortgage we were already paying on for the land and remaining building costs. The tea shop wasn't profitable either. It was more of a pet project than anything, one we could indulge in because Yasahiro already owned the building.

Maybe I should've been more generous. We weren't destitute, and we could afford to do more. But then I thought of the family farm, how we were going to buy it and make it a home for all of us.

I had worked so hard the last few months to let go of the resentment. I couldn't allow it to surface again.

"I bet Kumi and I could do a great job on the cookbook layout, and I'll look into selling it online, too, if you like." I kept my voice casual, hoping Mom would understand that this was the best I could do.

She lifted her chin. "That would be great, Mei."

Phew. Saved.

When would we arrive at the point where I wasn't worried about offending her all the time?

I knew it was *my* problem, but it felt insurmountable.

The front door opened again, and I looked at the security monitor, expecting to see Emi and Murata. Instead, I saw a police car pulled up to the curb, its lights flashing, and Goro standing in the front waiting area.

I shot up to my feet, almost too quickly for how tired I was.

"Mei!" Emi bolted into the back room. "Officer Hokichi is here, and he says it's urgent."

Mom and I glanced at each other, and she tucked Mari a little closer while jerking her head at the door.

When I stepped out of the back room, Goro relaxed. Shigimo and Hasé had paused their game of Go and watched me approach. Whatever was happening, I was sure it'd be gossip in no time.

"Mrs. Murata," I said, bowing. "How was your morning?"

She smiled as she hung up her coat. "Probably a lot less dramatic than yours."

I smirked at her before turning to Goro. "Goro, what's up?" I glanced past him to the lights on the police car. "You're going to blind half the neighborhood."

"There's been an incident out at your new house." He sighed while adjusting his belt. He had lost about four kilos in the last month from eating right and training for a marathon he wanted to run in June. It had changed the shape of his face too, along with the frown he wore. "I need you to come with me so we can sort it all out."

"An incident?" I grabbed my coat from the coat rack. "What kind of incident?"

He leaned close and dropped his voice. "We should discuss it in the car."

That wasn't good. "Okay. Just a second." I held up a finger as I returned to the rear of the shop.

"Mom, can you watch Mari while I go take care of whatever this is? Emi will watch the shop." I crossed the room to the fridge and opened it. "There are two bottles here, all ready to go."

My breasts would be sore later, but I'd deal with it. I always had bottles available because I never knew when my life would get busy. It was a good thing I was prepared.

"Sure. Warm it a little, right?"

"Right." I threw my scarf around my neck. "But she doesn't care if it's warm or cold. She only cares that it's food."

I swooped in and planted kisses in Mari's neck. She laughed, and my heart ached again. Motherhood was complicated.

"I'll be back soon."

CHAPTER
FOUR

"Oh no," I moaned as we approached the job site.

What now?

Already, the lot looked like a crime scene. Someone parked two police cars up on the curb, their lights on, and officers stood around, talking or waiting. An ambulance idled in the makeshift driveway that would someday be the real driveway. Right now, it was just a gravel entryway to the property.

My mouth dropped open as I climbed out of Goro's car. The whole site was in chaos, people everywhere, and a man laid on a nearby stretcher.

"Where's Yasahiro?" I asked, turning to Goro.

He waved down the street, and another police car approached with Goro's partner, Kayo, at the wheel and Yasahiro in the passenger seat.

"That's her!" Someone shouted in my direction, and I turned around slowly. "She's cursed this property."

Oh no.

Last summer, when I had been dealing with the missing persons case, I had also been dealing with a very arrogant and unhappy police officer, Kohei Watanabe. He had spread rumors around town that I was some kind of witch, and instead of debunking the rumors, I had piled onto them. Why? I still wasn't sure. It was an impulsive decision, something I did in the moment, and I didn't think it through. I owned the witchy stories and took control of the gossip. But it didn't stop people from thinking the worst of me.

The man pointing right at me seemed familiar. I tried to place his face or conjure up a name, but nothing. My brain was too foggy to concentrate.

"You should arrest her. Akira is injured because of her."

I blinked a few times before pulling my feet from where they tried to grow roots. All the officers on the street stared as I rounded the property line fence. I knew most of them, so I nodded at each as I slid past them to the ambulance.

The man on a stretcher, his leg twisted at an unnatural angle, was being loaded into the ambulance. His ashen face contorted in agony as the stretcher bounced its way in.

The other man who had been yelling at me approached. "You should be locked up," he said, pointing directly at me.

"What did I do?" I finally found my voice, and it was exasperated and cracked like it hadn't been used for two decades.

"I know what you did to Kohei Watanabe. And now you have it out for his friends, too?"

I looked to Goro, my eyes pleading for understanding. Kayo and Yasahiro trudged over the gravel to us.

Goro smirked and shrugged. "Your guess is as good as mine."

"I'm sorry." I shook my head and turned back to the irate man. "I don't mean to be rude, but I don't even know who you are."

"Don't play dumb with me," he replied.

Kayo pulled out her notepad. "This man is Daiki Wada. He's a plumber, here as a subcontractor."

A sinister smile lightened Daiki's lips. "I was with Kohei at the beer hall last summer when you threatened him with your witch powers."

I closed my eyes and sighed. I knew he looked familiar.

When I opened my eyes, Yasahiro was staring at me.

"What's this now? I married a witch?"

"I only use my powers for good."

Kayo snorted a laugh, and Goro rolled his eyes.

Daiki gestured to me. "See?"

I huffed, throwing my arms up into the air. "Why would I curse my own property? Huh? Why would I do that? Use your brain."

He took a step back.

"Why are Kohei's friends all the dumbest people I've ever met?" I grumbled under my breath.

The ambulance door slammed closed and pulled out of the property. I watched it go with a sinking stomach.

Masaru Imai, the foreman we dealt with daily, left the police officer he was talking to and joined us. He bowed to Yasahiro and then to me.

"What happened to him?" Goro asked, jerking his chin in the direction of the departing ambulance.

Imai shoved his hands into his pockets. "Well, I hate to mention these things, but... We arrived this morning, and things were not where we placed them the last night. Items have gone missing. Akira broke his leg stepping into a hole in the backyard that wasn't there yesterday. Daiki swears he saw something move in the house this morning when he showed up."

And I could have sworn something had moved in the house last night when we drove by. I glanced at Yasahiro, and he nodded.

"Sorry about all the racket, Mrs. Suga. I didn't realize Daiki knew who you were."

"Neither did I," I said, folding my arms across my chest.

"She has it out for us," Daiki said, his voice full of contempt.

"She said it in front of a dozen people at the bar last summer. If you don't believe me, I'm sure I can gather some witnesses. The bartender saw and heard it all."

"The bartender knows you were harassing me, so don't even try to use him to cover up your misdeeds." My voice growled with anger. Ichi, the bartender, was a Sawayaka employee, and he had seen enough that day to back me up.

Daiki stewed as my body heated with anger and embarrassment. I hadn't regretted that rash decision to make myself into the town witch until this moment.

"We *have* seen some bizarre things happening on this property in the last two weeks. I'm not saying it's you —" Imai raised his hands.

"It *is* her. Kohei Watanabe is in jail because of her."

"He's in jail for covering up a murder," Goro reminded him.

"We had the land blessed in the *jichinsai*, remember? You were here when we had the Shinto priest pray over the land only a few weeks ago," I reminded Imai. He had attended the ceremony in which we sat on our empty land and observed the priest chanting prayers over offerings, clapping his hands, and urging the spirits of our property to be at ease during the construction. We had invited the spirits to be present, then we cleansed the land with some handfuls of salt and drank saké before sending the spirits on their way.

That should have been enough.

Imai stepped forward, trying to halt the conversation with his body. As the foreman, he was keen to keep his people in line. "Is it possible, maybe, this land is cursed? Did you check to see if someone listed it as a stigmatized property?"

A few of the police officers whispered to each other behind their hands, and they stepped backwards towards the street. A wash of tingles rolled down my back.

"Of course I did." I huffed and tried to put as much disbelief into my voice as possible. "The listings from the previous owner and real estate agent said the property was fine. It's the law to disclose it."

And that was all I knew. This had been my first property purchase ever. I had signed the documents with Yasahiro, scouted the locations, and spoke to the neighbors. I thought I had been thorough. Should I have done more?

"Well," Imai said, shifting back and forth on his feet, "the law is that only the last tenants of the property have to disclose if it's stigmatized. It could be that there was a death or murder here farther back than one tenant. That's probably why you got such a deal on this property."

Goro chuckled. "That would just be your luck, Mei."

Kayo punched him on the arm. "Can you be a little more sensitive, please?"

Silence blanketed the group for a moment as I considered this new possibility. Perhaps the land was cursed? We did get it for cheap, and I thought that was due to the condition of the houses on the two lots, both of which had to be demolished. Other properties nearby were still listed for sale at twice what we paid.

"Yasahiro? Can I talk with you for a minute?"

Kayo and Goro looked at each other, and I could read their minds. *This is no good*, they said to each other with just a glance.

Yasahiro followed me a few meters away from everyone else. His lips twisted, trying to hide a smile.

"Don't you dare laugh," I mumbled through clenched teeth, and then I couldn't hold it in anymore.

The giggles began, and I couldn't stop them. They broke in my chest and burst from my mouth, so I rested my forehead on Yasahiro's chest and just let them go. This was all too ridiculous not to laugh at. It was a snowball that started out tiny but had rolled down the hill into a gigantic boulder to knock me sideways into a two-meter-high snow drift.

"Can you believe this?" I lifted my head and wiped away the tears of laughter. "Do you think we bought a haunted property?"

Yasahiro lifted his eyes to the sky. "I have no idea. I checked the papers from the two families we purchased from, and neither claimed the property was haunted."

"I talked with the neighbors, and they said nothing. Maybe I should've searched online databases, too?"

"I don't know. I didn't think of it."

I took a deep breath and let it out. "There must be a good explanation for this, but..."

I gestured to the foreman talking to his employees and subcontractors. They all had frowns and drawn eyebrows, and they stared at the half-erected house like it was going to jump out and bite them.

"But I get the feeling work will stop until we figure it out," Yasahiro finished, completing my thought.

I rubbed my tired face and tried to find the bright side. Couldn't do it. I thought of the bouncy chair I had tripped over this morning on my way to the couch, the overflowing diaper pail in the bathroom, the mountains of dirty clothes, and the stacks of cardboard boxes in every available corner. We had outgrown our apartment, as much as we loved the place.

"We need this house. If things had worked out, we'd be living..." We'd be living at 'home' which was no longer my home. My home, the place where I had grown up, didn't exist anymore.

Yasahiro stepped close and wrapped his arms around me. "This *will* be home. I promise. This is just another problem to solve. We can solve this one like all the other ones we've solved the last two years."

I inhaled and smelled cinnamon. I wondered what he had been cooking at Sawayaka before he ended up here.

"What should I do?" I asked, pulling away to look up at him.

"Nothing. Don't worry about it. I'll handle it."

"When?" I tilted my head to look at his tired eyes. "You're just as sleep deprived as I am, but you have a full-time job to attend to."

"As if you don't?"

I rubbed my face again to bring life back into it. I hadn't worn makeup in months. "We're both tapped out. But I have more freedom to leave the house and tea shop and come here to deal with issues. I'll handle this. It's my fault this happened, anyway. I was the dumb one that declared myself a witch. I'll have to find some way to exorcize the demons here."

I turned from him and swept my gaze over the muddy lot and the empty skeleton of a building. Something was going on here, and it was more than a ghostly presence.

And if I was going to get into my house by summer, I needed to figure it out. Fast.

CHAPTER
FIVE

I t was rare for me to go out at all, much less on a Sunday evening, but birthdays were for celebrating. My own birthday was July fourteenth, a few months away, but today we were celebrating Kumi's birthday just the way she wanted to. She insisted we should do something relaxing, easy, and close to home — a closed bathing session at the Kutsuro Matsu bathhouse then dinner and drinks at Izakaya Jūshi. In the days before children, we would have gone to Sawayaka, but tonight, Yasahiro was staying home with Mari.

I nearly fell asleep in the bath. Kayo, Kumi, and our other good friend, Akiko, exchanged stories about their weeks while I let my head loll back on the lip of the bath and closed my eyes. Bad idea. I jerked awake after only a few moments, and my sleepy eyes elicited a giggle from my friends.

Akiko laughed. "You look beat, Mei," she said from behind her hand. "Mari keeping you up at night?"

"She can't stop crying most evenings." I looked up at the clock on the wall. 18:23. Almost half past six? "She's probably screaming her head off right now for Yasahiro."

My heart raced as I imagined him pacing the apartment, stepping over baby toys and around towers of diaper boxes. I left our home a complete and utter mess to come here. I knew he didn't care about the mess, but I did. I cringed every time I saw another thing stacked against the wall, or the pile of laundry in the corner of the bathroom, or the never-ending tower of dishes. We had a dishwasher, and it was always in use, but some things like pots and pans needed hand washing. When did I have time for that? Never.

When I had lived in the city, in my tiny studio apartment, I'd been a bit of a slob. When I moved home, my room had always been a mess. But this was outrageously messy. Anxiety-inducing messy. Mom never came to our apartment anymore. The first two times she had come over after Mari was born, she fretted over the clutter. She kept trying to put things 'away,' but there was no place for them to go. She did dishes now and then, but she hadn't been in our apartment in a month. We met at Oshabe-cha instead.

Kumi cringed. "I wish I could help you. Taiga rarely cries unless he's hungry or tired. I never went through what you're going through."

"The car calms her down. Hopefully, Yasahiro will take her out if she needs it."

I had to restrain myself from leaving the tub to grab my phone and call him. My fingers ached from clutching the bath railing.

"You know, Mei..." Akiko began, and I cringed again. I knew what was coming. "You should consider hiring someone to help you out. Just for a few months."

I sighed and closed my eyes again.

"It's not a bad idea," Kayo insisted. "You could use the help, especially now with the house problems."

"House problems? What house problems?" Akiko's voice rose.

"Hey, I have an idea," I interrupted, lifting my tired head.

"Let's not talk about me. It's Kumi's birthday. Let's talk about something *she* wants to talk about."

Kumi looked sideways at me. "I agree with them. You need help."

I focused my eyes down through the water at my knees. "It'll get better. I'm sure it will. I don't need to hire anyone, except for Oshabe-cha. Emi will be gone in a few weeks, and I'll really need someone to take her place."

Or I'd be screwed. Because if things were the same or worse in two weeks' time, I would have to close Oshabe-cha. There was no way I could run it and do everything else I needed to do, much less do things I wanted to do like paint or spend time with my family and friends.

Everyone talked about owning your own business, but what happened when you couldn't physically run it anymore?

"Keep your ears open for someone who's qualified to work with the elderly. Emi had a year of volunteer experience working at an elderly care center before coming to work for me. Her high school was a lot better than ours. She's going to school to study elder care. I need someone like her."

"It'd be easier to hire a housekeeper or a nanny, Mei," Kumi said. She sunk farther into the water. "And a housekeeper would be cheaper than an hourly wage employee at the tea shop every day."

I fought this idea to my very core. My mother kept her house without a spouse for years with no problems. It had always been a point of pride for her. Sure, she hired people to help out on the farm. Minato Ohno was our last employee before having to sell the land, and he worked at Midori Sankaku now. But no one ever cleaned our house or made our meals but us. What would other people think of us if we hired a housekeeper?

"I'll think about it," I said, knowing full well I wouldn't think about it. I'd forget it and do my best not to consider it. I was already an undue burden to my town what with the witch rumors and the past problems with Amanda's murder. I wanted to get things onto a better footing now.

I wanted a little more respect, and I knew the only way to get that respect was to earn it. I wasn't going to earn respect by flaunting our wealth and hiring a housekeeper. That just wasn't our way.

"Call me if you want some help, okay?" Akiko made eye contact with me, and I nodded. "I have a busy schedule, but I'm sure I can drop by to babysit while you get things done."

"Thanks," I whispered, though I knew how busy she was since taking on extra clients at the assisted care facility. I doubted I would call her unless I was desperate.

"Now, what's this about your house problems?"

I glanced up at the clock. "Well, look at the time! If we don't get out of the bath soon, we're going to end up standing around at Izakaya Jūshi."

Standing up, I didn't wait for anyone to object. I couldn't afford another session of 'Let's figure out what's wrong with Mei.' I grabbed my tiny towel and made my way to the dressing room.

THANKFULLY, THERE WEREN'T TOO MANY PEOPLE AT Izakaya Jūshi when we arrived. As I opened the door for everyone else, I glanced up the street towards home. All the lights in the apartment were out, and our car was gone from the parking spot. Yasahiro was out driving Mari around. I struggled with the desire to go home. Home was where I belonged.

But I deserved to have a night out with my friends. I would stay for at least one beer and some food.

Kumi smiled and waved to everyone at the bar, and the owners, my deceased friend Etsuko's parents and brother, pointed to a table at the corner of the restaurant where they had placed a RESERVED sign for us.

As we crossed the restaurant and wove through the tables, my foot knocked against a chair, and the person sitting there jumped forward.

"Oh, I'm so sorry," I said before seeing the face that looked up at me. "Ah, Noriko! I'm sorry! How are you?"

Noriko Kubo, our small business coach and teacher, smiled, looking past me to our table. "Is that Kumi?" She waved, and Kumi waved back and bowed.

"Yes, it's Kumi's birthday, and we're out to celebrate."

"How fun! Please wish her a happy birthday from me."

Noriko hadn't answered my question. Instead, her eyes flitted to the man across the table from her. I glanced at him too, but he didn't say anything. He stared at his phone and ignored Noriko talking to me.

"Of course. I will. Sorry to bother you. I hope you have a good night." I bowed as I backed away from her table.

"You too, Mei." Noriko's smile was restrained. "See you tomorrow at Oshabe-cha."

"Yes! See you tomorrow. I know lots of people from class are looking forward to the extra session."

"Me too."

Her nod and smile urged me to move along, so I raised my hand in a small wave and made my way to the table.

"Who's that?" Kayo asked, leaning to the side to get a good look.

"Noriko Kubo. She's teaching the Small Business Success class at the community center that Kumi and I are taking."

"Hmmm." Kayo hummed while drumming her fingers on the table. "I saw her arguing with a young woman at the Lawson's convenience store over by the gas station the other day."

I shifted to the side as Hideo Hiyasa, Etsuko's brother, brought beers to the table.

"All right, everyone. Mom just opened a new batch of pickles, and the chicken meatballs are tasty tonight," he said, setting down the last beer. "We also have assorted tempura with fish, shrimp, and wild vegetables."

"Yeah, we'll take all of that." Kumi laughed. "It always tastes better when I don't have to cook it."

"Fresh udon noodles in soy sauce *dashi* stock too?"

We nodded eagerly.

He smiled, and it warmed my heart to see him happy. "Great. You're my easiest table tonight, as usual."

He winked at Kayo as he departed, and Kayo looked away. Akiko and I exchanged a knowing stare. Kayo had been coming to Izakaya Jūshi a lot. I wondered...

"What were you saying about Noriko?" Kumi returned to the earlier topic, and I sat back with my beer to watch Kayo squirm.

She glanced over at the bar again before picking up her beer. "I saw your teacher arguing with someone at the convenience store." Kayo took a long sip and set the beer down. "It was... uh, Thursday night." She looked up at the ceiling before nodding. "Yeah, probably around eight in the evening. I went in to grab a snack, and she was speaking to a younger woman, mid-twenties, very short, about not being responsible for other people's mistakes. The other woman mentioned somebody stole something. Maybe your teacher had stolen from her? I wasn't sure. They raised their voices, and the younger woman's face was bright red. She was pretty angry. I almost intervened, but they saw me standing there in my uniform, so they stopped and left."

I looked over my shoulder at Noriko talking to the man at the table. Their conversation was intense, and they passed the man's phone back and forth, scrutinizing whatever was on the screen. He rested his hand on her arm, and the gesture was intimate enough for me to believe they were close.

"She's coming over to Oshabe-cha tomorrow for a little break-out session with a few students from class."

I shifted my gaze from them to the kitchen doors. I needed food, soon. My stomach was an empty cavern, and I had nursed

Mari right before I left for Kutsuro Matsu. Calories were zipping in and out of my body lately at blinding speed.

"I'll see if I can get her to talk to me about what's going on. We're not friends or anything, but she lives in town now, and we know some of the same people."

I nearly jumped for joy when I saw the kitchen door open and Hideo approach with the first round of food.

"Good idea, Mei. Have a little chat with her tomorrow and see if you can figure out what's going on. If not, I'll try. I've enjoyed my chats with her, and we once had coffee together. I like her. And we can't have her miss classes because of some drama. I need to hear more about sales tax and bookkeeping." Kumi pouted. "I'm terrible at all of that."

Akiko patted Kumi's arm. "We're all terrible at it."

Not me, I almost said out loud. Thank goodness for business school!

Hideo left three dishes of food on the table. "Be right back with more."

"Okay, the Birthday Girl gets to eat first!" Kumi swooped in with her chopsticks and plucked a chicken meatball off the nearby plate. "Thanks for coming out to celebrate," she said, smiling at us. "I'm happy we're friends."

"Me too," said Kayo, tapping her chopsticks on her plate. "Now, let's eat."

Kumi chuckled as she dished out the food around the table, and we descended into talk about the latest TV dramas until I was so bleary-eyed I couldn't keep my head up. I had to stumble home, keeping my hand on the walls of the buildings between Izakaya Jūshi and the apartment so I wouldn't fall over. Not a bad way to spend the evening. Not at all.

CHAPTER
SIX

Bounce and walk. Pace up and down the length of the tea shop. Repeat forever.

Yes, I would pace the tea shop forever if I had to. Keeping my baby happy was my top priority.

Mari was having a rough morning, probably having more to do with me being gone most of the night than anything else. She had given Yasahiro quite a hard time until I arrived home at midnight. He was half asleep and feeding her a bottle when I slipped in the door. She collapsed into my arms and fell deep asleep once I held her to my chest. Yasahiro took one look at me and went to bed without another word. Yikes. Sorry. I supposed it wasn't the worst thing for your baby to be attached to you, but this situation was getting precarious.

The door to Oshabe-cha opened as I was making my way back from the rear of the store to the front. Kumi entered with a wave. She looked in much better shape than me. Her shoulder-length hair was sleek and her face shined with rosy cheeks. I was a mess with my hair in a ponytail, dark circles under my eyes, and my skin dull and gray.

It was Beauty and the Beast, for sure.

I smiled, a little flick of the corners of my mouth. Nothing more. "Kumi, how do you always look so radiant?"

"I have no idea." She left her bag at the table I set aside for everyone and came to kiss Mari's head. "Ah, I love the smell of babies."

"Do other people like the smell of babies? I'm thinking about selling this one on eBay."

Kumi chuckled and slapped my arm. "Stop. It's not that bad."

"I'm going nuts with sleep deprivation, my home is a disaster, and Yasahiro and I haven't had a night alone in months."

She frowned. "Chiyo babysat for us all the time when Taiga was a baby. Where is your mother?"

"That's a good question. I believe she's at home cooking and planning her new cookbook."

"Not now. Where has she been for the last few months?"

Mari stirred, so I continued my swaying and bouncing. "Doing the things that make her happy, which is what I told her to do when we lost the house. She has glaucoma, and she seems depressed too. I didn't want to burden her with more stuff. That and she won't step foot in my apartment with it a complete mess."

We had struggled enough. I had to accept Mom for the person she was, and she needed to give me the space I needed to be my version of motherhood.

Kumi's eyes spoke for her. She was disappointed in me, disappointed that I wasn't asking for more from Mom. Kumi had no problem asking for what she wanted from her own mother or Chiyo, but they weren't anything like my mom. Kumi's mother was a saint, and Chiyo was sweet, kind, and far too generous. My mother? She was as hard as a rock most days.

"Don't start," I snapped, and the rage lasted only a moment before I regretted it. "Sorry."

"It's okay." She placed her hand on my upper arm and squeezed gently. "Let's talk about this later."

Let's talk about this never, actually. What was there to talk about? The Mom situation wouldn't improve until she had her feet under her again. She needed to find her passion. And then the home and child situation wouldn't get better until Mari got through this irritable baby phase. I just had to hold out a little longer.

I could hold out a little longer.

Once Mari was asleep, I shuffled between the tea shop tables, helping customers, serving tea, and settling bills. Emi took care of my elderly clients on Monday mornings and would be in the tea shop at lunchtime, so I was on my own.

Today was a day for tourists, a treat for Chikata. Several Italian foreigners fawned over the bento boxes and bought tea to take home. They even posed for photos in the shop. Despite how tired I was, my smile couldn't be contained. I had spent weeks trying out different teas from farms around Kyoto, and this was my favorite thing to sell. I hoped those tourists went home, drank the tea, and thought of our small town.

While I took care of the shop, I waited on everyone from the business class to show up. Eight people, including Kumi, had paid for this extra breakout session where they'd learn more about sales taxes and selling goods at farmers' markets. By 11:00, everyone had arrived, and they were seated with tea.

I transferred Mari (very, very gently) to the bassinet in the back room and waited at the front door for Noriko to show up.

"It's so unlike Noriko to be late," one of the students said as she chewed on her pen. "She's always there before class starts."

"Did you see what happened after class the other day?" another woman asked. My brain was too foggy to remember everyone's names. "She had a huge fight in the parking lot with some young woman. I heard her say, 'I can't control other people!' and then she walked away towards town. The young woman followed her. They were both pretty angry." She flattened her lips before shaking her head. "Awful thing to fight in public like that."

I sat down at the table, eager to get off my feet for a bit. They ached right along with my hips and back. "Do you know where they went?"

That had been around 19:30, right at dinner time. We usually finished the Thursday class and went home to have dinner after because it ran from 18:00 to 19:30. Then Kayo had seen them at the convenience store arguing again at 20:00? The whole conversation from the night before was a little hazy, and my memory was shot. I had heard of baby brain, but I didn't think it would be this bad.

"Don't know, but they were heading for the parking lot."

"Maybe something's going on with her?" Kumi asked, her fingers drumming on her phone. She was probably itching to call Goro and ask him if he had heard anything.

My sixth sense for crimes and funny business prickled like it hadn't in some time, not since our trip to Kubako to visit Kayo's family last fall. Something was definitely going on with Noriko. This incident, combined with the tense conversation she'd had with the man last night at Izakaya Jūshi, seemed suspicious.

Or perhaps I was just paranoid, what with everything going on at the site of my new house. Either my life was quiet and comfortable or a hundred things happened at once, including a murder case to solve. It was never somewhere in between. Extremes at all times.

I listened while the rest of the classmates whispered about possible motives for someone accusing Noriko of suspicious things until I was sure something terrible had happened to her. Gossip became conjecture which then led to concrete theories in the span of twenty minutes. This group could talk!

By 11:30, Mari was making happy noises in the back room, and Noriko still hadn't shown up. When Emi arrived at 11:45

with Murata and we still hadn't started the class, I stood up at the table.

"Everyone, I'm sorry, but it looks like today's session is canceled. Unless we give Noriko a call? Does anyone have her business card?"

A chorus of nos rippled around the group until Kumi perked up.

"Oh! I do." Kumi dug around her bag. "I can't believe I forgot about it. She gave it to me because we talked about me designing a logo for her."

We had all been gossiping so much that we forgot to call.

Kumi dialed the number and waited. "Voicemail," she whispered, listening to the greeting. "Hi, Noriko. It's Kumi Hokichi. I just wanted to check to make sure today's breakout session is still on? It's 11:45 and we've been waiting here since 11:00. Please call either Mei or me to reschedule, okay? Hope everything is all right!" She left our numbers and hung up.

"I guess we should order lunch?" she asked, shrugging.

Everyone else stood up to go, but I shook my head.

"I can't. I need to head over to Sawayaka and talk to Yasahiro about house stuff."

And with Mari in a good mood after a decent nap, I could have Ana, the head greeter at Sawayaka, watch her for a bit.

I slipped into the back room, and Emi turned off the tap at the sink.

"How did the class session go?" she asked, wiping her hands on a towel.

"It didn't. Our teacher never showed up. She may have been mistaken about the date or time." Even though I had confirmed it with her last night at the izakaya.

"Oh, that's too bad." She crossed the room and opened her bag that sat on the table. "Mei, I want to say that it's been such a pleasure working here, with you and your clients." She approached me with a piece of paper in her hands, and my stomach sank. Extending the paper to me, she bowed. "I'm sad that I can't stay, but I really must get ready to go to school. This is my two weeks notice which we discussed before. I'm so glad I got the chance to work here. You're a great boss, and I've learned so much. I hope it'll be okay for me to visit?"

She kept her head down, and her hair swept across her face, but I could tell that her cheeks were red from embarrassment. She didn't want to disappoint me or cause bad blood.

I took the paper and returned the bow. "It's been great having you here, Emi. I'm so grateful that you were able to stay as long as you have. I don't know what I'll do without you."

She straightened up, and a wave of gratitude swept over me. I opened my arms and gave her a big hug. "Thank you. Thank you so much for your help."

"Oh," she squeaked as I hugged her. It was unprofessional, but I didn't care. She had become a valued employee in the last few months. "I hope you're not upset."

"No," I whispered, breaking away from her. I sat down at the table and placed her resignation letter in front of me. I couldn't read it, not now. My chest ached with sadness. "I'll miss you, definitely. You're always welcome here." I smiled at her even as my eyes stung with tears. "I don't know how I'll handle everything while you're gone."

Mari cooed in her bassinet, and I snapped into mom-mode. My hips objected as I rose from the chair and lifted Mari into my arms. "Hello," I said, smiling at her and kissing her neck. She replied with a smile and a giggle.

"Have you been looking for a replacement for me?" Emi asked, returning to the kitchen sink. "I wasn't sure if you wanted to come back here full time or not."

"I do want to work here full time." I grabbed the diaper changing pad from under the bassinet and placed it on the mattress. "I love this place. It's the culmination of everything I've worked for for the last two years." I paused while unsnapping Mari's onesie, remembering how poor Mom and I had been. We'd kept it hidden from everyone. Now, I had nothing to hide. "But it's hard balancing the house, the apartment, the tea shop, my daughter, and my husband. I'm always short a hand or two, or a few hours in the day. Having you here really helped."

Emi washed dishes in silence while I changed Mari's diaper.

Kumi stuck her head in the back door. "I'm heading out. Still no word from Noriko, so let me know if she calls or stops by."

"Sure." I sat down at the table to feed Mari. "Okay."

Kumi looked at me for a long moment. "Take care, Mei. Call me later if you need anything."

I nodded and closed my eyes as Mari latched on to feed. I could nod off right here.

"You know, Mei," Emi said, returning to the conversation. I opened my eyes to see her washing glasses and setting them aside. "You could hire a housekeeper for here and your house. That would give you a lot of freedom to take care of Mari and your clients."

I shifted my eyes back and forth. This felt like a trap.

"Has someone been talking to you about this?"

She looked over her shoulder and laughed at my drawn together eyebrows. "No. But I'm going to guess I'm not the only person who has mentioned it." She placed the last glass on the drying rack. "If you want to consider it, I have a friend from high school, a year older than me, who is looking to make some more money. She's going to college part-time and taking care of her sick father. She has the hours to spare for what you're looking for, especially if they're non-traditional office hours."

Hmmm. This was something I was more keen to consider than some fancy housekeeping agency out of Tokyo. The fancy agency would come with all the gossip. A young college student? I would be seen as helping someone else in the community.

"I'll consider it. Thank you, Emi." I smiled to let her know that my weary and tired voice had nothing to do with her suggestion. "Maybe I can talk to her later this week, after I deal with my house problems."

Yes, right now I had to concentrate on the problems at hand. I had to get this house situation under control before it sped away and left me with nothing but an empty lot and eyes full of tears.

CHAPTER
SEVEN

"What is going on here?"

Mari didn't answer, but I didn't expect her to. I rounded the corner onto the street where Sawayaka was located, and my jaw dropped. At least twenty people were waiting outside, on a Monday, *in early April*. The wind blew, and the sky threatened rain. It wasn't the best day to be standing outside waiting for a table at a restaurant.

As I glided by in the car, I craned my neck to see inside the front window. Maybe the place was closed because of a problem in the kitchen or a flood or something?

But no. The entire dining room buzzed with people, and every table was full. I brought the car to a stop at the intersection and glanced at my phone. No calls from Yasahiro.

Flipping on the turn signal, I circled the building and parked the car around the rear of the restaurant in Yasahiro's usual spot next to the dumpster. Mari squealed in the back seat, eager for the car to move again. I wished I knew what it was about the car she loved so much so I could replicate it at home.

I wrapped my coat around me tightly as I got ready to leave the car. The temperature was dropping fast. I hoped there was something warm inside for me to eat before I returned to work at Oshabe-cha.

In the back seat, I unlatched Mari's car seat and entered into the kitchen through the back door.

Everything inside the kitchen moved at lightning speed. All the chefs were hard at work, and Sadachi and Ichi were peeling and chopping vegetables so quickly I worried about their fingers.

"Mei!" Everyone cheered. Their energy almost knocked me over.

The door to the dining room swung open, and the cacophony of voices hurt my ears from across the kitchen.

"Wow." I blinked in shock. "What happened?"

In the last two years, I had only seen Sawayaka this busy on special occasions, holidays, or during catered events. But this busy on a Monday at lunch? What?

Mari began to fuss, so I set her car seat to the side and pulled her out. She was fascinated by all the kitchen hubbub.

"See Daddy?" I pointed to Yasahiro across the room, and my soul brightened to see her recognize him. She was beginning to hold up her head like a pro now, not as wobbly as last month. Yasahiro turned, saw us, and his face lit up. It was a defining moment, a milestone in our relationship when we really felt like a family.

I did my best to stay out of the way as we crossed the kitchen to talk to Yasahiro.

"What's going on?" I couldn't hide my smile now. The noise from the dining room was full of good cheer and a mix of languages.

Yasahiro flipped mixed vegetables in the pan and dipped his spoon in to taste the sauce. "We were so sleep deprived this weekend, we missed a few new stories about Sawayaka. We were mentioned on a Tokyo foodie blog on Friday, then some Instagram photographer posted about us to sixty thousand followers, *and then* another English language top ten organic restaurants list had us near the top. Ana's been turning people away all day, and there was a line outside when I showed up here this morning."

"Wow. That's fantastic!"

The excitement that flooded my chest bordered on panic. This was wonderful news for Yasahiro and our family. Restaurants always skated on the edge of profitability, and Sawayaka was no stranger to scraping by. Business had been good the last year, though, and I had been cautiously optimistic, knowing that any small slight could lead to imminent disaster.

I hadn't expected anything like this. I figured we were already at our peak since Yasahiro had earned a Michelin star. The restaurant was usually seventy to eighty percent booked during the weeknights and extra busy on the weekends. Now, it would be a miracle for locals to get in to eat.

The anxiety mounted as I watched Yasahiro work at the stove. He looked so... tired. When we first started dating, he was so energetic, his enthusiasm had bounced off the walls.

As he worked at the stove, I noticed all the ways he had changed since then. Under his handkerchief head wrap, his hair was longer and stuck up with wild abandon. I liked this new style, but he sometimes looked like he'd rolled straight out of bed, which he had. Tiny wrinkles creased the corners of his eyes, and he was seldom without a day's worth of stubble because he would forget to shave. His posture slumped forward, and he relieved pressure from being on his feet by swaying side to side.

I was just as much of a mess, if not more, so I wasn't going to judge. But I was his wife, and if he died an early death from overwork, I'd be one unhappy widow.

I shifted Mari to my other arm. "How can I help?"

"What?" he asked, transferring the vegetables from the pan to a plate and handing it off to someone for the main course.

"How can I help?" I repeated. "Do you need to be here more? Do you need me to help with the administration so you can keep working in the kitchen? I could hire someone if you tell me what you're looking for."

He stared at me for a moment while his brain caught up to my words. Then he smiled and leaned in to place his hand on my back. "You're a savior, of course." I imagined the kiss he would've placed on my cheek if he hadn't been in the kitchen. "Let's figure out if this will last before we do anything rash. Maybe we get a week or two of crowds, and then they'll be gone, or it might continue to grow. We need to do what's right for us. That could mean opening a second restaurant or any other number of decisions."

Mari grabbed at my shirt and smashed it against her mouth. Yasahiro smiled at her as she slobbered all over me.

"I should be getting back to the tea shop." I swept my eyes over the kitchen and everyone hustling to get meals cooked and out the door. So much for talking about the house or picking up lunch. They wouldn't be able to neglect paying customers to make me noodle soup. "I don't want to be in the way."

I stepped aside to let the two junior chefs scoot past as they hurried to the refrigerators.

"I'll be late tonight. Sorry." Yasahiro's face fell into a frown as he leaned forward to kiss Mari on the head. The baby got a kiss, but that was acceptable. I remembered when we once kissed in the kitchen, a knee-melting kiss that thrilled me to the core. But no one had been around, and we'd had the time and the space to be intimate back then. Times had changed.

I held Mari close to my chest as I wove through the kitchen and returned her to her car seat.

"Such a busy day," I said to her, strapping her in. "Let's go back to the tea shop and figure out how to spend the rest of the day together. Do you think Mommy can paint?" I smiled down at her. "Maybe?" She smiled back.

Maybe.

"Oh!" I remembered what else I came for. "Yasahiro!" I

waved to catch his attention. "I need the name of your photographer."

"My photographer?" he called out from the stove.

"Yeah, the guy who takes photos of Sawayaka and your food."

He hesitated as he threw vegetables into a pan. "Uh, top drawer on the right, in the office. In the stack of business cards."

I hefted Mari's car seat into the office and set her down next to the desk. Inside the top right drawer was a stack of business cards. I shuffled through them until I found one for Ryosuké Nagatomo, Photographer. I took my phone from my bag and snapped a photo of it for later. I would send him an email and see what kind of availability he had.

Before I could put my phone away, it rang in my hand, and I stared at the screen with a sinking feeling. It was Goro again.

"Hi, Goro. How are you?"

"I could be better. There's been another accident at your house. Some scaffolding came loose, and a man fell and broke his shoulder. Is it possible you can come by and deal with this?"

I sank into Yasahiro's chair and rested my forehead on the piles of papers on his desk.

"Yeah, sure. I'll be right there. I'm at Sawayaka, so I'll come by in about ten minutes."

"Okay. See you soon."

I hung up and tried to find more energy from somewhere deep in my body.

What else was going to go wrong?

CHAPTER
EIGHT

This time when I arrived at the work site, not only was there an ambulance parked outside, but a crowd of my new neighbors had gathered to rubberneck. Great. We were getting off on the wrong foot with everyone.

I huddled in the back seat of the car as I tried to get the baby carrier on and Mari into it. I was new to this, and my first attempts were always clumsy. Frustration ran my heart to racing speed, and I dripped sweat down my front as I held Mari to my chest and clipped the carrier at the back of my neck. I had to exit the car to pull the oversized fleece jacket around us, and as I closed the car door, one of the older ladies from across the street approached me.

"It's too cold out here for babies this small," she said, point blank. What was it about babies that brought out the worst in people? Around here, you either minded your own business to the point of exclusion or you minded everyone's business until you were deemed nosy. There seemed to be no middle ground.

I zipped up the coat and plopped the fleece hat on Mari's fuzzy head before turning to look at the lady. She was familiar, definitely a new neighbor.

"I'm so sorry. I've forgotten your name. I can only blame the lack of sleep," I said, bowing to her.

It was a low blow, but she had it coming.

"Asahara. Moeko Asahara. What's going on with your property? The police have been here twice in the last week." She pulled her jacket around her tighter as her short hair blew across her face.

I grabbed my bag from the top of the car and locked the doors.

"There have been some accidents on site. It's nothing much, but the police come whenever an ambulance is called." I looked sideways at her house across the street. "How long have you lived here, Mrs. Asahara?"

She huffed and pulled back. "What? Do you think I don't have the right to complain? I've lived here for thirty years."

"No, no. I understand that this construction and noise is an inconvenience, and I do apologize for that."

"It certainly is." She nodded once and swept her arm out at the muddy lot of mine. "And it's an eyesore as well."

I didn't have the time nor the patience for her attitude today.

"Listen." I stopped in my tracks and surprised her. "I've lived in Chikata my whole life, as have five generations of my family. Building this house here is good for this town and good for this street. I'm sorry about the noise, but we're doing the best we can."

Oops. That came flying out of my mouth before I could edit it.

"There's no need to get defensive about it." She rested her hand on her chest.

"I apologize again," I said, bowing. The words echoed from my lips, but I didn't feel apologetic one bit. "I'm only trying to build my house." I waited for her to acknowledge my apology and simmer down.

Once her shoulders dropped, and she nodded to me, I continued.

"Do you know much about the previous owners here?" I asked, walking towards the ambulance.

"Why do you care? You tore down their houses."

I stopped short. "For good reason. They were practically condemned."

She sighed. "I... I think I remember their names? If not, I can ask my husband when he returns home. Why?"

"I'd like to find out more about the land and what happened here in the past."

She pressed her hand to her chest. "Do you think the land is stigmatized?"

I shrugged. "I'm not sure." I dug in my bag for my business cards. "If you could give me a call soon, and let me know their names, I'd appreciate it."

She took the card while bowing. "I'll see what I can do."

Moeko crossed the street to make her way back home, looking over her shoulder when she reached the curb. I held a sigh behind my lips. My new life in my new home was off on the wrong foot.

I tiptoed up to the ambulance, afraid of who I'd find inside.

"You!" His ashen face contorted with pain. "Stay away from me!"

Yep. It was just as I feared. Daiki Wada laid on the stretcher in the ambulance, his arm supported and propped against his chest.

"Mei!" Goro called from the other side of the lot.

I paused for a moment to look at Daiki and decided not to say anything. Honestly, he was so frightened of me, nothing I could've said would've made him feel any better. I briefly considered chanting some nonsense at him or making some kind of sign with my hands, just to rattle him.

Bad, Mei!

I chuckled as I walked off.

"Sorry about this," Goro whispered as I approached. This time he was less amused by the situation. "Kumi said you were losing a lot of sleep over the house, so I feel awful that I had to call you out here again."

"What happened this time?" I asked, trying to fold my arms over my chest and failing because Mari was strapped there. I stuffed my hands into my fleece pockets instead.

"Mrs. Suga." Imai, the foreman, acknowledged me with a bow. "Some scaffolding collapsed and knocked Daiki Wada off a ladder. He fell right on his shoulder and fractured it."

"Did you check the scaffolding before working?" I looked at the house to determine where the accident occurred. It must have happened inside the structure because I couldn't see anything different from where I was.

Imai sighed. "We did check it, but we must have missed this one spot where the ground was uneven."

"Hmmm. Well, it sounds like an accident...?" The lift in my voice was unintended. I wanted this to just be an accident, but it was looking less and less likely.

Imai shifted his eyes down. A bad sign. "Well, whether it's an accident or not, my team has walked off the job, and they won't be returning until we get some answers about the land."

I huffed, and Mari blinked her eyes at me. "The land," I grumbled under my breath.

"Whether it's stigmatized or not. Now, I've worked on plenty of job sites in my career where contractors have been injured. It happens. Sometimes it happens three times in one week. Other times, we may have nothing bad happen at all. And normally, I would brush this off. But Wada insists that you're to blame. I'm so sorry." He bowed, covering up his unease about speaking so plainly. "So he's riled up the other men on the site and spoiled the lot of them. Again, I apologize."

While Imai was bent over in deference, I glanced at Goro. He sighed and stowed away his notebook.

"If I figure out what's going on with the land or whatever," — I waved my hand in a circle, not caring how informal I sounded —

"will you hire a new crew and return to finish the job? I really want my house. I have fought... so hard..."

And then the tears came. Ugh. I hated how they made me look. Like some weak, sniveling woman who couldn't control herself.

But both men were not embarrassed, thankfully. Goro did the decent thing and set his hand on my shoulder to steady me.

"We'll figure it out," Goro said, reassuring me. "And I'm sure Mr. Imai will find the right crew to be here and build your house. Isn't that right, Mr. Imai?"

Goro raised his shoulders and asserted his dominance, something I hadn't seen him do in quite some time. In his police uniform, he always looked like he had command of the situation, but now, with him staring down at Imai, his intimidating nature shone through.

"Of course. We want to build this house." He stood up straight. "The manufacturer assures me that this is a point of pride for them, to have one of their houses in this town, owned by a famous chef and his wife. We will get it done. This is only a small hiccup."

I bristled at the 'and his wife' comment as if I was a nobody, just someone's accessory. But it was not time to educate this man on the finer points of independent women. If Yasahiro's fame would carry us through this mess, then so be it.

"I'll get your answers, and I'll get them soon," I assured him.

As soon as possible.

CHAPTER
NINE

The sun set, and Mari lost her mind.

Again.

I literally looked at the ceiling and asked why? Why me? Why was my baby so angry with the night? She was so delightful most of the day, and I always considered it a blessing she gave me some time to get stuff done. And for a moment or two, I'd forget the hours of screaming and crying every evening.

This was my downfall. What I should've been doing each day was resting and saving up my willpower to deal with the nights. I had always considered myself a smart person...

And then I became a mother.

"There, there," I said, holding my baby to my chest and pacing up and down the length of the apartment.

I had the route memorized and could do it blindfolded. Three steps forward, half step to the left to avoid the giant boxes, step over the discarded baby toys, circle around the couch in a wide loop to avoid the empty cardboard boxes I didn't have time to break down for recycling.

The kitchen smelled. The bathroom was getting disgusting. I was at my breaking point, and Mari wasn't feeling any better.

I stared at the clock on the wall. Just after seven. It would be hours before Yasahiro arrived home. I needed to call Mom and ask for help. I didn't like to bother her, but I only had so much patience.

I deposited Mari into the swing and strapped her in. This completely pissed her off, and she brought her screaming to a crescendo.

"Oh. Oh no," I mumbled through my own tears. Pangs of sadness ripped through my chest to hear her so unhappy.

Once again, I went through the items on the checklist. Diaper? Fine. Temperature? Also fine. Nothing scratchy was touching her skin, and she had just been fed.

"Just... wait here a moment." Was I afraid she'd get up and leave? My mind was not what it once was.

I slipped away to the bedroom so I could make my call. I felt terrible for leaving her there, but what else could I do?

Mom picked up right away. "Hello, Mei! How are you?"

"Oh, I'm fine," I said, my voice wobbling.

"Are you upset? What's wrong?" I was grateful she was concerned and not angry.

"Mari won't stop crying. And Sawayaka is suddenly super busy which means Yasahiro can't come home. And the land for the house is haunted. And my house is a mess."

It all tumbled out of my mouth so quickly that the sob at the end surprised even me.

"Oh no," Mom said, and this time I noticed more traffic noise in the background. "I'm sorry, Mei."

"Me too. Um... I could really use some help. Can you come over?"

"Hmmm. Now? I'm actually in Tokyo right now."

I sniffed up and dragged my hand over my mouth. "Tokyo? What are you doing there?"

She chuckled. "Scouting out vegetable suppliers and picking up kitchen equipment. Chiyo and I drove in for the day. We have a reservation for dinner. I don't expect to be home until late."

I tried to concentrate on Mom's words, but it didn't make sense.

"Are you opening a restaurant?"

Mom was silent for a moment while a truck drove by on her end. "Mei, I'm beginning to worry about you. We talked about this the other day. I'm going to author a cookbook, remember? I need supplies so I can cook and test dishes and then have photos taken of them."

"Oh, right. Sorry. Sorry. For some reason, I didn't connect one thing to the other."

"You're tired. Try to get some rest. I can come by tomorrow."

"Okay. Yeah. Great."

Mari's cries in the other room reached a fevered pitch, and her throat sounded like it was cracking.

"Is that Mari?" Mom asked, jolting me back to the phone.

"Yes. Yes it is. I have to go."

I hung up the phone and gathered up more energy to call Akiko. But her phone rang and rang, and I hung up when the line clicked over to her voicemail. It was the evening so she might have been doing anything. My fingers hovered over the Line app as I considered texting her. Instead, I tossed my phone on the bed.

Okay, I was going to give this thirty more minutes, and if she didn't stop crying, I would drive to the nearest hospital, the one on the hill that Amanda had ended up in when she was attacked.

I hardly ever thought of Amanda, now that she was dead and gone. It was funny the way brains worked.

I swooped back into the room and smiled at Mari, trying to break her cycle of crying. This time I reached my finger into her mouth and felt along her gums too. Nope. No teeth either.

I picked her back up and did another five rounds of the apartment, and this time she was no less upset in my arms than she was in the swing. I tried nursing her, and that only made her angrier. Then I considered strapping her into the carrier again, but I had carried her most of the day, and I didn't want to have her in there twenty-four hours a day.

"Okay, sweetie. If you're going to cry in my arms or in the swing, you're going to cry in the swing while I get some house-cleaning done."

I wished I could pop in earplugs and sleep, but I felt too guilty doing that while she cried.

I strapped her back in the swing, looked around the apartment, and decided that the floor needed cleaning first. I was tired of constantly stepping on discarded pieces of paper or dirt.

I sprinted through the apartment, picking up anything on the floor I could find. Bags and boxes went on top of the table or on the couch. I threw Mari's toys and blankets onto our bed. She cried and cried, and I did my best to keep going.

I grabbed the vacuum cleaner from the utility closet next to the pantry, plugged it in, and started it up. It wasn't the cleaning that would make the highest impact on the state of our apartment, but it was better than nothing.

My mood lightened as I worked my way through the kitchen and into the common dining room. What was it about cleaning that made me feel better?

I turned around and faced Mari, expecting to see her contorted face. Instead, she was chewing on her fist.

Huh. She had stopped crying.

I kept going, hitting every corner and even vacuuming under the couch. Fatigue swamped me, but I was spurred on by the progress I was making while Mari wasn't crying.

Wow. Mari wasn't crying!

I finished up and turned off the vacuum. Maybe next I'd tackle some dishes.

Mari's face reddened, and she let out a peel of sadness.

"Wait! What did I do?" I asked, crossing the room to her.

I sighed as the impotent rage built up in me again. Why?

And then it hit me. I remembered an article I had read before Mari was born about what babies liked and didn't like. I had forgotten about it in my sleep-deprived state, and since I hadn't cleaned in over six weeks, it wasn't as if I had run the vacuum cleaner in ages.

Babies liked white noise.

At night, we kept a fan going in our room, and that provided quiet white noise for during the sleep period, but during the day, I had nothing going. Except for the car. And when Mari was exhausted, she was more sensitive than usual.

I jumped up, returned to the vacuum cleaner, and turned it on.

Mari stopped crying.

My cry of 'Why me?' changed to 'Why hadn't I figured this out sooner?'

I thought I was a good detective, and yet I had missed this.

I couldn't run the vacuum cleaner all day and night though. I'd need to come up with something else. But for now, it would work.

I gathered up the plastic rings Mari liked to stick in her mouth, brought her to the kitchen, and set her on the floor next to me at the sink. I left the vacuum cleaner running next to the kitchen island, and I got to work.

I was just about done with the dishes and high on the enthusiasm of having figured something out about Mari when I heard my phone faintly ringing.

I turned off the kitchen sink and looked around for my phone. Where had I left it?

On the bed! I tossed it there when I was done calling Mom and Akiko.

The missed call log showed that Goro had called, and instead of just listening to the voicemail, I called him back.

"Mei, how are you?"

"Much better now, thanks."

He laughed. "What happened? Sounds noisy there."

"I realized Mari likes the sound of the vacuum!" My voice contained a hint of hysteria. "I'm so glad she's not crying anymore."

"That's... that's great, Mei. You should really get out more."

"Ha. Get out? What's that? Anyway, I didn't listen to your voicemail. What's up?"

"I have some bad news, and Kumi is in hysterics. She told me to call you."

"What?" My heart beat hard in my chest. "Is it Taiga?"

"Huh? Oh no. But we found Noriko Kubo dead in the garden behind her house."

I blinked a few times, not processing this news. "What?"

"Kumi asked me to check up on her since she didn't show up today at Oshabe-cha, so I stopped by Noriko's house after my lunch break. Found her then. I was there all afternoon. Is there any chance you could call Kumi and talk to her? She's really broken up."

"Uh, sure. Yeah. I'll do that now."

"Okay. We'll talk tomorrow."

He hung up, and I stared at my phone.

Noriko was dead?

Thoughts of her flashed through my head, arguing with the young woman outside the community center and discussing something serious with the man at Izakaya Jūshi.

Noriko was dead, and I already had two suspects in mind.

I made sure Mari was okay (she was happily chewing on her rings), steeled myself, and called Kumi.

CHAPTER
TEN

The police station hummed with activity when I arrived the next day pushing Mari's stroller ahead of me at a brisk pace. Now that I knew she loved the loud white noise of the vacuum cleaner and being on the move, I felt like I could handle just about any situation. At least, until she hit another growth spurt and everything changed again.

Babies — unpredictable even at the best of times.

"Good to see you, Mrs. Suga," the uniformed officer at the front desk said as I parked my stroller there to sign in.

"You too..." I struggled to find her name in my addled brain. "... Miss Ueda."

Her smirk made my cheeks heat. "Rough night last night?"

"All my nights are rough nowadays, but I figured out Mari likes the vacuum cleaner, so as long as that doesn't break, I might get more regular rest."

She waved me through as the door buzzed. "Regular rest sounds like a myth, a story conjured up by fiction writers."

Too true.

Kumi sat at Goro's desk, her eyes rimmed in red and Taiga's stroller empty next to her. Across the room, Goro held Taiga while other people in the office fawned over him. Taiga was a big boy now, pulling himself up on everything and showing off his newfound baby muscles and sweet charm. He brought a smile to everyone's faces.

"Kumi," I whispered, settling my hand on her shoulder, "are you okay? You look worse than I do."

I parked Mari's stroller, unzipped her from her jacket, gave her her favorite bright and colorful toy, and sat down across from Kumi at someone's empty desk.

"I... I can't believe she's dead. I really liked her, trusted her." She shook her head. "I was up half the night thinking about her."

"What happened?"

She took a deep breath and let it all out. "I asked Goro to drive by her house and check on her. I figured the police would know where she lived, even if I didn't, so..." She shrugged. "Anyway, he finally got over there after his lunch break. He rang the door, and no one answered. Then he saw that the gate to her backyard was open, so he entered the property to make sure everything was fine, and he found her dead in her back garden."

She pointed to her own head.

"Hit over the head with a garden statue. It was broken on the ground next to her."

I winced. Bloody deaths were the worst.

"Do they know anything more? Like when it happened? Anything?"

Kumi shook her head. "Waiting on lab results and news from the coroner."

I leaned closer to Kumi. "Did you tell Goro about the young woman we saw her with after class the other day? Or the man we saw her with at Izakaya Jūshi?"

Kumi shook her head. "I mentioned the young woman but not the man. Totally forgot about it."

"Okay, I'll be sure to say something."

Kumi rested her hand on my arm. "Are you going to... take an interest?"

I held back a laugh as my stomach flipped over.

Last night, as I laid in bed, Mari slept, and Yasahiro finally settled next to me, I had weighed all the pros and cons of getting involved in another murder investigation. The cons were pretty highly weighted now. I was a mother with a baby, a tea shop to watch after, an apartment to maintain, a house to build. All of these things demanded my attention, and with Mari in the mix, I needed to be more careful than I had been in the past.

But the dream of solving another murder pushed its way into the forefront and jumped to the top of the list. I had known Noriko and liked her. She had died only a few hours after promising to be at *my* tea shop. I had solved other murders, and I would be doing her and her family a favor by helping with the investigation.

The compulsion to help was so strong, it pulled at my heart until I had to catch my breath.

"Am I going to take an interest? Are you asking? Or is it Goro asking?"

"Both of us." She leaned forward to whisper. "If we solve the case, the Chikata Police, that is, then it's possible they will promote Goro."

I raised my eyebrows as I looked across the room at him.

"With a promotion, they would put him on more high-profile cases throughout the local towns. A pay raise, too," she said, dropping her voice to a whisper.

I sat back in the seat and stared at her husband and son across the room.

"I want us to find Noriko's killer, but I also want this for Goro. Is that selfish?"

I thought about my ambivalence over Yasahiro's career shooting into space and becoming even more popular than he was now. I both wanted it and didn't. Was that selfish?

"Sounds human to me. I want to help out, Kumi. I really do. But I'm worried I'm being stretched too thin. The house building situation is out of control, and Yasahiro isn't around to help. I'm afraid my house will never be built at this rate."

Kumi drummed her fingers on Goro's desk.

"Maybe we should consider a switch. I'll help with your housing troubles, and you help out with this investigation. I'll even babysit."

My mind slipped away to a field of rice, the clouds opening to reveal a blue sky and sunshine, and I stood at the edge, basking in the warmth of a new day. Suddenly, my world looked bright and beautiful with the prospects of almost daily social interaction and time away from the routine drudgery of the mommy-cycle. No more constantly wearing the same clothes over and over. No more not bathing for three days straight. No more holing up at home.

Kumi waved her hand in front of my face, and I snapped backwards.

She giggled. "I swear that you are the queen of daydreamers. Where did you even go?"

"Someplace warm and comforting. I like your idea. It sounds like a good deal. I'll help you with the investigation into Noriko's death. You help me figure out what's going on with my house situation."

"Will we be ghost hunting?" she asked, perking up. All of her favorite dramas on TV revolved around ghosts and paranormal beings inhabiting old buildings or possessing people. "I've always wanted to go ghost hunting."

"Then it's your lucky day."

We watched a younger officer enter the bull pit, hurry across the floor, and hand a folder of documents to Goro. He frowned as he glanced at the top sheet, still carrying Taiga in his other arm.

"Maybe. Maybe not," Kumi mumbled as she and Goro exchanged frowns.

Certainly not for Noriko.

————

WHILE KAYO WAS OUT AT THE CRIME SCENE, CANVASSING the neighborhood and interviewing the people who lived around Noriko, I walked across town to visit Mom. Since Mom was uncomfortable in my messy apartment, she would usually come to Oshabe-cha, or I would come to her place. I visited her at least twice a week if not more.

"Hello?" I called out as I entered her apartment. I had a key which was good for days like this when I didn't want to wait outside with Mari for her to either show up or let me in. The kitchen hissed with the sound of high octane cooking. I couldn't see what Mom was making, but I could smell it. My nose told me she was frying onions on the stove, and my ears ached with the whir of the food processor grinding at full speed.

"Mei?" The food processor stopped, and Mom's head poked out of the kitchen. She smiled as she hustled across the floor to us. "I wasn't expecting you today."

I relaxed as she squeezed me in her arms. She smelled of home.

"I was out running errands, but I come with bad news."

Her smile faded. "Just a moment. Let me turn off the stove. Is it Yasahiro? Is something wrong with Mari?"

Mom swooped in from the kitchen as I sat down at the kotatsu with Mari and prepared to feed her.

"No, Mom. We're all fine. But Noriko was found dead early this morning in her back garden."

Mom's hand flew to her mouth as she gasped. I probably should have been less blunt with the news, but Mari was fussing and hoping to be fed. I took care of her while Mom reached for a tissue.

"What? How did it happen?"

"Not sure. It looks like it was murder though. She never showed up for the breakout session at Oshabe-cha yesterday, so Kumi asked Goro to check up on her. He found her."

I didn't want to give any more details.

"That's horrible. I'm so surprised. She seemed like such a lovely and talented woman."

I tried to relax while I fed Mari.

"I hope the police find out who killed her." Mom sighed as she looked down at her hands. "Will you stay for lunch? I was just cooking up one of my practice recipes. I'd love to know what you think."

She dabbed at her teary eyes as she rose from the heated table and returned to the kitchen. I scooted to the left so I could see her at the stove.

"Um, I suppose? What are you making?"

Mom knew I wasn't a fan of her traditional cooking. It had always been a sticking point between us when I was growing up. I'd wanted junk food, and she cooked only the stuff that was good for me.

She glanced over her shoulder at me and smiled.

"Ramen. Homemade noodles."

"Oh. Well then, yes, please." I loved ramen so that would always be a yes.

"I'm testing out a pork and onion broth. Easy to make, simple, not too challenging for the aspiring chef."

"Sounds like fun. And it smells great too. I told Emi that I wouldn't be back to the tea shop until later today. I wanted to get cracking on the murder case."

Mom paused, pulling her noodles out of the hot water bath.

"Oh no, Mei. You're not going to get involved in this mess, are you? What about Mari?"

I looked down at my daughter, nursing at my chest, and I had a pang of regret for telling Kumi I'd help her.

"Well —" I began, but Mom continued.

"Sometimes these investigations can be dangerous. You were almost burned alive. And then that man..." She paused to remember his name, a name I'd never forget.

"Fujita Takahara," I filled in.

"Yes, him. He attacked you. And what about the bear incident?"

She slipped the batches of noodles into bowls of broth and garnished the tops with sliced green onions and bits of pork.

"I forgot about the bear," I mumbled.

Oops, Mari had fallen asleep at the breast. Her little mouth laid open, dribbled with milk. Sigh. I'd do anything to sleep that peacefully. I slipped my shirt down and tucked myself back into my bra.

"How could you forget about the bear?" Mom asked, setting the bowls on the table. She saw Mari and lowered her voice. "Really. It's just not safe, and you have a family now."

Mom was right, of course. These were all concerns I'd had the moment I found out Noriko was dead.

I decided to switch tactics with Mom.

"You're right. Absolutely. It isn't safe to do any investigations on my own like I have in the past."

Mom blinked. "I'm glad you can see reason on this."

She hustled back to the kitchen to grab our chopsticks. I had a pair I kept at Mom's, a new pair I'd purchased after the flood to replace the old ones lost in the disaster.

"This is why Kumi and I have decided to tackle this case together." I leaned forward, gently so as not to wake Mari, to inhale over the bowl. Wow. That smelled like a proper bowl of ramen.

"Mei," Mom admonished me, "you know that's not what I meant."

"I really want to help. And besides, if Goro can solve this case, then he's next in line for a promotion." I raised my eyebrows. "With a pay raise and everything. Not only would it be good for the town and the police force to solve this case, but it would also be good for our friends."

Mom thought about it for a moment as she swirled the soup in her bowl. Oil from the broth dotted the surface and mixed in with the noodles. She hummed with pleasure. There was nothing better than a well-made meal for my mother. It was something she looked forward to with every step into the kitchen.

I decided to put my cards on the table and bare all.

"Mom, I want to repair my reputation with everyone in town."

She stopped blowing on her noodles to look at me.

"I know how upset you were with the rumors last year. I know that I can help make things better for me, for my family, for you too, if I can show I'm useful in situations like this."

"You don't have to do this for me, Mei." Mom's voice was quiet and soft, and I knew I had said the right thing.

"I need to find my calling, Mom. I've been lost since I moved home. I thought it was the tea shop, and I love helping the elderly, but that's not it. It's not being married with a family, although that's pretty great too."

"Then what?"

I shrugged. "I don't know." I gestured to her. "Think about your life. Farming was what you did to keep us afloat, but your passion has always been cooking. Cooking and sharing your knowledge has always been your calling. What's mine?"

Suddenly, a moment from when I first arrived home popped into my head. "Mom, remember when I moved home, and we were working in fields, and I was despairing about my life?"

Her smile was full of sarcasm. I plowed on.

"You said this was a detour and I should get back in my studio and paint." I closed my eyes and remembered that moment before everything went wrong. "That I should work out my feelings until I found my path, and you would be happy with whatever I decided on."

"I remember." And though her voice was easy and non-confrontational, I detected a small sigh, almost as if she regretted being reminded of her words. "Do you think your calling is in investigation work?"

I relaxed a little now that I felt she was helping me, not questioning me.

"Maybe? I think, if I can make a difference in this case, even with a baby in tow, I'll know for sure."

Mom stirred her bowl of noodles while she thought about this.

"You'll promise to be careful?" She leaned over to look at Mari asleep on my lap.

"Of course," I whispered back and punctuated it with a smile.

"I'll take her so you can eat first." Mom held out her arms, and I paused with surprise.

"No, I can hold her. You eat."

"Mei, give me my grandchild," she insisted, and I gave in immediately. Gently, and with as little movement as possible, I transferred sleeping Mari into Mom's waiting arms. She stirred but didn't wake. A successful move!

"Oh, before I forget." I leaned to the side to grab my bag from the floor and find my phone, so I could show her the business card of the photographer. "I found that photographer, Ryosuké Nagatomo."

Mom took my phone and looked at the card while I stirred up my soup to taste, adding a little seven-spice chili powder to give it a kick. My belly growled, and I worried that I would eat all of this food and want a nap. I couldn't afford to rest today.

I needed to return to the tea shop, speak to Emi about her last days of employment, and think about how I would get by without her. Inventory needed to be done, and new teas and snacks had to be ordered. There was so much to do.

Mom handed my phone back before I could eat.

"Will you call him for me? I'm... I don't feel right intruding on his business."

"Mom, it's his business to be a photographer and get new clients." I tried to push her hand away, but I didn't want to jostle Mari.

"Please? Just the initial contact. Be my personal assistant so I sound important enough to work with."

Oh boy. Mom's ego was flaring.

"Does this personal assistant job have a paying salary? Or is it an honorary title?"

Mom's smile bordered on wicked. "That will all have to depend on how well you do the job."

I see. Slave labor, then, I thought, keeping it to myself.

I grabbed a spoon and lifted the soup to my lips for a slurp. Salt and fatty pork burst across my tongue, and I murmured with pleasure.

"Delicious."

Switching to the chopsticks, I tasted the noodles, and they were perfect, not too soft, and they held their shape well.

"Great job, Mom," I said around a mouthful of food, my hand hovering over my lips.

"I'm glad you like them."

She leaned back in her kotatsu seat and held Mari to her chest, smiling as I sucked down the whole bowl without stopping.

CHAPTER
ELEVEN

With a belly full of noodles and a happy baby, I returned to Oshabe-cha after lunch in a pleasant mood. It was amazing what good food and a few hours of sleep could do for me. Would I get that lucky again tonight? Last night, Mari spent the evening happy with the sounds of the vacuum cleaner and then slept peacefully, probably, if I had to guess, because she didn't spend five hours screaming at the top of her tiny lungs.

Inside the shop, the atmosphere was bustling, all the tables were full, and Emi spoke to tourists who had stopped in for tea on their way up the mountain to the local temple.

"Mei!" Murata cheered as I walked in the door. "There you are. I was hoping I'd see you and Mari today." She sat in a comfortable spot, away from the door, a steaming cup of tea in front of her, her tablet propped to the side, and a blanket across her lap. I had convinced her to buy a reading tablet to get her news and stop delivery of the newspaper. Though the screen was too bright for her sometimes, she could increase the size of the text and read a lot easier.

I pulled Mari from the stroller, folded it up, and shifted it into the stairwell up to the apartment.

Murata opened her arms. "I've washed my hands recently," she said, wiggling her fingers for my baby. I melted a little as I deposited my baby into her arms, and Murata gave her a metal spoon to touch and gnaw on. Mari's hand-eye coordination got better every day.

I sighed as I fell into a spot opposite her at the table.

"How long have you been here?" I asked, pulling my scarf from around my neck. The weather was cooler today, and the sky threatened rain again. I was sick of the clouds. Where was the sun? Still, the walk from Mom's apartment to the tea shop had been nice. It was a good fifteen-minute walk across town, the perfect distance to walk off a heavy lunch.

"Since late morning. I was hoping I'd catch you today." She bounced Mari on her lap while holding her upright and against her chest.

Mari lifted the spoon to show me her prize. "Look at you! You have a spoon!" I cooed at her. She smashed the spoon into her mouth.

I stretched my shoulders and arms. They both ached from all the baby carrying, lifting, pushing and pulling I had been doing lately.

"I plan to be here for a few hours. There's a mountain of paperwork for both the tea shop and the house I have to sift through." That mountain of paperwork was sitting on the table in the back room. I'd give myself a few minutes of rest before I went to get it.

"Emi told me she gave notice of her last day." Murata looked behind her at the register where Emi was attending to a few customers.

"Yes. She'll be with us for about two weeks and then she's off to school. I'm glad she's continuing with her education, but we'll miss her around here."

Emi bid goodbye to the tourists as they left the shop, waved hello, and slipped into the back room.

Murata leaned forward and dropped her voice. "What are you going to do once she's gone?"

"I'm not sure what you mean?" I dug around in my bag for my phone, suddenly sure I had left it at Mom's place. Nope. But it was dead. It was a good thing I had a phone charger in the back room, not far from the mountain of paperwork.

"Mei, I'm really proud of you for opening this tea shop and taking charge of your life, but you have gone from 'no work' to 'too much work' in the span of a year. Add in the baby and a husband, and you look manic half the time I see you. Exhausted the other half."

I burst into a laugh, and Murata nodded her head.

"See? This is what I'm talking about. Even your laugh is bordering on psychotic these days."

I pressed my hand to my mouth, chastened. I was sure I seemed a little unhinged to everyone around me.

Emi emerged from the back room with a stack of paper and sat down at the table across from me. "So, it's time to go over some details I don't want to be missed when I leave here in two weeks."

My stomach sank, and my scarred back tingled as she started with the invoices, the bills, the calendar, and the correspondence I had to pick up again. Funny that five months ago, we were in opposite places, and I was handing these tasks to Emi. I had done these and more before I had a baby. Now, I wasn't sure when I would fit them in. Maybe I could set aside twenty minutes every night to go through the most critical tasks first? Considering most nights I went to bed right after Mari, that would be difficult.

Murata watched us both from the corner of her eye as the pile of papers grew in front of me. I placed my hand on the top of it and sighed.

"Are you sure you can't stay, Emi? I really need an employee around here."

Emi smiled. "You know I wish I could, Mei —"

I lifted my hand. "Say no more. Your education is important. I'm just feeling a little... a little overwhelmed."

Mari banged her spoon on the table a few times. We all watched her be happy for a moment.

"Would you like the contact info for my friend I mentioned the other day? I checked with her to see if she had availability and she does." Emi pulled her phone out, and I realized again that my phone was dead. I should've plugged it in before we started on this meeting.

I took Mari from Murata's arms so she could drink some tea.

"Are you hiring someone new, Mei?" Murata asked, pleased with this development.

"Oh, I don't know," I said, brushing it off. "I really need someone to take care of the tea shop. Not a housekeeper."

"A housekeeper?" Murata sipped her tea. "Well, that sounds like a better option than finding someone to replace either you or Emi. Both of you are irreplaceable."

"Thanks," Emi said, blushing. "But my friend is especially efficient, and she loves to help. I think she'd make a great addition to your team, Mei."

I hesitated and didn't respond.

"Just think of all the things she can do for you, at home and here. She can run to the store or pick up boxes from the post office. She can clean your apartment or make lunches or take Mari out for walks in the stroller. She could even help clean here in the tea shop, do dishes, or whatever. I bet she could free up enough time for you to pick up all of your duties here and still spend plenty of time with Mari."

Okay, yes, this sounded like a good idea... an excellent idea, even.

"I like this idea, Mei," Murata prodded. "You could use the help, and I think you'd be happier working more here again."

"Okay. Okay." I relented, but I laughed at the same time. "You all really know how to wear someone down."

"Let me send you her information." Emi turned on her phone. "Oh, I forgot to mention that she's into art, so I think you'll have a lot in common."

"Great! I love talking to other people about art." I picked up my phone and stood up. "Send it my way, but my phone is dead, and I need to go plug it in before I get to all the paperwork."

"I'll take Mari," Emi said, wiggling her fingers at us. I handed the baby off, and Emi slowly walked her around the room.

In the back, I plugged my phone in and waited for it to charge for a few moments before powering it on. The sink was piled with dishes, but Emi would handle that, and my recent painting sat unfinished. Would I ever have a few hours straight to work on it again?

My phone buzzed with new messages from Kumi. *"Call me when you get this."*

Oh, I wonder what this is? Information on Noriko? My land?

I moved closer to the wall so I wouldn't pull the cord out of the socket, and I dialed up Kumi.

"There you are. I was wondering why you weren't texting back," Kumi said.

"I forgot about my phone, and it died. Sorry. What's up?" I let my gaze wander around the room while I waited for Kumi's answer.

Yes, I needed someone to help me handle the place. Three large cardboard cartons of bento boxes against the far wall needed to be unpacked and inventoried, and the baseboards needed to be scrubbed. I imagined what my life would be like with extra time, real extra time. Emi had been a great addition to the tea shop, but now that she was leaving, I was in a real pinch. There was so much to do in so little time and with too few hands.

And then I realized Kumi had been talking for a whole minute and I missed everything she said.

"Wait, wait, wait. Sorry, I missed that. Say it again?"

"Mei, pay attention!" She admonished me. "Kayo and I are coming by around five to get you. Our first stop tonight will be to Izakaya Jūshi so we can gather information from Hideo about the man Noriko ate with the other night."

Five o'clock was edging on the unhappy hours for Mari, and that made my stomach tighten. But maybe being out and about would distract her from her transformation into Baby From The Underworld. I wasn't sure. This five-hour screamfest every night had only been happening for just over two weeks, and I was hoping that it would end by her three-month growth spurt.

There was only one way to find out.

"Sounds like a plan. I'll be here at Oshabe-cha, closing up."

"Sure. We'll see you then. Maybe we can grab dinner out too?"

"Anything's possible," I replied.

"That's the spirit," she cried into the phone before she hung up.

CHAPTER
TWELVE

Kumi and I parked our strollers to the left of the door as we entered Izakaya Jūshi. Mari and Taiga looked at each other, each fascinated with the other baby in the stroller.

So far, so good. I fed Mari right before we left, and she was in a happy mood. I hoped it lasted for an hour or two.

Kayo led the way to the bar. We hardly ever sat there, preferring to sit at a table when there were a bunch of us. But we weren't there to eat.

"Hi Kayo, I wasn't expecting you today." Hideo's smile was bright and familiar, and once again, my instincts buzzed. Something about him was different when he talked to Kayo now, softer, happier.

I glanced at Kumi, but she was intent on the matter at hand.

"Sorry to drop by out of the blue," Kayo said, "but we have a few questions for you we think you may be able to answer."

"No need to apologize. I'm always happy to see you all." He turned his smile on Kumi and me. I smiled back.

"The other night, when we were here for my birthday, there

was a woman and a man, sitting over at that table." Kumi pointed to the table Noriko had sat at. "Mei had stopped to talk to them briefly. Do you remember them?"

"I do." Hideo reached under the bar for three glasses and filled them with water, setting each in front of us. "I know them both. The woman, Noriko Kubo, moved to town about six months ago. I think she's teaching classes at the community center."

"That's how we know her." I pointed between Kumi and me. Kayo jotted down something in her notebook.

"She's dead," Kumi said, shocking Hideo. He pulled back with wide eyes.

"No. When?"

"Possibly Sunday night or early Monday morning. We're still waiting on the autopsy report." Kayo shifted into one of the bar chairs and sipped at the water. "But, it's my guess, as well as Goro's, that she was killed not long after she was here."

"Where is Goro?" he asked, glancing towards the door.

"In a meeting with the chief." She pulled her phone from her pocket and glanced at it. "We're going to meet him soon. So, I was wondering if you knew the man who was with her on Sunday night? He may have been the last person to see her alive."

"I do know him — he's from around here — but Mom knows more about him than I do. His name's Yutaka Mikami. He has a reputation for being someone who invests in businesses. Independently wealthy. But, I don't know. He's always been a little shifty. Hold on."

Hideo left and disappeared into the back, then returned to the front with his mother. She bowed to us and tried to smile through her unease. Ever since her daughter, my friend, Etsuko, had died, she'd been wary of the police. When Kayo visited, not in uniform, Hideo's mom's posture relaxed, and her smiles were more generous.

"You're asking about Yutaka Mikami? Yes, I know him. He

invested in my friend's internet startup, some technology that helps restaurants in the city connect with farmers."

This piqued my interest. "Oh really? For what purpose?"

She rested her hands on the bar and looked at the ceiling. "Hmmm, I believe it helps restaurants buy local produce and plan out what to buy for their menus. I have a business card for it if you're interested."

"Yes, this sounds like something Yasahiro would be interested in. Thanks."

She relaxed a little more. "Anyway, this is what he does for a living now. Small time venture capitalism. He invests a sizable sum in a small company and then makes back that money, usually. I've heard he's had bad investments now and then, though." Her cheek twitched.

Kayo leaned in. "And what happens when his investments don't pay?"

"Well..." Hideo's mom shifted back and forth. "It's just rumors, but I've heard things. Property damage. Harassment. Those types of things."

"Hmmm." Kayo scribbled in her notebook again. "I'll look him up at the station and see if there are any outstanding complaints about him."

"What's going on?"

We explained about Noriko and her eyes filled with tears. "So much death in this town. This is what happens when strangers move here."

"Mom." Hideo's voice was full of warning. "It's been good to see Chikata revitalized. Think about how many new friends we've made in the last two years, how prosperous the izakaya has been."

She shook her head and left, saying nothing else.

"She misses Etsuko. We all do. But I'm happy to see new people here. I guess some things come at a price."

I looked over to the door and our babies cooing at each other from the strollers.

Hideo was right about that.

"So where can we find Yutaka Mikami? Does he live in town?"

Hideo pulled a white towel from behind the bar and wiped the condensation from the surface of the glasses. "He does. He lives in an old house, recently renovated, to the rear of the train station. Nice place. He inherited that from his family as well as his money. His father was a banker, I think." He shrugged.

"Thanks," Kayo said, flipping her notebook closed. "I may send Mei or Kumi back to ask more questions later."

Hideo grinned. "Calling on the local experts to help out?"

Kayo returned his grin, and this time her eyes crinkled at the corners. "The chief has always believed that we should call on the community for help in cases like this. When we work together, we keep the town safer for everyone. Of course, the chain of evidence must be maintained, and searches must be legal, but otherwise, we can always use the help."

"I'll keep my eyes and ears open for you."

"Ask your mom to get me that business card when you get a chance, okay?" I said, stepping away from the bar.

"Sure. I'll bring it by Oshabe-cha for you." Hideo nodded as he cleared our water glasses.

"Thanks for your help, Hideo," Kayo said, and this time, Kumi poked me in the side. She saw the sparks between these two as well! It was subtle, but there was something brewing.

"Let's head to the station and find out what Goro is up to." Kayo ushered us away to return to the strollers, and Kumi and I raised our eyebrows at each other.

Nothing like a little budding romantic relationship to keep everything interesting.

———

If I thought the police station was busy on a regular day, it was always in overdrive when dealing with a murder investigation. The bullpen teemed with people, officers and staff, and someone had set up the community whiteboard with all the details of the case so far.

Kayo, Kumi, and I walked in and tried to stay out of the way, difficult to do with two strollers.

I inspected the board, laid bare with the intimate details of Noriko's life. She had been thirty-six years old when she was killed. She had been married and divorced. She had a sister in Nagano, but they were from Hokkaido, and Noriko had lived in Tokyo for ten years before moving to Chikata. Her in-laws and former husband lived in town as well. Presumably, she had moved here when she was still married to the ex and had decided to stay? The timeline wasn't clear.

I released Mari from the stroller and held her as I approached the whiteboard. She was getting fussy and needed to be at home, but I was hoping to hold off another twenty minutes, if possible.

"What do you see, Mei?"

Goro approached and stood with me at the board.

"Hmmm, I see the fall of a successful woman."

Looking through the timeline of Noriko's life, one thing became clear. She'd had it all and lost it, despite the way she presented herself to her students.

Until two years ago, she had worked in Tokyo as the marketing director at a media firm. She'd been married, but they had no children. Her life had been one upward step after another from college onward until one day when it all fell to pieces.

I pointed to the board. "What do you think happened here?" I shifted Mari from one arm to the other, and she clutched at my shirt.

"Don't know yet."

The board read, 'Left job. Divorced.'

"Did she leave the job? Or was she forced out? What did her husband do?"

"He worked for the same company. Chief Technical Officer."

He pointed to the man's name on the board, Takuma Kubo.

I nodded, a picture forming in my head. The scene was patchy and full of conjecture, but I thought it held merit. Something happened between Noriko and her husband, and because he had been in a position of power, he divorced her and pushed her out of the company.

"I'd check on that first. If she left the company of her own volition, then she might have been happy to find a quieter life here in the country, away from Tokyo, though I'm not sure I'd move to my ex-husband's hometown. If not, if she was forced out, then she was here and bitter about it. I'm going to guess the latter is true."

Goro smirked. "One mind, you and me. I had the same thoughts."

"Have you found the woman she was with on Thursday evening? After class, Kumi, Mom, and I saw Noriko speaking with a young woman, and the conversation looked quite aggravated." Speaking of aggravated, Mari was getting fussy.

"This the same woman Kayo saw her with at the convenience store?"

"I think so? I can't be sure, but the description sounded the same."

Goro nodded as he flipped through his notebook. "We're looking for her. Can you give me a description? Anything you noticed about her? I'll add it to the report."

I thought back on those few moments I had seen them both and tried to call up as many details as I could while Mari whined and squirmed. I looked at the clock on the wall and it read 18:28, time for both of us to head out before Mari's screamfest.

"I'm sorry," I said, sighing and flipping Mari over onto her belly to carry her like a football. "I wish I could help you more, but Yasahiro won't be home from here to eternity, and I have to take care of this fussy baby on my own. I don't know how much help I'll be on this case."

I glanced over my shoulder at Kumi. She was talking to Kayo, and they were both looking at Kayo's notes.

"Kumi was really upset about Noriko's death. How is she?"

"Determined," Goro said with a huff. "She was working on getting Noriko into classes in Kawagoé. Kumi has a college friend who was facilitating the deal."

I looked at Kumi again. I had missed a lot while birthing and taking care of a baby.

"What was it about Noriko that inspired Kumi to help her out?"

Goro folded his arms across his chest. "I'm not sure. They met at Kutsuro Matsu and hit it off right away. Despite Kumi making a lot of effort to spend personal time with Noriko, though, they only met for lunch once or twice before the classes started." He shrugged. "You know Kumi. She sees the best in people, seeks out those who need help, and then latches onto them. Happened to you." He uttered a wry chuckle.

"Happily," I replied. I turned back to the board. "So, the ex-husband, Takuma, is the prime suspect, right? There's bad blood there, and it's possible he killed her for something in their past relationship?"

"Exes are always the prime suspects. But there could've been more going on, especially with what you learned at Izakaya Jūshi. Yutaka Mikami is not a man we look upon as honest and forthright. He's put a lot of people into debt, lost a lot of respect with people here in the community. He makes me cautious."

The door to the chief's office opened, and Chikata's mayor, Shin Tajima, exited and nodded to people as he passed us and walked out of the police station. The chief, Naito Ohashi, got up from his desk and closed his office door.

Goro leaned in. "He's been on shaky ground since inviting

Midori Sankaku into town to do business here. Tourism has increased, and the real estate business is thriving. But crime is up too. Obviously."

"Obviously. And no one likes that."

"No one. Even Mom was complaining about it the other day, and you know how she feels about all the new business. She loves it."

"It's a sword that cuts both ways," I said, shrugging. "All the crime keeps you busy and away from her, away from her family, too."

"What can I say? I'm loved." He broke out in a belly laugh and threw back his head. Mari let out a wail in response.

"Oh no. My humor is lost on babies."

Across the floor in Kumi's arms, Taiga laughed and clapped, waving to his father.

"Not all babies." It was tough not to feel sad about that. Why was my baby so unhappy?

"She'll grow out of it. I promise," Goro said, reaching over to pat Mari on the butt. "What's this about Yasahiro not being around?"

"Sawayaka is too busy for him to leave. Drop by and ask him yourself."

I walked away from the board to get Mari into her stroller and out of the station before she distracted everyone.

"Mei," Goro called, trotting after me, "would you like a ride home? You look exhausted."

I joined Kumi, and she held the stroller while I strapped Mari in.

"No thanks. I don't want to take you away from the case. I'll walk her home. Maybe it'll calm her down."

I got us both bundled up, and Kumi handed me my bag.

"Tomorrow, let's go visit your new neighbors and ask about your property before we get involved with this case again. Okay?" Kumi squeezed my upper arm.

"Yeah, sounds great." My voice was weak with fatigue, but I managed a small smile.

I looked back at the room on my way out, and everyone was busy but Goro and Kumi who watched me all the way to the door. I couldn't help but feel they pitied me right then. Maybe they did.

CHAPTER
THIRTEEN

Yasahiro groaned, stumbled out of bed, and tripped on the vacuum cleaner in the other room, swearing loudly. I opened my eyes to slits to see if the commotion had woken Mari, but she was out. Could I close my eyes and sleep some more? Maybe. My husband ground coffee beans in the kitchen and kept my conscious thoughts churning. I wanted to spend time with him, but I also wanted to stay in bed. He had worked late last night, and I hadn't even heard him come to bed. I had been dead asleep when he'd arrived back home.

"Hey," I said, emerging from the bedroom and shifting a throw blanket around my shoulders. I gently closed the bedroom door behind me. "Morning."

His face softened. "Morning." He yawned as he turned on the extravagant coffee maker. I only knew how to work one function on it. Hot coffee. "The place looks different."

"It looks clean, you mean. I figured out that Mari won't cry for hours on end if the vacuum cleaner is running. And with her not crying, I can get a lot more done."

He leaned against the counter and rubbed his hand over his chin. "That explains so much, including my stubbed toe."

I nodded, my head bouncing to a slow beat, which was all my body could take. "She even falls asleep sooner and sleeps better."

"So, you've been busy cleaning?" He tried to hand me the first cup of coffee, but I waved it away.

"I'm going back to sleep. I just wanted to see you. Yes, I've been cleaning the last two nights."

"I'd prefer it if you relaxed. You always look so tired."

"I believe it's a rite of passage to be tired as a new parent." I shrugged. "But this is why I'm going back to sleep."

He shut off the coffee maker and crossed the room to me. "Any word on the house? The property?"

"No. Hopefully later I'll know more. Kumi and I are going to talk to one of the new neighbors and go to the city offices to see the property registry. We only ever got the names of the last previous owner, and I'm hoping we can get more information by going to the source."

"Mei," he said with a sigh, "it's silly to go through all this work for land we own, for a house we've already paid for that hasn't even been built yet. There are no ghosts on our land."

I yawned as I bopped my head back and forth. "I know that. I don't believe in ghosts, but something is definitely going on there, and it's best to figure it out before we have to hire a whole new crew. And I don't want to be labeled as the town witch for all eternity."

I lifted myself from the chair, and he set his hand on my shoulder, leaning in for a kiss on my cheek.

"No, we can't have that. Go back to sleep and call me later. I'm going to set aside a table for you and Mari tonight. Come and eat with me. Don't worry about her being fussy. If she likes the white noise of the vacuum cleaner, then the restaurant will be fine."

"Will do." I waved as I shuffled off to bed.

———

WE KNOCKED ON MY NEW NEIGHBOR'S DOOR, AND KUMI gave me a confident nod. We were here to get things done, make some progress. First, we'd talk with her and see if she knew anything about the property, then we'd head to the town offices. I told Emi I'd show up at the tea shop around lunchtime. That would give us plenty of time to get the initial research done. I adjusted Mari in the baby carrier as she gnawed on the strap.

The front door slid open, and Moeko Asahara pulled up in surprise.

"Mrs. Suga, I wasn't expecting you this morning."

I bowed and held out a box of fresh-baked donuts that Goro picked up for us this morning. In true police officer fashion, Goro knew where all the good bakeries were in town. He didn't eat the baked goods, since he was watching his waistline, but officers who spent hours on patrol always knew the best places to eat.

"Sorry to bother you. But I wanted to come by and apologize again for all the trouble." I handed the box over. "And I was hoping we could talk about the neighborhood more."

Moeko's eyes widened. "Whatever's inside here smells good."

"Fresh donuts," Kumi interrupted. "Hello, I'm Kumi Hokichi. I'm a good friend of Mei's. I'm sure you'll be seeing a lot of my husband and me once Mei and her family has moved into the new place."

"Oh." She shifted back and forth. "Please come in."

We slipped into the front entryway and left our shoes on the cold stone floor.

"I think I've seen you before," Moeko said, gesturing us inside. She shuffled ahead of Kumi, leading us to her all-purpose room.

"Me?" Kumi pointed to herself. "Maybe so. Have you ever been to Kutsuro Matsu? My mother-in-law and I own and run the bathhouse."

"That's it!" She set the box of donuts on her low central table. I was surprised she didn't have a kotatsu, especially in this old and drafty house. But running a kotatsu cost money in electricity or gas. Moeko's tattered clothes and bare home spoke of a low-income livelihood.

"Let me put water on for tea." She made her way into the kitchen while Kumi and I sat at the low table.

"It's cold in here," Kumi whispered.

I nodded as I pulled Mari out of the carrier and propped her on my lap.

"I'm glad I left Taiga with Mom. Two babies in here would've probably have been a mistake. Mari is enough for us both." She winked and tickled Mari's chin.

While Kumi played peek-a-boo with Mari, I examined the room. The whole place was like something out of a time capsule. The television in the corner was at least fifteen years old, and there was a stack of second-hand DVDs piled up next to the console, a strange sight when almost everyone streamed content from the internet now. The *washi* paper in the sliding doors dividing up the room was yellowed with age, and the tatami mats were frayed on the edges. The room felt vacant, almost devoid of any character. Only a few framed photos were placed to the side of the family's personal shrine.

"Here we go," Moeko said, depositing mugs on the table and a box of tea bags. "Let me grab the hot water." She returned with an electric tea kettle moments later.

"I'm sorry again for all the noise and hassle of the last week. I know what an inconvenience it is to live with construction." I bowed from my sitting position and Mari cooed.

"Thank you for mentioning it again, but it's no bother. I was just worried about all the police activity."

"That's something you don't need to worry about," Kumi interrupted. "My husband is on the police force here, and he assures me there's no real problem and the police won't get involved again."

I didn't know this. I tried to hide my surprise behind my baby.

"Have you seen anything strange happening at the job site lately?" Kumi asked as she leaned forward to prepare cups of tea for us all.

"My husband and I came by a few nights ago, and I swore I saw something moving on the property." I left my mug where it was to cool down, which would be quick in this drafty house.

Moeko nodded as she dunked her tea bag in the hot water. "Last night, I was putting the trash out to the curb when I heard something happening over in your lot. It sounded like something had fallen over and was being rolled around?" She shook her head. "I ran right back inside because it spooked me, especially after you asked me if the property was stigmatized."

Kumi bounced lightly. "Do you think maybe it's haunted?"

I smacked her on the arm. "Do you think maybe you could sound less excited about that?"

Kumi chuckled. "I can't help it. I love ghost hunting."

This made Moeko smile, the first I had seen from her. "Well, I've always had a feeling the property was haunted. For the past year, strange things have been happening there. The front gate would sometimes be open, or I'd hear the sounds of howling, or a baby crying." She shivered, and it wasn't because of the chill in the air.

She paused, and my daydreams kicked in. A ghost mother, wearing a robe and slippers, paced the halls of the house we knocked down, holding her baby and singing lullabies. Maybe they had both died in some tragic accident? How long ago had it happened?

In no time, I had convinced myself the property was haunted, even though just yesterday I was blowing off this idea.

I sighed, disappointed with this turn of events. How would I fix this?

"Did you know the previous owners?" I slipped Mari to the

side so I could sip at the warm tea and not worry about her grabbing for the mug.

"Yes, I did, which is why I find the whole situation strange. They were good people, never any problem to us or the neighbors. Their children are still alive and well, living in Tokyo, I think."

"Yes. We met them when we bought the land."

She shook her head. "Then the other land you bought, those were also good neighbors. Never any problems. But I never saw or heard anything from that land."

We had purchased two adjacent lots with condemned homes, so this escalated the problem two-fold. One house had been occupied as recently as two years ago but damaged by a typhoon; the other had been abandoned for ten years. We knocked both houses down, and our main house would take up most of one and a half lots with a planned garden that would wrap around the house to give us privacy. Our connections with city hall and the town planning board made getting the permits easy, but we still had to conform to a lot of crazy building codes. With all the preparation work we had done, I wanted the house to get back on track.

"Do you remember anything about any of the previous owners before the recent ones?" I pushed the mug out of Mari's reach.

Moeko shook her head. "Sorry, but that was before my time. My husband and I moved here about twenty-five years ago. I'm originally from Shikoku, and he's from Aomori. Neither of us wanted to live near our families, so we chose a spot in between."

"And what does your husband do for a living?" Kumi asked, trying to keep the conversation going.

"He sells insurance." She waved a hand. "A boring but steady job, and he likes being out and talking with clients day after day. I used to teach primary school." She pressed her hand to her chest with pride. "And I did that for years after my children were born, but I retired ten years ago. Now I just garden and cook."

I summoned a smile up from deep in my stomach. "Well, my husband cooks, and I'm the gardener in my household."

"Mei doesn't enjoy gardening, but she has a green thumb. Everyone is jealous of her."

I rolled my eyes. "There's not one person on this planet who is jealous of *me*." I turned back to Moeko. "I helped my mother for years on her farm, so I know what to do and what not to do, but it was always a childhood chore—"

"And an adult chore," Kumi said.

"Yes it was," I affirmed. "I helped my mom until we sold the land late last year. Our house was destroyed in the typhoon."

"That typhoon was one of the worst I have ever seen," Moeko said, shaking her head. "A tragedy. I lost one of my favorite trees."

Kumi's phone buzzed, and she glanced at the screen. "Oh, look at the time. We should get moving if we're going to go to the city offices before lunch."

Moeko popped in surprise. "Leaving so soon? I haven't served the donuts yet." Her hand hovered over the box.

"Oh no, don't worry about that." I held out my hand, palm out, to stop her from fussing. "You and your husband should enjoy them. We're sorry for taking up your time this morning."

"It was no bother." Her face brightened with a new smile.

Considering that just yesterday she was yelling at me for having my baby out in the cold, this was an excellent turn around for our soon-to-be neighborly relationship. Donuts and tea could solve world peace, I was sure of it.

"What will you be doing at the town offices?" Moeko asked as she escorted us to the door.

"Kumi figured it was a good idea to research the past owners of my properties. If we can find the names, then we can do further research online or in the local newspaper archives."

"I can also run the names through the police's database and see if anything comes up," Kumi added, handing me my jacket after I got Mari back into the carrier.

"That's a smart move. I hope you get answers to your questions. I'll keep my eye on your property for the next few days."

"Thank you," I said, bowing. "Please feel free to call me if you see or hear anything. You have my card."

"I do." She jerked her head at the small table in her entrance hall where my business card sat in the open. Perfect.

"What will you do if you find out the land is haunted?" she asked, holding the door open for us.

"I'm not sure." I shrugged and pulled the hood up over Mari's head. "But I'll figure that out if I need to. Maybe get the land blessed again or call in an expert?"

"There are experts in stigmatized properties?" She laughed, wrapping her sweater around her frail figure tighter.

"It's the twenty-first century," I said with a wink. "Anything's possible."

CHAPTER
FOURTEEN

"I'm so glad that was a lot easier than I thought it would be," Kumi said with a sigh as we left the city administration building. Chikata was a small town, and I had built up quite the reputation as a helpful citizen (though a bit nosy) over the last few years. Between Kumi's pull as the wife of a police officer and my fame as a budding detective, we obtained the property records easily. Plus, now that I owned the land, I had every right to know who had owned it before me.

"I think I was owed the information, so I had a feeling it would be easy to get." I pushed Mari in the stroller as she snoozed away. Her late morning naps were always peaceful, and she took them on the go in the stroller, carrier, or car. I had about another ten minutes of peace before she woke up starving. Plenty of time to walk with Kumi to the police station.

Kumi glanced over at me. "So, before we get to the police station, Goro and I were talking the other day about something."

"What's that?"

"Well, we'd like to offer you and Yasahiro a date night."

I slipped her the side eye. "What's a date night?"

"Ha. No, really. I think the two of you could use a night out, away from work and the baby."

I walked in silence for a few moments while Kumi waited for my answer. But I just didn't have it in me to be deferential and kind. Not today. Not for a while.

"Come and talk to me again in a few months. Yasahiro can't take even one night off from the restaurant now, and Mari is a mess almost every evening. There's no way I'm going to subject you to that."

Kumi tried to skip ahead by a pace or two so she could get in my eye line. "In a month or two, you'll be completely broken in half, Mei. You don't want to fall into the same trap so many couples in this country fall into, right? We've talked about this."

Yes, we had talked about how men and women in Japan got married, had kids, and barely ever saw each other again. They fell out of love. Their relationships crumbled and died. Granted, some of the younger generations now got married and actually cared about work-life balance or made sure both parents took on the burdens of home life. But that was *if* they got married and had kids. I knew more single people than married people, and I doubted that would change with age.

Tears pooled in the corners of my eyes as I stalked along pushing Mari's stroller with aggressive forward momentum.

"Don't be upset," Kumi whispered, grasping my arm. I shook her off.

"Look at us," I blurted out. "Where's Taiga?"

The corners of her lips sunk in. "With Chiyo." She sighed.

"And where's my mother? My mother-in-law? My help and my family? I don't have it. Mom's eyesight is not that great still and asking her to watch Mari more would only frustrate her and make her angry for encroaching on her time. Plus, she won't set foot in my apartment with it looking like a bomb hit it. I can get her to come to Oshabe-cha a few times per week and watch Mari for an hour, but that's it."

"I'm sorry," she said, directing her eyes to the sidewalk in front of us.

"Don't be," I said, calmer now that I had put those words in the open. "It's not your fault. It is what it is. Yasahiro's parents live an hour away, and they only drive here three or four times a year, and then we go there too. Still, they're getting older and don't like to be in the car for long distances. My brother's family? I don't even want to see them after what happened with the house though I'm trying not to be bitter about the whole situation." I sniffed up and took a deep breath. The police station was only a block away. "I just have to deal."

"Let me help. I have my mom and Chiyo, and Goro has mostly regular hours."

I was determined not to be a charity case. "Mari is a joy during the day but a challenging baby at night, Kumi. She cries for hours every evening." I couldn't yet let myself believe I had found a solution with the vacuum cleaner. Any day now it would stop working, and Mari would go back to screaming for hours on end. I was sure of it.

Kumi shrugged. "So what? Babies cry. I'll deal with it."

I sighed. "You're not going to let this go?"

"Nope," she said with a bright smile. "I've even recruited Akiko and Kayo to convince you."

"Ugh. Fine. If you want this to happen, then talk to Yasahiro, and good luck convincing him to walk away from a packed house with a line out the door."

"I have my ways." She opened the police station's door for me, and we rolled into the outer office.

"Seito," she said, approaching the man at the front desk, "can you please find an open room for Mei to feed her baby while we wait for Goro?"

As I sat in someone's empty office and fed Mari, I stared out into space and tried not to get angry. Why was everyone butting into my life? I was struggling to keep my life together, and all these people wanted to poke their fingers in and find all the weak links. Or I was being ignored. It was always one of two extremes.

I closed my eyes and tried to imagine a date night out with Yasahiro. We'd had those before the baby was born, but now I couldn't picture it. So much had changed in the last six months. After I returned home from my girls' weekend away in Kayo's hometown, Yasahiro and I had spent plenty of quality time together before I became bedridden. He'd been able to hire a few extra people so he could stay home more and even plan for our future. We hadn't expected Sawayaka to get so much attention. That hadn't been in the long-term plans.

The situation would only get worse. People came from far and wide to eat at his restaurant, to eat food prepared by *him*, not someone else. I had to share him with all the thousands of people who would come in and out of the restaurant. I was still struggling with that realization.

It was all the more reason for me to have my own hobbies, my own businesses and social life. Sadness flooded through me as I contemplated not being able to share those things with Yasahiro because he would be too busy for me.

Don't cry, Mei.

The hormones after birth were still as bad as while pregnant.

Mari pulled away from my breast and looked up at me, happy and content. Ah, there was nothing like her smile to put me in a better mood. I covered myself up, smoothed down her wild hair and kissed her cheeks and neck before bringing her up to my shoulder for burping. This whole motherhood gig was pretty great when I got past the sleepless nights and constant state of exhaustion.

It will get better. It will get better.

I just had to repeat that in my head a billion times a day, and I'd believe it.

Someone knocked on the door and cracked it open slowly.

Seeing I was finished feeding Mari, Kumi opened the door all the way.

"We ordered lunch. Pizza and salads. Let's go eat. I need to leave in about forty-five minutes to meet Chiyo and Taiga at the bathhouse."

In a rare display of camaraderie, the chief made eyes at Mari and offered to hold her while I ate. She smiled at him like he was the best thing she had ever seen, and he melted like a snowball on a hot summer's day.

"Aw, I miss having children this small," he said, holding her at the conference room table and allowing her to bang a plastic spoon on an empty plastic container.

"Do you miss the sleepless nights and constant anxiety?" Several people around the table either laughed or raised their eyebrows. There were plenty of reasons I didn't conform to Tokyo corporate life, and I had been let go from many jobs in a row. Being late to work was one of them. Having a loose tongue was the other.

He clutched Mari as she leaned forward. "It was *a lot* of work and many sleepless nights, to be sure," he answered. "But I promise it'll be worth it."

I smiled, reassuringly. "That's what I keep telling myself."

I ate two slices of pizza though I could've eaten the whole pie myself. Hunger plagued me constantly, despite trying to use mind over matter and not care about food so much. I had quelled my appetite during the months of poverty I experienced the previous year, but that was before I had a baby to feed from my own body.

As the chief handed Mari back to me, the door to the conference room opened, and Kayo entered with a sheet of paper in her hand.

"Here you go, Mei," Kayo said, handing me the paper. "I looked up all of those previous owners for you, and only one came up in the police database."

Surprised I had the data I needed so quickly, I held the paper away from Mari's grabby hands and scanned down the list of information. The only person that the database had recognized was someone who lived on the property from 1974 to 1976. In the spring of 1975, the property owner, a man named Taizo Nogami, called an ambulance to the house to report a child who slipped while climbing the rocks in the house's outside garden. The little boy fell, hit his head, and became unresponsive.

I covered my mouth with my hand. The child had died in the hospital the next day.

"Oh no," I breathed out. "This is awful."

I passed the paper to Kumi, and after a moment, she gasped. "Oh no."

Goro inhaled the last of his pizza crust. "What's going on?" He beckoned for the paper. "Well, looks like your property *is* haunted, Mei," he said, trying to keep his smile undercover. "Maybe the dead child has returned and doesn't want anyone else moving in?"

I rolled my eyes. "There have been three other property owners since he passed away. I doubt this child's ghost suddenly cares now." But a gram of doubt clawed at my calm. What if a ghost had been wreaking havoc on the property for the last forty years, and that's why it was sold to us?

I didn't want to admit in a room full of police officers that I was afraid of ghosts. I wasn't afraid of ghosts... But as I bounced Mari on my lap, I had my doubts. It wouldn't be the most unusual thing to have a haunted property. I fully believed that we turned to spirits when we died, and I also believed spirits would want to hang out in the places they knew best. There was probably a world of spirits right behind the world I spent my time in.

A blast of cold air rushed over my back as the conference room door opened, and I shivered. There were probably hundreds of spirits hanging out in the police station.

"You look a little worried," Kumi said, snapping me out of my daydreams of the spirit world.

"Maybe a little, yeah." I turned Mari around so I could see her happy face. The pain of those parents, the ones who lost their own child to an accident, sat heavy in my heart. I was a new mom, and I hadn't gotten the hang of it yet, but I definitely loved my little girl. I didn't want anything bad to happen to her.

"What should I do?" I asked Kumi before bringing Mari's face to my lips for a kiss.

The tightness around my heart eased somewhat as she giggled.

The rest of the officers cleaned up the conference room table and prepared to go back to work as Kumi leaned closer.

"What if you did a little research on what happened? If we know more about them, we can ask a priest to bless the land again. Ask their spirits to give your property back to the living?"

My logical self wanted to brush aside this idea. Why couldn't this be easier with fewer trappings of superstition? I didn't have the time to be chasing down this lead with everything else going on in my life right now. I had to take care of Mom's photographer situation, the tea shop, my overtired and unhappy evening baby, and a ton of other things, including helping with the murder case happening around me.

I glanced out the conference room window to the whiteboard the officers were standing around. Noriko's life was fleshing out with more details added to the board. I squinted my tired eyes and took in the smaller details in the section entitled 'Students.' Were there any names there I knew besides Kumi and me?

As I pulled my eyes away from the board, a new idea bubbled to the surface of my scattered brain.

"Oh, I have an idea." I grabbed the last of my water bottle and stored it in the diaper bag I carried with me everywhere. "I should contact Sakiko Yoshida, that private investigator I met when I was working on Ria Fukuda's case. She's been working in this area for a long time. I bet she would know more about these people."

Goro handed the paper back to me, and I added it to my diaper bag. Mari began to fuss, so I grabbed a colorful toy and gave it to her.

"Good idea, Mei," Goro said, stepping to the side to let me through. "We'll have our hands full in the coming days with this murder case. I don't think I could spare anyone right now to look into this for you."

"Don't worry about it." I squeezed Mari's bottom, and yeah, that diaper was full. "I'm going to change Mari and head back to the tea shop. I have so much paperwork to do."

Goro checked his phone. "Are you sure you can't spare an hour? I was going to go corner Noriko's ex-husband. My officer on the scene says he's due back from lunch soon. I thought we could ambush him outside of his office."

I looked from Goro to Kumi and thought of everything I had to accomplish, but the pull of the investigation was too strong. Emi was handling the tea shop, and I needed to take advantage of these last few days of help.

"Go with him," Kumi urged me. "I need to get back to Kutsuro Matsu. Chiyo has to run errands, and I haven't seen Taiga all morning."

I sighed. "Okay. Fine." I laughed and shook my head. "It's ridiculous that my weakness is questioning suspects."

Goro handed me my bag. "I'll be waiting for you out in the car. Your stroller holds the car seat, right? We'll strap it in, and I'll put your stroller in the trunk."

Okay, then. Another detour, and then hopefully I'd be getting back to my life.

CHAPTER
FIFTEEN

was always pleased and slightly amazed that I could tag along for witness questioning, but I guess I had earned the privilege after helping with a few investigations. In the beginning, the police told me to stay home and stay out of the way. It was the same attitude I had witnessed in Kayo's hometown of Kubako when we traveled there last autumn. But community policing has always been the way of Japan. We watch out for each other. I believed I only ever got shut out because I hadn't been an actual part of the community for several years. Now that I was in, *I was in.*

Goro and I approached the small, squat, practically ancient building on the edge of town with some trepidation.

"Are you sure this street is even in Chikata?" I asked, looking up and down the long avenue. "We're so far from the center of town, we're almost in the next prefecture."

I kept Mari in the carrier, strapped to my chest, this time and left the stroller behind in the trunk of the police cruiser. She was quiet, but her eyes scanned the surroundings like the curious little being she was. I often wondered how the mind of a baby processed what they saw and heard. What would she remember of this time we spent together? Probably very little. Some people remembered details from their toddler years, but that was rare.

Once again, my mind was wandering.

"We're right on the edge of town. Low-rent district." Goro craned his head back to look at the signs on each building as we passed.

"What did you say this guy does? Wasn't he the CTO of a big media firm? What's he doing in a run-down building in Chikata?"

"He *was* the CTO of a big Tokyo media firm, but he left that place at the same time Noriko did. I have a feeling they were both forced out though no one is talking about it. Now he runs a web design agency." He stepped back from one of the buildings and nodded. "This is the one, Tokoro Media."

The roof's shingles were cracked, and rust coated the two street-facing windows. If you opened a dictionary and flipped to 'dilapidated,' there would be a picture of this building.

Goro tried to open the front door, but it was locked. He rang the bell and knocked. No one answered.

"An officer was just here forty-five minutes ago and said he went to lunch. He may not be back yet."

"Are we going to hover until he returns? Do you think we could do it in the car?" I shivered as a cool breeze swept up the street. It still wasn't beautiful every day like we all wished it would be. Some days the sun would shine with a blue sky, and yet, it would still be as cold as a brick outside. Very deceiving.

"I'd rather be here to jump on him when he comes back. If he makes it inside, he could just shut us out."

We moved into a pattern of shuffling feet and humming to keep warm.

"Have you gotten any more information on the time of death from the coroner?" I asked, trying to keep my mind sharp on so little sleep.

"Oh yes, I meant to call you. The coroner said that with the ambient temperature of that night and the cold stone Noriko laid on, she estimates the murder occurred around three or four in the morning. No earlier."

"No earlier? Hmmm. Someone woke her up in the middle of the night to kill her?"

Goro shrugged. "Our coroner is one of the best around. She serves most of this side of the prefecture. She said the body was too warm to have been out there all night."

Okay then. Three or four in the morning.

"So, did Kumi mention our idea to get you and Yasahiro a date night?"

I tried not to groan. I really did. My humming took on an aggressive tone instead.

"She might have mentioned it, yeah. I just don't see how I'll make it happen. Mari cries for hours every single night. I can't let you guys be subjected to that."

I didn't mention the new vacuum cleaner revelation. It could have been a fluke, anyway.

Goro waved away my worries. "Babies cry. I'm sure it's not that bad."

I tipped my head to him. "Look at my roots. I'm sprouting gray hairs so quickly I'll never keep up even if I get my hair colored every month. This is what five hours of crying every night does to a person. I'm literally two night's of broken sleep away from cowering in a corner and mumbling to myself."

"All the more reason to get away and give yourself a break." He shrugged. "Besides, Kumi insists, and she won't let this idea go. If you have any warm thoughts in your heart for me and my sanity, you'll do it to save me the constant discussions and nagging."

Movement up the block caught my eye. Saved by the witness!

"Look, I think he's coming."

It had to be him. The block was quiet and empty with hardly anyone around. Not a lot of foot traffic to this part of town. His stride was full of purpose, getting back to the office, and his eyes were trained on his phone instead of the path ahead of him.

We stood and waited, and he was so engrossed with whatever was on his phone that he almost ran straight into us.

"Oh! Sorry," he said before he registered Goro's uniform. "Can I help you?"

His face fell into a deep frown, and he took a small step back, signs he wasn't happy to see us.

"Takuma Kubo? I'm Goro Hokichi with the Chikata Police Department. We need to ask you a few questions. Can we come inside?"

"Who's she?" he asked, jerking his chin at me.

"This is Mei Suga, my assistant."

A laugh burst from my lips, and I covered it by coughing. His assistant? Was this the new cover story?

"All right there, Mei?" Goro gave me a slap on the back, and Mari squeaked.

"I'm fine." I shot lethal daggers at him with my eyes.

Takuma's eyes focused on Mari, and I said, "The police department has a great working-mother program."

"Can we talk inside?" Goro gestured to the door, and Takuma sighed and pushed past us to open the door and beckon us in.

"Fine." He sighed. "How long will this take? I have a lot of work to do."

He led us down a long hallway to an office in the back of the building. The place was as cold as it was outside. When he flicked on the light, a small space heater hummed to life, and a few computers booted up.

I could understand shutting off a space heater while out to lunch, but all the computers as well? Only if I really had to save money on electricity. And, yes, this was something I did when we went through that period of poverty last year. I unplugged everything we weren't using all the time.

"So?" His behavior was aggressive as he threw himself into a creaking office chair. "What's this about now? Who's complaining this time?"

Goro and I glanced at each other.

"Because if it's my upstairs neighbor, they have no right to tell me not to walk around my home at night. She said she'd call the police, but I didn't think you'd actually follow up on it."

"Do you have regular complainants?" Goro asked. Per usual, he didn't help himself to a seat, but I had no issue with planting my butt someplace. I turned and found a threadbare couch, set my bag on it, grabbed my notebook, and then sank into the sad cushion with a sigh. I supposed if I had to be an 'assistant' I should play the part and take notes. Mari grasped my cheek and squeezed. Ow. Man, her grip was strong.

"Who doesn't complain nowadays? Oh! Let me guess. My next-door neighbor has had it with my recycling situation?"

Goro shook his head. "Nope."

"Ah, then it must be the jerk who owns this building. I've only ever missed one rent payment. So what if I never put the garbage out in time for pickup? If he continues to complain about the excessive garbage in the storeroom, I'm going to find another place to keep my office. He's lucky to have me in this dump."

Bluster. Something told me he couldn't afford to move his office, and there was no way he could pay for anything better.

"Sorry. We haven't had any complaints about you," Goro said, not sounding sorry at all. "What is it you do here?"

Takuma removed his phone from his pocket and placed it on the desk next to him. "I build websites for companies. Nothing fancy but I've had some big profile jobs."

Goro glanced at his notebook. "That's a hefty step down from the CTO of a Tokyo media firm."

Takuma paused. "Yes, it is. Why are you here?"

I wrote in my notebook that he had avoided talking about his work.

"When was the last time you spoke to your ex-wife, Noriko Kubo?"

"Her?" His eyes lifted to the ceiling. "Three or four weeks ago? Wait. I saw her at the Midori Sankaku sometime last week, but we didn't speak. I'm not even sure she saw me." He shrugged. "Why?"

"We regret to inform you that she was killed two nights ago."

I waited for the reaction. Sometimes people found out about the death of a loved one, and they entered a state of shock, a state of disbelieving. Like they didn't know if they misheard what was said.

"What?" He jumped to his feet. "What?" he repeated.

Goro stood his ground and stared at Takuma. I was impressed. Goro had changed a lot in the last two years, and this was a sign of his maturity. He used to talk first to cover up his insecurities and then fix things later. Now, he waited for the other person to blink first.

"Where were you two nights ago? Sunday evening?" Goro kept his eyes on Takuma while he waited for the answer, his pen poised over his notepad. I bounced Mari lightly in the carrier from my seat on the couch.

"Where was I? You don't think...?" Kubo's face flattened. "Why would I possibly want to hurt Noriko?"

Goro cooly glanced at me. "When did he leave the media firm in Tokyo?"

I closed my eyes for a brief moment and pictured the board at the police station. "Three years ago. The same time Noriko left the firm."

"Hmmm," Goro said, returning his attention to Takuma. "You both left at the same time and divorced a month later. Why is that?"

"That's none of your business," Kubo spluttered, but his face was as white as snow. "I'm sure it has nothing to do with her death."

"He hasn't answered the question, or any questions, yet," I pointed out to Goro and turned my stare on Takuma. He squirmed under our combined gazes. "Where were you the night Noriko was killed? Sunday night."

"Out. Drinking," he spat out finally. "There's this izakaya I like that has great drink specials. I go there all the time."

"How late were you there?" Goro scratched information into his notebook.

"Around one in the morning. My girlfriend and I took a taxi home afterward."

"Your girlfriend? I'm going to need a name." Goro's eyebrows climbed. A girlfriend made things interesting. If he had moved on from Noriko, that made him less of a suspect.

"Erina Ichisé. She lives in Kawagoé."

"Do you have any photos of her?" I asked, finishing off my notes.

"Uh..." He glanced at his phone. "No, actually. She hates having her picture taken."

This statement sounded genuine to my ears. His voice dripped with disappointment like he wished he could prove she existed. I asked for her phone number, and he recited it off to me from his phone.

"Anyone see you after you got home?"

Takuma shrugged. "Probably not. My girlfriend slept over, and she was there with me all night. Then I was here the next morning."

There was a quiet moment where Goro scratched away at his notebook, and I let my attention focus on Takuma Kubo. From his down-turned eyes and hands clutched together, he was obviously upset.

He looked up and saw me watching him. "I can't believe she's dead," he said, his eyes watering.

"She is. I'm sorry." I rested my chin on Mari's head for a moment. "How long had you known her?"

"My whole life." He looked from me to Goro. "Is there anything else? I should really contact Noriko's family."

"Just a few more questions. Tell me about your dismissal from the Tokyo media firm."

Takuma's face hardened. "Why? What does that have to do with her death?" He huffed. "You cops are always trying to dig up old dirt for no reason."

"Okay," Goro said, and I thought he was going to end the questioning. "So, next, I'm going to go digging into why both you and Noriko left the media firm. I'll call your old bosses, your old colleagues, your friends, your family, your neighbors... I'm going to speak to every person who knew you back then until I get the information I need."

Takuma groaned. "That will ruin me. I'll never find work again!"

"Then maybe you should just tell me what happened and anything you know about what Noriko has been up to since then."

Takuma sighed, rubbed his face, and planted his hands firmly on his knees before he started talking. He and Noriko had been married a few years, working different jobs, before they both got hired by the same firm. He was hired first, and she came on board at the firm a few months later. They had been there together for two years when things began to fall apart. He cheated on Noriko with another woman who also worked at the same firm, and when Noriko complained to the CEO, the whole situation deteriorated from there.

"They let her go first, and she was livid. Absolutely enraged." Takuma got up from his chair and crossed the room to a small refrigerator. Grabbing a bottle of green tea from the shelf, he unscrewed the cap and chugged it down. "She drank every day, sometimes during the mornings too. I stayed away from home because she was mean when she was drunk."

He set the green tea bottle on his desk.

"I filed for divorce a few months later. She didn't contest it. She showed up, signed the papers, and left. Didn't even ask for anything."

He threw himself back into his chair.

"Gotta say, though, I was surprised to find out she moved here from the city. It's *my* family that's here, not hers. But one of her friends got her on this small business classes idea, and some Chikata city official talked to her landlord to give her a discount for a year to stay and offer classes. Guess she couldn't pass that up."

I wrote everything down, craning my neck to look past Mari's head as she looked around the room.

Cheating husbands. Jealous wives. It was the usual suspects for murder.

"What happened to the woman you had an affair with?" I asked, flipping back in my notes.

Takuma shrugged again. "Didn't last."

"Sounds like you still have plenty of reasons to hate Noriko. You lost your job because of her, lost your livelihood." Goro's eyes traveled around the room, taking in the shabby office space. "She moved to your hometown." Goro's voice rose along with his eyebrows.

"If you think I'd murder her because she moved to my hometown, you're crazy."

"Maybe, maybe not. She seems to be doing a whole lot better than you," I said, and I knew I was being confrontational. My conscience cringed, and I immediately wanted to apologize. But it was true. In all the time I had known Noriko, she was always put together. Her outfits were neat, tidy, and fashionable. She drove a new car and owned a new phone. Sure, all of those things could've been a smokescreen. I never did see her home. But something told me she had bounced back faster and easier than Takuma.

"Yeah, about that. I know she's not making a ton of money, so where did the expensive bags and brand-new car come from? I saw her driving around town."

Takuma's question caused Goro to pause.

"You should go speak to that business partner of hers. What's his name?" He twirled his hand in a circle. "Yutaka Mikami. Not me. If anyone is a killer, it's that man. He has quite the reputation."

Goro put his notebook away. "Thank you for your time," he said, bowing. "We ask that you go nowhere for the next two weeks, at least. We may need to question you again."

I stowed my notebook away in the diaper bag and stood up, bouncing Mari a little and keeping her entertained.

Takuma's lips twitched. "Fine."

Though I doubted he had anywhere to go.

"I guess I have a funeral to attend, anyway," he said to our backs as we retreated from the office.

Yes, a funeral. I was sure Kumi would want to attend, and I always did my best sleuthing at funerals.

A funeral sounded like a morbid but good idea.

CHAPTER
SIXTEEN

My eyes blurred as I tried to concentrate on the papers in front of me. Five hours of sleep and running around all morning had drained me of every last vestige of energy I had. Mari was asleep in the bassinet in the back room of Oshabe-cha, and her nap gave me time to get some paperwork done while talking to my favorite client, Murata. Sometimes she asked me to call her by her first name, Yomé, but I couldn't shake the habit of deference with her.

"Mei, you should go take a nap. When Mari sleeps, you sleep. Isn't that the general wisdom on babies?" Murata sipped her tea and stared me down from across the table. At this point, she was like a second mom to me, watching everything I ate or did. Thankfully, she was a lot less judgmental than my own mother. Regardless, I loved them both and what they did for me.

"Do you know one person, one parent in all of history, who has ever taken that advice?" I asked, keeping my eyes on the columns of numbers. This looked right. I needed to restock the tea from my distributor, and the tea prices, in the thousands of yen, were swaying in front of me.

"Not one, unfortunately," she grumbled.

I lifted my eyes from the papers, rubbed them, and sipped my tea. I needed more caffeine.

"Did you follow that rule when your kids were small?"

Her smile was bittersweet. "No, I don't think I did. It was a long time ago though."

I thought about Mari snoozing away in the back room, and how she would soon wake up, and then the evening would be upon us. I dreaded it.

"Speaking of my children, I was talking to my son the other day…"

"How is he?"

"He's just fine. He's worried about me, but then again, he always is. He says thank you again for helping me out."

I smiled at her. "Of course."

"You and Emi have been a big help. I'll be sorry when she's gone."

"Yes, me too."

"Anyway, my son brought up an idea, and I wanted to run it by you, see what you thought of it."

"Okay," I said, trying to concentrate.

Murata looked around the tea shop, but it was just us in here for now. Shigimo and Hasé both left an hour ago after another game of Go, and Emi was out running errands.

"I was considering, just considering, moving to the new assisted living building on the north side of town. You know the one."

Now I was really paying attention.

"Yes. Yes, I do know that one. Akiko works there sometimes. Well, she has some clients who moved there, so she does house calls to the premises."

"I think…" She traced the lines on her palm, one of the things she did when she was worried. "I think, maybe, it might be good for me. There are a lot of stairs in my apartment building, and well…"

I dipped my head to make eye contact with her.

"I worry something will happen when I'm alone there, and I won't get help in time. I'm ninety-four now, and I'd like to live another few years. I want to see my grandchildren more."

"But you don't want to move to the United States." It wasn't a question. She missed her son and his family, but she would never be comfortable in the States like she would be in Japan.

"Yes." She worried her hands together. "I'm not sure what to do."

I thought for a moment while I strained my ears to hear if Mari had woken up.

"I think you already know what to do." I reached across the table to pat her hand. "It's a good idea. I certainly would worry about you a whole lot less if you were there. Akiko says the place is great. They have a caring and attentive staff. They even have robots!"

She laughed, and her eyes shone with life. She still had plenty of years left in her, I was sure of it.

"Robots? Well, I guess if they're helpful and not nosy, then I should be fine with them."

I shuffled the papers and looked at what I had to do next. More order forms and inventory. I sighed and rubbed my eyes.

"Maybe you could use a robot, Mei."

I popped a tiny smile. "I don't think I could afford a robot unless I got one of those that did nothing but vacuum. Even then, Mari loves it when I run the vacuum cleaner, so I'm not sure I want to give up that advantage."

"Emi was telling me that she recommended someone to help you out."

I groaned and dropped my forehead to the table. Murata laughed.

"Have you been hearing the same things over and over?"

"Everyone is on me lately. Mei, you should get more sleep. Mei, you should take a break. Mei, can you help us with this murder investigation? Mei, you should really not have your baby out in the cold weather. Mei, you should go out on a date with your husband."

"Oh, that's a good one. You should definitely go on a date with Yasahiro."

I lifted my head from the table. Tears burned in my eyes, and I pulled from my last reserves of strength to keep them there.

Murata's face fell into a worried set of lines.

"Honestly, Mei. Hire someone. You need the help."

"I know. I know I do. I need help like a person crawling across the desert needs water. Finding the time to even *think* about getting help is just impossible. Whenever I have a spare moment, it either flits on by along with a few more brain cells of mine or someone needs me."

Once again, I strained my ears to gauge if Mari had woken. The back room was silent.

Murata reached across the table and gently pushed the stack of papers aside.

"Call now. Go on. I have tea to drink." She picked up her tea, sipped, and turned to stare out the window.

I nearly burst into tears at her kindness, but I kept them inside.

My bag sat on the bench next to me, so I grabbed my phone, found the text from Emi with the young woman's information in it, and dialed. *'Nahomi Shimizu, twenty-one years old, student, long-time friend. You'll love her,'* is what Emi had texted. Okay, I hoped so!

The line rang only twice and then someone answered.

"Hello?"

"Hello. Is this Nahomi?"

"It is."

"Hi, this is Mei Suga. I'm a friend of Emi Asano. She gave me your number because she said you were looking for work?"

"Oh, hi! Yes, yes. Your name sounds familiar now."

I immediately liked her voice, and it brought a much-needed smile to my face.

"I was wondering if you had time soon to come by my tea shop. I'd like to meet you and tell you about what I need help with. We could see if it's a good fit for you and your schedule."

"I would love to!"

My lungs lightened, and my shoulders straightened. Suddenly, I was more relieved than I had been in weeks. I had been carrying the weight of doing everything myself for so long, the dark cloud of responsibility had become second nature.

It was a short conversation, but we exchanged more information, and I invited her to come to Oshabe-cha the next day to meet.

"See? That wasn't so hard," Murata said, slapping my hand playfully.

"I feel inspired to do more!" I swiped through my phone and found the photo of the business card for Yasahiro's photographer. "I'm going to call this photographer for my mom. She's writing and designing a cookbook," I said, my chest swelling with pride. I dialed up his number, confident I would be happy to get even more tasks off my to-do list.

The phone rang a few times before someone finally picked up.

"Hello?" The voice on the other end was tentative and quiet. A woman, unexpectedly. But maybe she was an assistant?

"Hello, I'm trying to reach Ryosuké Nagatomo. I was interested in hiring him for a photo shoot?"

"Oh. Oh, I'm sorry. I regret to inform you that he died four months ago."

"Oh no." The dark cloud descended back on me. Murata's eyebrows furrowed. "I'm so sorry to hear this. You have my condolences."

"Yes, thank you. It was a bit sudden. I'm sorry I can't help you."

Maybe this was his wife or daughter, and the call had been forwarded to her. Either way, it felt impolite to ask or pry now.

"That's okay. I'm sorry to have bothered you. Please have a nice day."

"Thank you. You as well."

I ended the call and set my phone on the table, only to stare at it for a long moment.

"The photographer is dead. Died a few months ago. So I guess that's not going to work out."

"Oh, that's too bad. Well, you've had a fifty percent success rate today. I guess that's not horrible."

"It's not great either." I paused as I heard Mari wake from sleep with a few grunts and a tiny wail.

I sighed and groaned as I lifted my tired and worn-out body from my seat at the table.

Back to square one with Mom. I'd have to call her later and let her know. I shook my head as I left the front room.

"It's always something," I said, shrugging my shoulders.

CHAPTER
SEVENTEEN

When I opened the door to Sawayaka, the clamor of voices blew me back. Several people in line out the door murmured and grumbled as I walked past, carrying Mari's car seat in the crook of my arm. People waiting for dinner packed the front vestibule, and every table but one in the dining room was occupied.

"Mei!" Ana, the head waitress and greeter, smiled and waved as I tried to get past everyone. "Sorry," she said, leaning in to give me a quick hug. "The place is a bit noisy for a baby." She turned her smile on Mari. "Hello, sweet Mari. How are you today?" She reached into the car seat and lightly brushed Mari's cheek. Mari smiled back.

I held my breath for a moment and wondered how long I had before the screamfest began. It was nearing five-thirty, and the beginning of the unhappy hours. But Mari's eyes merely searched the surrounding room, what she could see from her spot in the car seat.

"She's such a doll," Ana said, smiling at me. "What a lucky mom you are."

I heaved a sigh of relief. Even though I struggled with Mari, she still managed to be a perfect baby in public. I was sure this wouldn't last into the toddler years when I'd be dragging her from stores kicking and screaming.

Ana turned to deal with an irritable customer, so I set Mari's car seat down and pulled off my coat. Ana and her husband did not have kids, yet, but she had said they wanted them. Maybe it would happen for them soon.

Ana waved over a server and passed my coat to him. "Can you bring this back to the office for Mei, please? Come, Mei. Let me show you to your table."

"Hey," an older man stepped in front of us. "We've been waiting for twenty minutes, and the line is out the door. You're going to give her a table?"

"Excuse me," Ana said, asserting her authority by standing up straight and looking down her nose at the man. "This woman is a principal investor in the restaurant and has been waiting weeks for her dinner here. Please step aside."

He dipped his head, chastened, and allowed us to pass.

"Wow. People are getting testy here." I kept my voice down but couldn't whisper with all the noise in the dining room. Really, the place needed carpet or wall hangings or something to dampen all the sound. I would have to speak to Yasahiro about that.

"It's been a trying week," Ana said, pulling out my chair and the one next to me for Mari. "The crowds are insane. We've been thinking about making dinner reservations-only to make things easier, but I know how much this would upset the locals. They love having Sawayaka here for a quick dinner."

I nodded as I sat down and turned Mari towards me. "I'll talk with Yasahiro. There has to be something we can do."

She skipped giving me the menu but passed the daily specials slip instead. "We have some delicious specials tonight. Have a look, and I'll let the boss know you're here."

I held my breath as I glanced at the specials menu. I loved my husband and his organic, all local produce, slow food restaurant, but what I needed was a giant, greasy burger, some fries, and something decadent, preferably filled with chocolate or sugar. Or both.

I knew I was better off eating healthy, but that didn't negate the years I lived off convenience store food and loved every moment of it.

My breath leaked out slowly as I scanned down the menu. Okay, I would start the meal with a salad, and the Moroccan beef stew with rice sounded tasty and filling. Dessert was red bean ice cream, but that wasn't a favorite of mine. I would instead break into my stash of chocolate at home that I kept next to my stun gun in the linen closet.

Yasahiro emerged from the kitchen, and more than half the heads in the dining room swiveled to watch him. It was a strange sensation, knowing my husband was popular and sought after. I watched him take in the stares and let it buoy him up. He was never embarrassed, so I tried not to be as well. I was sure he saw Mari and me sitting near the kitchen door, but he bypassed us to do a quick tour of the restaurant.

I leaned close to Mari and whispered, "You have a very popular dad." She raised her sleepy eyes up to mine, and she smiled. What was it about her smile that made my heart ache? What was it about her attention that made my life seem more whole? It was a curiosity.

I unstrapped her from the car seat and lifted her into my arms so she could watch Yasahiro do his thing. Cooking and running the restaurant weren't the only tasks for a successful chef. A lot of the job was being charming and making connections. I didn't know many reclusive chefs. Sure, some of them stayed in the kitchen, but many more were out talking to customers, patrons, and suppliers instead of slaving away over a hot stove.

"Hello, my darlings," he said, finally making it back over to our table. Everyone was watching him now, and I did my best to ignore the many dozens of pairs of eyes trained on us.

Yasahiro reached down and picked Mari off my lap while smiling at me. I thought this was all the affection I'd get in public, but then he surprised me by bending down and kissing me on the cheek. I gasped and closed my eyes because I didn't want to see the crowd's reaction.

Sometimes Yasahiro surprised me, like when he took my hand at festivals or when he knelt down on the sidewalk outside of Izakaya Jūshi to propose to me. I had to remind myself constantly that those years in Paris made him a very different man from those I had grown up around.

"How are my ladies today? Hungry?" he asked, sitting down across from me with Mari in his arms.

"Always," I said, trying to cool down my body and ignore the murmurs rumbling through the dining room. "I was lamenting the lack of burgers and fries on the menu only moments ago."

Any other chef in his position would've been horrified, but he only laughed.

"I'll pick up ground beef and cook some at home tomorrow."

I blinked in surprise as he made funny faces at Mari and she tried to pull his bottom lip off. One of the waitstaff delivered a bottle of saké to the table and two glasses.

"You'll be home tomorrow night? How is that even possible?" I jerked my head at the overflowing dining room.

"Michio said he'd cover for me for the evening, and tomorrow I'm interviewing two possible new chefs to train under him. It only took two crazy nights here for me to see the light. There's no way I can work these hours and live a happy life."

I was both mortified and impressed. The Japanese way of life was to work until you die, practically die at your desk or in the fields. But the life Yasahiro lived in France counteracted that at a fundamental level. The French were almost our polar opposites.

"That's great!" I blurted out with a relieved sigh. "I was afraid I'd never see you again."

"Same. Both you and Mari." He bounced her on his lap.

"And with the house in crisis, and you helping with the murder investigation too, I felt I should be around more to help with Mari."

I was this close to tears. *This close.*

How did I get so lucky? I'd always been such an unlucky person, so I wasn't surprised when we started having troubles at the house building site. And other events in my life had left an aura of unluckiness about me.

But I was lucky in love. It was my one saving grace.

"That would be great." It was hard to push the words out through the lump in my throat.

"I have some ideas besides the extra staff I want to run by you, but let's eat first and talk about your day."

He waved over one of the waitstaff, we ordered our food, and then we served each other saké.

While we waited for the food to arrive, I filled him in on the murder investigation and the interview with the ex-husband earlier in the day. Yasahiro laughed at me being Goro's assistant, and I couldn't blame him. I was the furthest from being anyone's assistant. I could barely hold together the tea shop on most days. Granted, I had done better with it before Mari was born. But now? I was a wreck.

"Isn't it usually the ex-husband? I mean, when it comes to murder suspects, I feel like that's a given."

He sat forward to fill my cup.

"Only a little for me," I said, holding my hand over the cup. "I still have to feed Mari in the middle of the night." I yawned, and she yawned too. "Here, I'll take her."

The restaurant was still noisy, and Mari wasn't screaming her head off. I was beginning to see a pattern here.

I took Mari into my arms and bounced her a little. Her eyes drooped, so I shifted her into her car seat, tucked a blanket over her lap, and draped another one over the top of the seat.

"That's amazing," Yasahiro said, his eyes wide. "It's like you've become Super Mom in the last three days."

"Oh stop." I was afraid I'd blush again especially with some alcohol in me. "I think it's the crowd noise. We should record it and play it at home."

Our salads arrived, and as I picked at the greens, I moved back to the original conversation.

"It *is* almost always the ex-husband, at least according to Goro. But I'm not sure he has much of a motive to kill her, and he has an alibi for the time of the murder. If anything Noriko had a motive to kill *him*. He was the one who cheated on her and caused her to lose her job."

"You have a point there." Yasahiro finished his salad in only a few bites. "I'm starving. I've been on my feet all day." He pushed his plate away. "So, if it's not him, then whom?"

I shrugged. "I don't know. My gut tells me it's someone she slighted. Someone she hurt enough to kill her. Maybe the guy who invested in her or one of her students?"

"Do you know anyone in your class who could be a suspect?"

"No. Someone after class, though. Maybe."

Our main courses arrived at the table, looking splendid and larger in portion size. Ana dropped by and peeked in on Mari.

"She's dead asleep," she said, her voice rising in surprise. "With this noise?"

"She seems to like it. Are you to blame for the larger portions tonight?" I asked. She had been smiling at our plates as she approached.

She winked. "You both look too skinny. Enjoy your meals."

The beef stew was rich and hearty with carrots and potatoes and a red wine sauce. Just what I needed to get me through the evening. Eaten with local white rice, slivered almonds, and golden raisins, I felt like we were back in Paris instead of Chikata.

"This is delicious." The food hit my stomach and warmed me

from head to toe in blood sugar. I was more hungry than I had thought.

"I'm glad you like it." Yasahiro glanced around at the dining area and I followed his gaze. People were inhaling the specials, and no dinner or appetizer plate was left untouched. A good sign. Pride blossomed up from my chest. My husband was so talented.

"It looks like everyone likes it." I smiled at him, and he smiled back.

"And I think I can bring this food to more people," Yasahiro said with a small smile. This felt like a confession, so I set down my spoon to concentrate on him.

"How? I think you're well at capacity here. A new restaurant?" My stomach flipped over, and I wished I hadn't just filled it with stew. Could we afford a new restaurant?

"No. A food truck." His eyes lit up, and I chuckled.

"A food truck?"

"They're all the rage now." He sat back in his chair and folded his arms over his chest. "After all our ideas for your mom's farm were set aside, I started thinking of other ideas we could borrow from other countries. I thought then that a food truck, maybe even two, would be a good addition to our business. Then I saw a news story about parts of Tokyo that aren't served well by restaurants for people who work there, and food trucks have filled those gaps."

I imagined a Sawayaka Express truck with a few daily specials and how popular it would be. People would wait in lines for it to show up, the social media photos would be spectacular, and it would take the pressure off the main restaurant.

When I didn't respond because I was daydreaming, he continued.

"The initial investment is pretty small, and I can hire a few people to take charge of it. What do you think?"

I pushed my saké cup to him. "I think we should toast your ingenuity! This is a great idea. I love it."

He filled my cup with a smile, and we toasted and drank.

"I love how supportive you are," he said, and his warm eyes melted my heart.

"You too."

We drank again, and he cleared his throat.

"Not to change the subject, but tell me what you found out about the house and the land this morning."

My good cheer evaporated in a blink.

"That bad, huh?"

"A child died. Fell while climbing in the garden and hit his head." I didn't know this child, but his parents lived in my daydreams, inconsolably sad, angry, and despondent. They had purchased the house to give their child a life away from the city, and instead, it had killed him. It was every parent's nightmare.

I tried to concentrate on my dinner, on the rich sauce of the beef stew and the individual grains of rice, instead of on my teary eyes. People were still glancing our way, star struck by Yasahiro, and I didn't want them to think we were fighting or anything. Public perception was very important.

"Oh no. That's so tragic." Sadness filled Yasahiro's voice. "They must have been devastated."

I shrugged and continued on with my meal. "Most likely, yes. They sold the house and land only a year later. There have been several owners since which is why we weren't warned about the property." I sighed, and my shoulders fell. "I'm not sure what to do now that I know this."

Yasahiro thought for a moment while he finished up his meal. Someone immediately came to take his dish away.

"You don't believe in ghosts, though," he pointed out.

"I don't, but..."

He smiled. "But. I had a feeling that was coming."

"But even if I don't believe in ghosts, the men who work on our property do."

"Ah." His eyebrows climbed as he sipped his saké. I reached

across the table and filled his cup back up. "Thank you. Well, I see the problem here. It's not really about what you or I believe in; it's about everyone around us."

Yasahiro waited while I continued to eat. There was a time in my life when I devoured everything and moved on to do something else. Now, I was slower than a sloth because I was so used to being interrupted every other second.

But it gave me some time to think. My whole life had been about compromise. I had compromised most of what I'd wanted from my life, especially after moving home, so that I could serve my mother, my family, my friends, and my community. Not that there was anything wrong with that. But, most days, the effort felt very lopsided, like I was giving ninety percent and only getting ten percent in return. And why? Because my pride got in the way.

I lifted the spoon from my bowl of stew slowly and asked myself one fundamental question. Was it worth it? Was all the bending-over-backwards favors and subjugating worth my health and happiness?

I had two choices. I could continue to put everyone else's wants and needs first, above Yasahiro's, Mari's, or mine. Or I could assert boundaries and rules for the sake of our sanity.

Thankfully, I knew Yasahiro was on my side.

"Do you have ideas of what we should do to fix this situation?" he asked, leaning forward with his elbows on the table. "Because we should fix it and get on with our lives. I don't like how this construction crew has held our future hostage."

"I have an idea," I said, pushing my plate away from me. "And since you've told me about Sawayaka, here's what I want to do with this task. I'm going to ask Sakiko Yoshida if she'll investigate the people who lost their child. I'll text her later tonight and see if she can come by Oshabe-cha soon for a chat. If I can find photos or a relative to be there for another cleansing ceremony, I think I can convince the workers to come back and pick up where they left off. But that doesn't stop the actual accidents that are happening on the property. So, it'll cost us a few ten-thousand yen, but I'd like to buy a remote, wireless security system with several cameras so we can observe the property when we're not there — for when we get electricity on the property. But for now, I'll buy game cameras and cover the construction site."

"Game cameras?"

"Yeah." I took a sip of water to calm my racing heart. I loved a good mystery. "They're motion-activated cameras that run on batteries and can either broadcast their photos or videos or store them on a memory card. Wildlife enthusiasts love them."

Yasahiro stared at me.

"I've been doing research while Mari's been sleeping."

"You should be sleeping while Mari sleeps," he said, calling one of the waitstaff over.

"You and Mrs. Murata should spend more time together. You two are practically one-mind about this."

I smiled as I looked across the dining room to the waitress crossing to us, and my eyes caught sight of a familiar face. I concentrated on her for a long breath, my brain burrowing back through memories new and old. Where did I know her from?

She laughed and then listened intently to the person across the table from her, and I finally saw her in my head... standing in the hallway outside of class, talking to Noriko.

This was the woman who had argued with Noriko, and Kayo had seen her with Noriko only a few hours before Noriko died. How had I not seen her earlier? Maybe she had come in when Yasahiro and I had been deep in conversation.

"I... Um..."

I reached for my water glass, bumped it, and caught it just before it tipped over. The silverware on the table jumped and knocked against my plate.

"Oops. That's okay," the waitress said, pulling a cloth from her pocket and mopping up the mess I made. "Let me get that."

I lowered my eyes and furtively peeked around the waitress to look at the woman. Was it really her?

Our eyes locked on each other, and yes, it was her.

Her stare was piercing, and even though we had never met, she knew who I was. I'd been standing in that same hallway with my mom and Kumi when this woman had confronted Noriko.

My gaze flinched from hers, and I chastised myself for being intimidated.

"Is something wrong, Mei?" Yasahiro asked.

I ignored him and bent over to check on Mari. She was fine, of course, sleeping soundly, but I needed a moment to collect myself and figure out what to do.

I kept my eyes on my own table and switched from checking on Mari to grab my bag instead.

Ugh, where was my phone?

"Mei?" Yasahiro was getting worried. I couldn't ignore him, but I also couldn't ignore this situation. Last I checked, Goro and the rest of his team didn't know who this woman was. And she was right in front of me.

Well, she was across the dining room. Close enough.

My hand made contact with my phone, and taking a deep breath to slow down, I pulled it out and dialed Goro.

His phone rang and rang, but no one picked up.

"Come on, come on," I urged the universe.

Yasahiro had quieted and watched me intently. I made stern eye contact with him. It was my 'I'm serious' face that hushed even the most ardent of people.

I got Goro's voicemail and cursed under my breath. My instinct was to hang up and dial again, but I left a message first, just in case.

"Goro, I'm at Sawayaka having dinner with Yasahiro, and the

woman who was last with Noriko before she was killed is here. Right now."

Stupid me. I looked up.

She was still watching me, and this last eye contact was enough to spur her into action.

"You or Kayo have to come here. *Now*," I demanded into the phone while simultaneously watching the mystery woman give out brief excuses, dump a pile of cash on the table, and grab her coat to make her way out.

I cursed again and fumbled with my chair while trying to get out of my seat. I couldn't let her get away.

"Where are you going?" Yasahiro's voice finally broke into a panic.

I looked around. "Ugh, my coat. It's in the office."

No time.

"Watch Mari. I'll be right back," I said and bolted from the table.

I stumbled to get through all the tables without knocking into anyone or causing a ruckus. The last thing I wanted was rumors I had left Yasahiro to chase after someone even though that was precisely what I was doing.

"Where are you going, Mei?" Ana asked as I bolted past her.

I turned and smiled. "Left something in the car! Be right back!"

Through the door and onto the sidewalk, the frigid evening air hit me like an anvil.

Oof. I gasped and pulled my thin cardigan sweater closer while looking up and down the sidewalk. There was still a small line of people waiting outside, so I approached one of the men at the front of the line.

Quick! Come up with a good lie, Mei.

"Excuse me. My friend just left here. A young woman, dressed in a gray coat. Did you see which way she went? She left her phone." I showed him my phone.

"That way." He pointed to the left and down the street. "I think she turned at the second corner."

"Thanks!"

I ran off, trying to catch up with her. It was stupid of me to leave my coat behind on such a cold evening, but I had to act fast. My legs burned as I raced up the sidewalk, and my lungs ached from the bitter night air.

Was the fact that she ran a sign she was guilty?

Obviously, I couldn't base anything on her behavior, but still. It was suspicious.

I turned at the second corner, and no one was there. No! I stomped my foot on the sidewalk. If only I had been faster. If only I hadn't acted so shifty! It was my fault she got a vibe off of me and recognized me from Noriko's class.

Not to be deterred, I hustled to the next corner and looked up and down the block. Nothing. And it was too cold to keep going.

I'd lost her.

Well, I'd tried. There was only so much I could do once she had fled from Sawayaka. I turned and hurried back. Ugh, I couldn't believe how close I was to figuring out the identity of mystery woman!

My phone rang in my hand as I re-entered Sawayaka, and Goro was on the other end of the line.

"Mei! You found her? Is she still there?"

I rubbed my arms and paced up and down the front vestibule of Sawayaka before heading back to the table.

"No. She saw me and bolted."

I stopped dead in my tracks, lifted my eyes, and the table the young woman just left was right in front of me.

Her friends were still there.

Goro sighed on the other end. "I'm only five blocks away. I got in my car as soon as I heard your message. Sorry. The chief had called a meeting, and my phone was off and —"

"Goro, get here quickly. You're in luck. She's gone, but her friends are still here."

Goro laughed and whooped on the other end of the call. "Mei, that's the best news I've heard all day. Now, we're finally making progress! I'll be right there."

CHAPTER
EIGHTEEN

We had found Erina Ichisé. The woman Takuma Kubo was dating and the woman who had hounded Noriko before her death were the same person. I looked at Goro's text on my phone and tried to focus my eyes after a broken night of sleep. Our dinner had ended in good spirits while Goro sat with the mystery woman's friends across the dining room and asked them questions.

But near nine o'clock, Mari jolted awake and began to scream, so we dashed home before we bothered everyone in the restaurant. I nursed her three times during the night, and Yasahiro paced her to sleep with the sound of the vacuum cleaner around four in the morning. My phone alarm scared the daylights out of me. Seven had come too soon.

Pulling my phone away from my face, I realized Yasahiro wasn't in bed, and Mari wasn't in her bassinet. Had I fallen to sleep before they had? And where were they?

Erina Ichisé.

Goro's second text read, *"I've got Kayo on the lookout for her outside of her apartment and another officer on her place of busi-*

ness. Hopefully, we'll talk to her by the end of the day or tomorrow."

"Okay," I texted back. "*Let me know if you need me.*"

Erina had bolted from Sawayaka at the mere sight of me which made her level of guilt rise in my eyes. She had only ever seen me in that hallway outside of Noriko's class, and now that night was associated with a fight between them. So unless she knew me by reputation alone, she was trying to avoid me because of that fight. It was the only explanation for her behavior. We had witnessed her fighting with a woman who was dead two days later.

The word 'guilty' flashed in my head over and over.

I closed my eyes and rolled over onto my side. Why had I set my alarm again? Oh right. I was going to handle more paperwork this morning and order the security cameras.

My phone buzzed.

"*Need you? I could always use your eyes. We're going to go over the crime scene again today. Want to come?*"

I sighed. Wasn't I going to cut back on my obligations to other people?

But the pull of the mystery was strong, and I hadn't been there for the first inspection of the crime scene. Maybe we wouldn't find anything more, or there could be something hidden in her garden or the house. It was worth a shot.

"*Sure. Though I need to make sure Yasahiro can stay home with Mari.*"

"*Pick you up at nine.*" He didn't even wait to see if I could come. He knew Yasahiro would approve.

I fell back to sleep for twenty minutes, and when I emerged from the bedroom, Yasahiro was passed out on the couch, and Mari was sleeping swaddled in the portable bassinet on the living room floor. I tiptoed to the bathroom to shower, hoping they'd get a little more sleep. And then I would be off for more clue hunting!

———

As we approached the side of Noriko's house, I went over the details of the assault in my head and snapped on my crime scene gloves. Someone had attacked her in the back garden, and no one had seen anything. That was basically all I knew. An officer in a police car parked outside waved to us as we walked across the front lawn, and we waved back. Yellow and black caution tape still enclosed the garden gate, and a police notice hung on the front door. The murder was fresh on the books, and it would be a while before the owner could clean this place up and sell it off. It would end up a stigmatized property as well. Too bad. It was in a great location.

Goro and I stood in the garden of Noriko's house for a minute before he pulled a few photos from an A4 envelope under his arm.

"Okay. She was lying right here when I found her." Goro pointed to the spot and handed me the photo. Noriko's body was face-down, the back of her head bloodied. It wasn't too gruesome except for the pool of blood next to her body.

I tilted my head at the photograph and held it out to compare it to the blood-stained stone patio in front of me.

"Did she have abrasions on her face? From the fall or a fight?" I shifted around until I had the right angle for the photo in my hand. Whoever attacked her stood where I was standing if she had been whacked over the head and fell right there.

"Abrasions on her face. Yeah." Goro handed me another photo, and this one was taken in the morgue. Ugh. I closed my eyes for a moment before studying it. "Consistent with a fall. Abrasions on her knees too. Kayo believes she was hit over the head, fell to her knees, and then forward. She was found mostly rolled on her side."

I nodded, picturing the assault in my head. My daydreaming

skills were strong, but this was one occasion when I wished my brain could be a little vaguer.

I thought about the scene and looked again at the photo of Noriko on the ground.

"Is she... wearing pajamas in this photo?"

"Yeah. Good quality pajamas. And slippers." Goro pointed over my hand holding the photo to Noriko's feet.

Turning around, I looked at the door to the rear of the house then back at the photo.

"Hmmm."

"What do you see, Mei?" Goro watched me as I processed the photos.

"Okay. Here's my theory. She was home and ready for bed. It was three in the morning, right?"

"Yeah."

"Hmm, okay. So either she was asleep, and this person woke her up, or she was an insomniac and maybe watching TV or on her computer or whatever. Someone tried to get her attention, either through the back door or..." I glanced up at the second floor where I assumed a bedroom was. "Or he or she tossed something at the window to wake her. Noriko then came out to talk to him or her."

I acted it out, walking from the door to the spot on the patio where she perished.

"They had a conversation. Something quiet because no one heard anything, right?"

Goro nodded. "Not at the time of Noriko's death. The neighbor on this side" — he pointed to the next house over — "was letting out her dog that morning when she thought she heard or saw something here."

"What did she see?"

Goro shrugged and checked his notebook. "Her statement was, 'I heard some rustling around in the bushes and thought it was an animal. When I turned to come back inside, Noriko's garden gate closed, and I thought I saw the silhouette of an adult walking swiftly away from the house.'" He closed his notebook. "She thought it might have been Noriko or a delivery or something. She didn't investigate and didn't check on the garden. I was the one who found the body."

"Typical. Anyway, Noriko and her assailant argued, she turned to go back inside, and *that* was when she was hit over the head. She was facing the back door when she went down. So she knew the person who attacked her."

"You're sure? Chief thinks it could be random."

"I'm sure. If she hadn't recognized the person trying to break into her house, she would've called the police right away. Or if she was stupid, which I don't believe she was, she would've come out with a weapon. You didn't find any weapons, did you?"

"Just the small stone statue that killed her, identical to that one." He pointed to a gnome statue on the opposite side of the garden. Cute little thing, but deadly. Goro's eyes skirted over the shrubberies around the perimeter. "The neighbor heard a rustling in the bushes. Let's look through the underbrush and see if we find anything. I'm not sure how thorough the crime scene team was."

I let my mind wander again as we each took sections of the garden to examine. She knew the person who had killed her, so whoever it was had a clear motive, a reason to keep her quiet. Had she done something else to her ex-husband to make him want to kill her? Or had she swindled her student out of a job or money? Or did she owe capital and interest on a dodgy loan and the investor had come to collect?

"Goro, what about Yutaka Mikami? Have you spoken to him yet?" I pushed aside the leaves of a tiny bush. Nothing there.

"Not yet. He's on my list for today, this morning hopefully. There's the funeral later, but I have to be at the station."

"Oh yeah, right. The funeral." I sighed as I straightened up and stretched out my back. "Is Kumi going?"

Goro continued to poke around in the weeds. "Of course."

"I guess I should go too. I almost forgot about it."

"My mom and Kumi are going together. Your mom was going to catch a ride with them." He squatted down to lift rocks along the border of the greenery.

"I'll call Mom and offer to drive."

I bent over again, and this time something caught the light, deep in the bushes. "Oh, look!"

I pointed to the spot sparkling in the morning sun, and Goro came over to inspect it.

"What's this?" he asked, reaching in to grab the shiny object.

A thin silver chain with a heart charm tangled with the bush, stuck in its scraggly branches. Goro pulled it out slowly, careful not to break it.

"Hmm." He held it up to the light. "Does it look familiar?"

"I'm not sure." I closed my eyes and tried to picture Noriko as she had been in our classes, but the necklace didn't stand out in any of my memories. "Sorry. I don't remember. She may have had it on under her shirt, so it's not like I would know for sure. Ask Kumi."

Goro pulled an evidence bag from his pocket and dropped the necklace in. He handed it to me and used his phone to snap photos of the bush and the surrounding area where we found it.

I held the bag up to the light and looked at it. The necklace was shiny and bright. Silver didn't react well to the elements and tarnished easily. If it had been outside for a while, it would've looked worse for wear.

"What else?" Goro asked, folding his arms across his chest. "Anything else stick out to you?"

Turning around, I scanned the garden, but nothing seemed wrong. There was a set of table and chairs that looked relatively new, like no one had sat in them in a while. A hose was curled up next to a garden tools trunk. An umbrella for the table rested against the back wall. All in all, a typical garden.

"Can we go inside?" I asked, eyeing the back doors. "Do we have time?"

He checked his phone. "We can spare ten minutes."

Goro opened the door and led us inside to the kitchen. I nodded while scanning the layout, pleased with the design of the place. It was a clean, modern kitchen with a built-in breakfast nook, not typical of a Japanese house, but this place had obviously been renovated in the last ten years. I walked around the kitchen island and noticed the dirty dishes stacked in the sink. Inside the refrigerator door, Noriko had kept a small selection of fresh vegetables and a stack of takeout containers.

"The team has been through here and taken photos." Goro wandered the length of the kitchen. "They went through her bedroom upstairs and took her computer and her bag. I believe the second round of evidence gathering will be later today. The team has been stretched thin lately."

Between the kitchen and living area was a small transitional space with an old-fashioned wooden roll-top desk. I stopped here, attracted by the antique design and the neat stacks of papers.

"Wow, I haven't seen a desk like this in a long time. Akiko's dad had one when I was a kid, but they sold it off at some point." I ran my fingers along the wood, and they came away clean. No dust here. Noriko had used this desk.

I swept my gaze over the whole desk before starting. Along the top, someone had turned a few framed photographs down, so I glanced at them. They were photos of Noriko and Takuma, her ex-husband. Hmm.

Moving on, I sorted through the papers, most of which were utility bills and invoices for work she had done. The roll-top area had lots of little cubbies, spaces in which Noriko had stuffed receipts, greeting cards, more photos, money envelopes, party or wedding invitations. I found her bank statements and noted her balances. She was making good money doing what she was doing. Probably a lot more than her ex-husband.

A notebook buried under a pile of bills was interesting. I sat down to flip through it with Goro over my shoulder.

"Look. She had several websites she was administering." Listed in the notebook were project names with web addresses, FTP addresses, usernames, and login credentials. I recognized database names, too, and their login credentials. Each website was for something different, and it looked like the projects had gone back at least three years. I leaned in to read Noriko's tiny handwriting. There were no client names for any of these. Maybe she kept that information somewhere else.

"I think I remember her saying in class that she built online stores for other people. I wonder if she learned that from her ex-husband?" I handed the notebook over to Goro.

"Maybe so. I'll take this down to the station and have the guys look at it." He dropped it into an evidence bag.

I opened a few drawers, only finding things like pens and pencils and stationery before opening the bottom drawer and hitting the jackpot.

"What do we have here?" I asked the bundle of envelopes. There were at least fifty letter-sized envelopes all tied together with string. Next to them in the drawer were two jewelry boxes. I pulled them both out and set them on the desk.

But the letters were too juicy a clue to set aside. The top envelope had been sent through the mail to Noriko here in Chikata from a post office in Chikata. I raised my eyebrows, wondering what was inside.

"Oh boy," Goro said, peering down at the envelope. "That top one is dated only three months ago."

I stood up with the bundle. "Can we open these?"

"Hmm. Put them back in the drawer where you found them."

I followed his instructions, and he took photos of the letters in the drawer. Then he took the letters out of the drawer and over to the kitchen nook. He set them on the table as he dialed up the precinct and asked to speak to the chief.

"Hey, Chief. Mei Suga and I are over at the Kubo residence, and we've come across a bundle of letters in the bottom drawer of Kubo's desk along with some jewelry boxes. I've taken photos, and we're going to open the bundle, take photos of the top ten letters, and put them into an evidence bag."

I heard the chief murmur through the phone.

"Understood. I'll bring them right in as soon as we're back at the station." He hung up. "Chain of evidence," he explained, not really explaining. But I knew what he meant.

Sifting through the top ten letters, we placed them on the table and photographed each. They were love letters, and the intimacy surprised me. They were sweet mostly, but some bordered on creepy, talking about Noriko in intimate settings, her body and having sex with her. None of them were signed except to say, 'Yours forever.'

I took photos of them so I could zoom in and read them. I hoped I would find details that would help me determine where they came from. A shiver crawled up my back as I considered that *I* was the creepy stranger taking these photos.

Goro counted them all to the last envelope which was dated a little over a year ago. "There are forty-two letters here, and the latest one was three months ago. It looks like they averaged about one a week? If my math is right. Some aren't even open." He tilted the stack so I could see. There were unopened envelopes in the middle of the pile.

He dropped them into an evidence bag and sealed it up.

I handed him the two jewelry boxes, and he opened them. One had a gorgeous diamond and sapphire ring, the other a diamond bracelet. Both looked expensive and brand new.

Goro hummed. He snapped the boxes closed without further comment and dropped them in bags as well. "We should get going."

As he ushered me out, I looked over my shoulder at the rest of the house. I wanted to stay and snoop around some more! But I knew we had a long day ahead of us.

Goro pulled the back doors closed and stopped next to me before we left.

"Anything else out here pique your curiosity?" he asked, but no, nothing outside was as interesting as what was inside.

I looked at Goro, waiting patiently for my response, and my brain ticked over.

"Tell me something, Goro. Why do you value my opinion?"

He raised his eyebrows.

"Seriously. I'd like to know." I paused for a moment and felt I needed to justify my question. "I was a failure back in Tokyo. I couldn't hold down a real job to save my life. And now, I've got Oshabe-cha, and a great husband, and a sweet baby, yet I feel like I'm struggling with everything. That I'm not really good at anything. I'm passable at a bunch of small things, and it's enough to hold my life together, just barely. So...?"

Goro nodded, looked at his feet, and started pacing in a circle. This was one of his many thinking postures.

"You know, I've been in the police force for a bit of time now..."

I smiled because I knew he had been a police officer for ten years.

"And I've been in and out of a lot of precincts, met a hundred officers and detectives and managers." He waved his hand in a circle, noticed his discarded coffee cup from earlier, and picked it up. "I can immediately tell the good cops from the bad ones. I'm not talking they're bad people, or anything. Not like Watanabe. I'm talking good at their jobs. Instinctually. They have the nose and the gut for this line of work. They were made for it."

He chugged down the last of his cold coffee.

"You, Mei Suga, are in the wrong line of work. You have the nose for this." He tapped his own nose. "Maybe not a lot of guts, but I swear that your suspicions are always dead on."

I squirmed, uncomfortable with the praise. He noticed my dancing feet and threw his head back in a laugh before pointing at me.

"And that's how I know it's for real. You don't take pride in your gift. A shame."

I sighed. "It's too late for me to think of a career change. I'm married with a family and a tea shop, and I have a mother who both is ashamed of me and needs me. Can you imagine what she'd say if I told her I wanted to be a detective?" My laugh was rueful and bitter. I thought of my conversation with her just the other day about finding my calling. "When I told her I was helping with this case, she got seriously worried for me."

But then she had accepted that maybe I was good at this investigation thing. Would she approve of me wanting to be a detective? Or was she humoring me?

Goro shrugged. "When has that ever stopped you?"

My scalp prickled with intense fear, fear of upending my life for a dream that bordered on stupid.

Goro took a step back. "Just think about it. If not the police academy, then something else similar. You already have the support of the chief."

"A private investigator?"

Goro avoided my eyes. "We should clean up here and head back. I'd like to get the necklace into evidence. Maybe ask Kumi if she saw Noriko wearing it." He looked around and grabbed his bag.

"You didn't answer my question," I said, following him out of the garden.

"Did you really have a question?"

I guess not.

"How much longer do I have you?"

I glanced at my phone as we approached the car. A text from Yasahiro read, *"Can you be back by 10:30? I have interviews at Sawayaka at 11."* I checked the time, and it was only 9:45.

"An hour tops."

"Great. Let's go talk to the investor, Yutaka Mikami. I bet he'll resist questioning, and we'll be done with him in only a few minutes."

"What's the point then?" I slid into the car and buckled up.

He flashed his most devious of grins. "I like to put the fear of jail into people like him. Keeps them on their toes and makes them do stupid things."

He threw the car into gear, and we sped off.

CHAPTER
NINETEEN

Yutaka Mikami was not happy to see us. Yes, it was the same guy from Izakaya Jūshi, though he was a far cry from the man who sat across from Noriko as they looked at something on his phone together.

He was a mess at almost ten in the morning, an acceptable time to be up and on one's way to work, if not already at the office. His hair angled in a hundred different directions, and his eyes were bloodshot. He appeared to be three days into growing a beard too. I caught a whiff of old alcohol and winced. He might've even been still drunk.

This was almost a different man than the one I saw only a few days ago.

"What do you want?" he grunted at us.

Goro kept his cool. "We're here to ask you some questions about Noriko Kubo. Can we come in?"

"No. Go away."

He slammed the door on us, and we both blinked a bit at the rough dismissal. Who spoke like that to the police? No one I knew.

Goro sighed and knocked on the door again. He raised his

voice. "I could go talk to your neighbors instead! Find out the names of all your business partners and talk to them? Would that be better?"

Sneaky, Goro. Usually, a good public shaming was the best way to motivate a witness to talk.

I counted to six before he reopened his door.

"You can't come in. Ask your questions from there."

Okay then. It was impolite and suspicious not to invite the police in. Another strike against him.

"Sure." Goro pulled out his notepad, and I grabbed mine from my bag.

"We're here to ask questions about Noriko Kubo, who we believe you knew. She was found dead Monday morning in the garden of her home," Goro began.

I kept my eyes on Mikami. His face flattened. "Yes, I know. I was planning on attending the funeral later today."

Oh, good. I would see him there and have more of a chance to observe him in public. This rendezvous was less telling than how he would act around other people.

"How did you find out?" Goro asked.

"I, uh, came by her house the other afternoon to talk business and the police were there. Someone told me."

Goro wrote this down. If the information surprised him, he gave no sign.

"So, talk business, huh? What kind of business did you do with Noriko Kubo?"

He let the door open a little more while leaning on the door jamb, and I peeked past him to see the inside of an immaculate and stylish home. He had money. That was for sure. His appearance was the exact opposite of the way he lived.

"She was interested in starting an online correspondence course in business basics for Japanese women. You know, for moms and the like." He huffed and looked at the floor. "Despite thinking it was a losing prospect, she showed me all the numbers and the data from the previous in-person courses she'd done. The people she'd helped. It seemed like it would make money."

He stopped to blink his eyes hard and pinch the bridge of his nose. From the wrinkles at the corners of his eyes, I guessed he was fighting off a headache.

"Had you invested in any of her other business ventures?" I asked, butting in.

He shook his head, but his eyes darted from me to Goro. That gave me doubt.

"Nope. She was a new business client. She had done her research and asked around town until finding my information and calling me. We met about a year ago for the first time, but only started doing business together recently."

I wondered how honest this was. The way he spoke about her seemed off. Maybe they had only done business recently, but they had known each other for a year? How well had they known each other?

Maybe he wasn't as much into his businesses as people in this town believed him to be. If he had known Noriko a year, then he would have known she was building her life around small businesses. That would've been a good investment for him right from the beginning. He seemed like a slacker, still in his pajamas and half drunk, but it was possible he spent hours every evening out with clients. I couldn't base my thoughts and feelings on this one interaction.

"Do you know anything about Noriko Kubo's other projects or her students?" Goro waited with his pen poised.

Mikami cleared his throat. "Um, well, you see... I tell my clients that I like to keep things confidential, you know? We sign contracts that prevent us from disclosing details."

Goro stared hard at Mikami.

"But," Mikami said, standing up straight with his hand on the door, "that doesn't stop me from giving you a name. As long as I make it clear I didn't divulge any business information."

"Go on," Goro growled and then sighed. There were days I thought of him as a big bad wolf. Today, he was bordering on being just that.

"Erina Ichisé. The name came up a few times in conversation. According to Noriko, Erina had a business she was getting off the ground, a lucrative subscription box sent to people overseas. Really hot right now. The businesses doing these subscription boxes are making big bucks."

"Yeah. I've heard of them." I thought of all the subscription box advertisements I ran across on social media every day. It was the newest trend.

"Well, Noriko fostered this student all the way to helping her with the storefront and everything. But I guess it wasn't working out so well for Erina and she blamed Noriko for all her troubles..." He shook his head.

"Wait. Was it a subscription box for Japanese candies?" I had flipped past that information in Noriko's notebook earlier today.

"Yeah. Yeah, it was." He seemed taken aback I had knowledge of the situation.

"What happened with Erina?" I prodded him.

"She was furious. I think she blamed Noriko for her faulty website design?" He shrugged. "I guess the store got hacked and everything went south really quick. Noriko was her teacher, a person she trusted. The whole situation did not go over well. Noriko told me all about it a few weeks ago."

Finally, new information! We had been chasing our tails for the past couple of days, wondering what Noriko had been saying to Erina that night we saw them together in the hallway after class. Erina had been pretty aggressive when she was arguing with Noriko at the convenience store. Kayo had felt it from across the store.

Now, we had a suspect *with* a motive, and my mind immediately set the stage. Erina had killed Noriko over a failed business venture. She had come to Noriko's house to confront her about it after they'd already fought. When Noriko asserted that the failure wasn't her fault, Erina had killed her.

Bam. Just like that.

Goro was talking to Mikami while my mind played out the murder in slow motion, over and over. Erina, a tiny, young woman, wielded a heavy garden statue and bashed Noriko over the head.

A heavy garden statue.

That short woman?

Really?

After seeing it a few times in my head, the scene felt wrong. Out of balance. I would need to see the photographs of Noriko again, and that was the last thing I wanted to do.

Did people really kill each other over stolen business ideas?

I supposed anything was possible.

Looking at Mikami, his disheveled appearance and remembering the way he slammed the door on us, I couldn't believe he had given us this information without us having to coax it out of him. He offered us Erina on a platter, and that didn't sit well with me either.

"Thanks for your help. I may send my partner by in the next day or two to ask a few more questions. Here's my business card." Goro handed it over with both hands and a bow. Mikami received it in the same manner, more at ease now than he was before. "If you think of anything else, please let me know."

I pulled on a polite smile and bowed as Mikami shut his door, and we walked away.

Checking my phone, the time was just after ten. Good. I would be home soon, and Yasahiro would have plenty of time to get ready for his interviews. He needed these new employees, and I didn't want to make that hiring process difficult since I would benefit as well.

"Good stuff. Don't you think, Mei? I had no idea Mikami knew Ichisé. This is the link we were looking for."

I nodded my head absently as I stared at the sidewalk, and we made our way to the car.

"Except, it feels wrong, doesn't it?" Goro asked, stopping next to his police car.

"What?" I lifted my eyes from the sidewalk. My thoughts had already moved on to everything else I had to do that day including fitting in a funeral. The hours stretched in front of me like a marathon I had to run, and I could barely accomplish a walk around the park.

"It's too convenient, isn't it?"

I brought my thoughts back to the case. Yeah, Mikami connected the dots between Erina and Noriko pretty quickly.

I huffed a small laugh. "Are you living in my brain? How did you know that's what I was thinking?"

"Because I'm thinking the same thing." Goro turned and looked at the house we just came from. "Did you notice the shadow of the beard and the red eyes?"

"Yeah, but I smelled alcohol, so I thought... Wait, do you think he had been crying?"

"From everything I know about the man, he's usually well-dressed and groomed. He prides himself on looking tip-top at all times."

"Even when people show up at his house in the morning?" I didn't think it was fair to judge the man when he was hungover and pounced upon without prior warning.

I turned around to look at Mikami's house. It was the picture of perfection. The grounds were meticulously groomed, there wasn't a leaf out of place, and his BMW in the driveway sparkled like Mikami had just washed it. Goro was right. This was someone who was first class at all times.

"He's known Noriko Kubo for a year, and they recently

started doing business together... Does that sound familiar to you?"

Goro stared right at me.

Yasahiro's face flashed before my eyes.

"They were dating," I said, convinced. "They've been dating for some time."

Once Yasahiro and I were in a serious relationship, we considered business ventures together, like the tea shop.

"Why didn't he say so?"

"Trust me, Mei," Goro said, opening the door to the car and removing his hat. "He doesn't want us to know. Who are always the top suspects in a murder case? The lovers, past and present."

He rested his arm on the roof and stared at the house.

"Bet he doesn't have an alibi, and he's freaking out. But *that* is a man who is grieving. He's trying to play off Noriko's death like it's nothing, but my gut is telling me different."

Hmmm, I still had a lot to learn.

CHAPTER
TWENTY

"Thank you for the ride," Mom said, opening the car door and sliding inside.

Yasahiro had walked and taken the bus to Sawayaka today so I could have the car. It was easier to go places around town with the car when I also had to take Mari along with me. So I offered to give Mom a ride. She didn't have a parking spot at her new apartment, so she didn't purchase a car after the typhoon last year. Eventually, when she lived in our apartment, she could get one again, if her eyesight cooperated.

"I'm happy to drive you when I can, Mom." I smiled across the car to her and glanced in the rearview mirror to see how Mari was doing. Her eyes were pointed out the window, taking in the beautiful blue sky and sunshine. After a cold night and blustery morning, the weather had turned and warmed up.

Mom relaxed back into her chair. "You seem cheery for someone heading to a funeral."

"I am? Hmmm. I'll try to be a little more sullen."

"No, don't," Mom insisted. "It's nice to see you with a smile on your face. What's going on?"

"Nothing really. Nothing you don't already know. Still

working on getting the house cleared. Still looking for an employee for me or the tea shop. Still trying to find Noriko's murderer."

Mom nodded as I put the car in gear and headed to the opposite side of town to the local funeral home. I had been there for funerals a few times already.

"Any progress? On Noriko's murder?"

"Actually, Goro and I had a great morning. We uncovered more evidence, and we interviewed the venture capitalist who was investing in Noriko's businesses. It was a very enlightening interview."

Mom was quiet for a few moments. "Who watched Mari?" she finally asked.

"My wonderful husband did." I smiled at the road as I drove along. The beautiful day had brought more people out to the sidewalks, and each intersection we passed was crawling with pedestrians.

When Mom made no further remarks, I looked over at her. Her eyes were on the road (more than mine were), and her face was passive.

I cleared my throat and went for it.

"So, Mom, I had an idea I hope you'll be on board with."

She grunted a bit in acknowledgment.

"It has to do with our conversation the other morning. I was wondering if you could babysit Mari two or three mornings a week. You could come over to the apartment or I could bring Mari to you. You could cook and work on your recipes, involve Mari in your cooking and baking, and give me some time off to do more... stuff."

She looked at me sideways, so I rushed on.

"I have so many projects going on right now. Between Oshabe-cha, the house, and then these other investigations I keep getting pulled in on, I need some free mornings."

I remembered Goro and Kumi talking about how their

parents always chipped in to help them with Taiga whenever they needed it.

I had to ask for what I wanted. Mom wasn't a mind reader.

"I think it would be good for you to spend some time in our apartment. I know it's been especially messy these past few weeks, but I promise I'll get it under control. I'll clean it to a state you'll be comfortable in. You can come and get to know the kitchen and think about what you want to do with the place once it's yours."

Hint hint. We are giving you a place to live in. How about a little help in return?

"So, have you found your calling then? What do you want to do on your mornings off?" Mom asked, and I blew out a slow breath.

"I have a few ideas besides dealing with the house." And here I took my biggest risk. What would Mom say? "I'd like to see if there are any opportunities for learning more about the law and investigative work." I swallowed hard and turned the car down the last road to the funeral home. "Goro seems to think I have a knack for police work. It's obviously too late to think about going to the police academy or anything like that."

I snorted at myself and waved my hand, swatting away any ideas of doing something that rash.

"I am definitely not cut out for the police academy." I looked down at my soft belly. "I need to get back into shape."

We pulled into the funeral home's parking lot, and I grabbed a parking spot close to the door. I was unsure of how many people would even show up. Noriko hadn't been a member of the community for long, and Goro had spoken little of her family. She was originally from Hokkaido, but the police briefings hadn't mentioned her parents. Perhaps her parents had passed on already? I knew she had the one sister who lived in Nagano. That bit of information had been on the board at the police station.

I looked over at Mom, and her eyes filled with tears. Uh oh. I was afraid it would come to this. She was angry with me, upset for bunking the status quo.

She turned, and her face broke into an unexpected smile.

"It's a dream come true," she said, and I pulled back in shock. "Mom?"

"You were such a lively and curious child. Always observing, always listening. Remember how you said you wanted to go into law, help people?"

"No...?" My thoughts drifted away. Okay, maybe as a kid, I did dream about myself arguing cases in court or solving mysteries. I had been really into mystery novels for a good number of years.

"I didn't show it... or I tried not to. But I was disappointed when you sold yourself short for a degree in business. You're good with business, sure. You have a sense of what works and what doesn't. But you should've been a lawyer or a police officer or" — she threw up her hands — "whatever."

My cheeks heated at Mom's confession. She must have been holding it in for years.

"Why didn't you say anything the other morning? You could have urged me forward then."

She clicked her tongue. "Mei, *you* had to figure this out for yourself. Me telling you what to do is never going to work. You have always done the opposite of what I suggest."

The blush I had gained elevated to maximum levels. Me? Contrary?

Okay, yeah. I was always doing the opposite of what she suggested.

Ugh. I was a horrible person.

"Are you disappointed in me? In my life?"

"No," Mom said, definitively. "You've made a good life for yourself. You have a loving and successful husband, a great tea shop, and a beautiful baby. You'll understand how I feel someday." She glanced back at Mari in her car seat. "You'll have dreams for Mari, and you'll compromise those dreams for the things she wants. It's just the way of life."

I could only imagine the kinds of dreams and daydreams I would have for Mari as she grew up. What would she want to do with her life? How would I feel about it?

I gripped the steering wheel hard and asked, "So, you'll help me? Because I don't think I can do this without you. Yasahiro is so busy, and there's Oshabe-cha, and —"

"Say no more. Yes. If it helps you finally reach this dream, I'll be happy to help."

"Mom —"

She raised her hand to stop me.

"Only after you get your house in order, though. I cannot spend more than three minutes there now without going out of my mind. Your home is a pigsty. I cannot abide it."

My joy turned to anger in a flash.

But I took a deep breath and nodded. I couldn't argue with her. It *was* a pigsty. It wasn't what I wanted, but that didn't stop the place from being a fire hazard.

Mom inhaled through her nose. "But I will help you with the cleaning, if you need it."

Wow. This was a big concession on her part.

"Got it. It'll be clean. I promise. Mom," I stressed, "I don't think I can go to law school or anything like that." She tilted her head and waited for me to continue. It was time to say it out loud. "I was thinking about becoming a private investigator. You know, handle local cases, nothing too strenuous like these murder cases, though I'm sure the police would ask for help if they needed it."

"I think this is a great idea." Her voice was light and breathy, and she cleared the tears from her eyes.

I was both warmed by her enthusiasm and frightened by it. How long had she been waiting for me to step up and take control of my life?

A lot of our problems from the past few years shifted into

clearer focus. Even though we had been working on being more understanding of each other, she had never mentioned this dream she had for me... and probably for a good reason.

A car pulled up next to us, and Kayo, Kumi, and Chiyo waved.

"We can finish up this talk later." I wanted to move on from all the questions I had about Mom's behavior. "But, I have some bad news. We'll have to continue the search for your photographer."

I opened my door and came around to get Mari out of the back seat.

"Oh, yeah? Did Yasahiro's photographer not want the work?"

Pulling Mari into the baby carrier, I grabbed the diaper bag and slammed the door shut.

"Uh, well, there's no nice way to put this." I glanced up at the funeral parlor's sign. "But he died last year."

"Oh."

"Yeah."

"That's unfortunate. I'll pray for him today too."

"Prayers sound like a good idea to me."

I smiled at Kayo, Kumi, and Chiyo and followed them all inside.

CHAPTER
TWENTY-ONE

Turned out Noriko had very little family. In the greeting area of the funeral home, an older woman stood by a photo of Noriko and welcomed each mourner as they approached. This woman's husband and two children stood next to her, each of them deferential and obedient, not broken up or in tears. I waited my turn to speak with the family and express my condolences then asked, as politely as possible, how they were all related. The woman was Noriko's older sister, and their parents had been dead and gone five years. Noriko didn't have any other family.

Except for her ex-husband, of course. But divorce was a strange beast in Japan. Most people washed their hands entirely of an ex's family members, even if children were involved. I thought of Yasahiro's family, who had become my family too over the last year. I couldn't imagine just cutting off contact with them if we were to divorce. There were so many things I did not understand about my own society.

In the banquet room, several people were already sitting at tables, eating small crudités, and drinking saké. I scanned the room as I crossed to the buffet table. Noriko's ex-husband, Takuma Kubo, stood with his back against the wall, drinking saké and keeping his eyes on everyone. It was a defensive posture, something one used to keep enemies in sight at all times. What was he doing? Watching the crowd to find Noriko's murderer? I thought about our interview with him. He had been angry but brushed off her death except for that moment when he confessed he had known her all their lives. In that one moment, I had witnessed the hurt in his voice, the pain in his eyes. It was brief, but it had been there.

I kept my eyes on him as I bent over the table and tried to get a few snacks with Mari in the carrier in front of me.

"What do you think?" I asked her, quietly. "Should I eat everything?"

My baby stared up at me like I was the center of her universe. I kissed the top of her head and sighed.

Mom came up behind me and set her hand on the small of my back. "Can you get me a few things? I'll grab us a table."

"Sure," I said, adding vegetable sushi rolls to my plate. They had a nice spread of food, nothing too extravagant. I wondered how many people they expected to show up today.

Just as I resumed my observation of Takuma Kubo, his eyes flicked to the door, and his nose flared. I turned to see who had caught his attention.

Erina Ichisé.

Takuma's girlfriend and one of the last people to see Noriko alive had shown up for the funeral!

And Takuma Kubo looked angry that she was there.

My brain tumbled as I connected the dots. Noriko and Takuma had been married, then they divorced when Takuma had cheated on her. They both also lost their jobs. Noriko had done well for herself with a consultation and teaching business and online businesses too while Takuma had done poorly for himself. Had Erina been the woman that had split them up? Did Takuma suspect Erina of killing Noriko?

Where did Yutaka Mikami, the investor and possibly Noriko's boyfriend, fit into this?

I hurried to the table and slid the plate in front of Mom.

"Can you take Mari, please?" I pulled Mari from the carrier, gave her a set of brightly colored plastic keys to play with, and set her on Mom's lap. "Be right back."

Erina spotted me from across the room and did her best to avoid me. As I walked along the near wall, she walked in the opposite direction along the far wall. Well, at least she wasn't going to run for it. But she remembered me from Sawayaka.

Kayo and Kumi were finishing up their condolences as I entered the first room again. We had arrived at the funeral parlor at the same time, but they had used the bathroom first and then got into a conversation with someone they knew. They ended up farther back in line.

I frantically waved to them and ushered them into the front vestibule instead of into the banquet hall.

"Did you see who's here?" I asked, my voice rising with giddiness.

"I did." Kayo's eyes were shining with glee.

"Who?" Kumi asked, grabbing both of us.

"The mystery woman, Erina," I blurted out. "The woman we saw outside of Noriko's class, the last class we all attended."

Kumi's mouth dropped open.

"And she's dating Noriko's ex-husband," Kayo said, checking her phone. "Goro is on his way. The officer we put in charge of watching her house followed her to this part of town, so I had a feeling she would be here. This could be the break we need. Maybe she'll do or say something, confess even. Funerals do strange things to people."

Kumi squeezed my hand. "I have a feeling she did it."

I shook my head. "I don't know. I'm not so sure she hurt Noriko."

Kumi's hand squeezed mine harder. The door opened, and we stepped aside to let someone into the funeral parlor, bowing and excusing ourselves.

"How can you say that, Mei? She's so obviously guilty. She was fighting with Noriko, and now she's romantically involved with Noriko's ex?"

I shrugged at her and Kayo. "I think she's associated with Noriko's death somehow, but did she kill her?" I shook my head as I tried to play that scene through again. Noriko towered over Erina. Where had the final, crushing blow landed? "I don't know. I really need to see the photos of Noriko from the crime scene again."

It was one thing to visit the crime scene this morning with nothing else there. But I needed more details, and I hadn't looked hard enough at the photos the first time.

Kumi paled. "How can you look at those?" She wasn't judging. She was curious about how I'd gained the guts to do such a thing.

Kayo stepped in for me. "When you look at enough crime scene photos, you become immune to them. In a way, the more you look, the more attuned you become to the details of a murder. Mei is tough." Kayo gave me a reassuring nod.

Kumi heaved a huge sigh. "Goro has said this before as well. But I feel weird talking about this at her funeral."

I touched her shoulder and smiled reassuringly.

"Let's go back inside, and we'll see what happens."

Kumi was right. We needed to be more deferential during this mourning period for Noriko and her family.

Except, when we returned to the banquet room, the mood had changed drastically since we'd left.

Mom's eyes were wide as she wrapped her arms protectively

around Mari, and Chiyo covered her mouth with one of her hands.

"You killed her!" Takuma Kubo shouted at Yutaka Mikami.

Oh, boy.

It wasn't Erina we had to worry about, it was the two men from Noriko's life facing each other across the room.

Mikami had finally shown up. He looked marginally better than he had that morning. He had showered and shaved, maybe even caught a nap, but he still was not at his best.

And the rage he held in check was enough to make him pink with anger.

"I *loved* her, which is more than I could say about you."

Suspicions confirmed. Mikami and Noriko *had* been dating, and those red eyes and scruffy cheeks this morning had been more because of grief than a bender at the local izakaya.

The funeral parlor staff were frozen in place, just like everyone else in the room. Erina stood at a spot near to Takuma Kubo, her mouth covered in horror. Mom and Chiyo were enraptured. Never before had something this dramatic happened at a local funeral.

Takuma swore, and several people gasped. "That is one of the biggest lies I've ever heard." His eyes were wild and crazy. "You killed her. Smashed her head in. How could you?"

"Exactly," Mikami said, a cold calmness coming over him. "How could I? Why would I? We were in love. She was going to move in with me! You have no real reason to suspect me except for your jealousy."

Takuma paused. His eyes darted left and right. "Me? Jealous? She was going to get back together with me! You were the jealous one!"

"You're delusional. She would never get back together with you."

Kayo's eyes were slitted and staring hard at Takuma Kubo.

She was in her casual clothes, but she pulled her police badge from her back pocket and stepped forward to present it.

"Takuma Kubo, I'm taking you down to the station for questioning."

"Why me?" His voice squeaked, and he pulled away.

"All of you." Kayo's hard stare landed on Erina, Mikami, and then on Takuma again. "Causing a public disturbance at a funeral? You all must be mad."

The door to the banquet room opened, and Goro entered with another police officer. He took a read of the room immediately and joined Kayo.

"What's going on here?"

"These two have been yelling at each other and disturbing the peace." Kayo gestured to the two men. "I want them all brought in for questioning about Noriko Kubo's death."

"You can't detain me." Takuma's voice rose in indignation. "I didn't hurt Noriko. I was in bed and asleep when it happened." He looked straight at Erina, and she paled by three shades of white.

She whispered, "He was with me." We all stared at her. "We've been dating for months."

Her hands shook as she considered reaching out for Takuma, but she pulled them back and squeezed them together.

"We can and will detain you," Goro informed Takuma, "as long as we need. You have questions to answer."

Mom stood up from her seat and crossed the room to me. Mari reached for me, so I pulled her into my arms.

"It was madness, Mei. They saw each other across the room and just started yelling," she whispered. "Never have I ever seen such a poor display of character at a funeral before."

We watched Kayo, Goro, and the other officer speak in low voices to the three. Erina grabbed her bag from a chair, and Mikami stepped to the side to get his coat. But Takuma continued to argue with Goro, and I wished I were closer so I could hear what they were saying.

"She was my wife!" His voice was broken, and his eyes filled with tears. Erina dropped her head to stare at the floor. She was ashamed. But of what exactly? Takuma's continued devotion to an ex-wife? His behavior in the funeral parlor? Or maybe something else?

I didn't know.

But I would find out.

CHAPTER
TWENTY-TWO

Erina's actions at the funeral played over and over in my head as I waited for Nahomi, the young woman who came recommended by Emi to be my housekeeper, to arrive at Oshabe-cha.

Why had Erina acted so ashamed? Wouldn't an ardent lover jump to her boyfriend's aid in a tense situation? I was surprised by how docile she was around Takuma Kubo. She was not the same independent young woman who had run away from me at Sawayaka. There was something below the surface there that poked at my instincts, and I wasn't sure what it was.

I stared out the window and sipped on a cup of tea until I saw Nahomi arrive. I figured it was her. This young woman was the right age and arrived at the tea shop on her own, unlike the other tourists or elderly customers who always seemed to appear in groups.

Edging around the other customers, I approached the young woman.

"Nahomi Shimizu?"

"Oh! Yes, yes. Hello. Are you Mei Suga?" She almost gave me a hug, but she pulled back at the last second. She was exuberant which was a nice change of pace from the dour faces of the funeral.

"I am. Welcome, welcome. Please call me Mei. Thank you so much for coming into Oshabe-cha today."

I sat us both at a table near the back of the tea shop next to Mari's car seat stroller. She was fast asleep in there, taking her afternoon nap.

My first impression of Nahomi was solidly in the likable camp. Her eyes were alert, and her expression conveyed a certain amount of wonder. She was in her early twenties, but she seemed a lot younger, like she had just stepped out of elementary school into the big bad world. Her smile was friendly, her lips colored pink along with her rounded cheeks.

I remembered being that young. I had been in school at her age, going to classes, drinking beers with friends in the evening, and eating cheap food from back-alley dives in Tokyo. Ah, those were the good ol' days.

Even if she was young, Nahomi knew her manners because she bowed first before taking the chair I offered her.

"Thank you for having me here, Mei."

"Be sure to thank Emi, too. She spoke very highly of you."

"Oh, she's too kind, as always."

"I'm going to keep this short because I spent most of my day at a funeral, and now I'm tired." I glanced at my phone to check the time. Yasahiro would be upstairs in the apartment soon, and we would tackle Mari's evening screamfest together with some burgers and a glass (or two) of wine.

"Oh no. I'm sorry to hear that. Was it someone you were close to?"

I relaxed back in the chair and looked over at Mari. Her breathing was a steady metronome.

"Yeah, a bit. I only knew her for a month or two. She taught a small business course here in town. She was killed earlier this week."

Nahomi gasped and covered her mouth. "Do murders happen here? I thought this area of Japan was safe."

I shrugged. "All of Japan is safe compared to the rest of the world. We've had some crime here but nothing more than usual."

Don't mention the other previous four murders and the serial killer, Mei. I wanted this young woman to work for me and feel safe and happy here, not run for the hills.

Nahomi nodded eagerly. "I've never left Japan. The world is too scary for me."

"I completely understand," I said, reassuring her. Did I understand? Yes, I did. Did I agree? Not anymore. I got my passport recently so I could fly to France with Yasahiro for our honeymoon. I had never been so excited to have that document, to open it and see the immigration stamp, and to use it and know I was going places. Someday I would travel the world.

"Anyway, I think you'll like Chikata. And the people who come here to the tea shop are pretty great too. Did Emi tell you what I was looking for in an employee?"

Nahomi relaxed and opened a small notebook she had grabbed from her bag.

"Yes, she did. She told me you need a basic housekeeper? Someone to help keep your apartment clean and organized, do laundry, that kind of thing. Is that correct?"

"Yes." My shoulders lightened hearing she already knew what the job would entail. "I think I'll really need you to help me get rid of stuff in the apartment first. There's just no room up there anymore. I'd also like some support here in the tea shop too with organizing and cleaning. You wouldn't have to help customers as I'd like to hire someone for here full time, but maybe once a week I'd have you here to work as well."

She nodded and scribbled away in her notebook. "That all sounds doable." She set her mechanical pencil down on top of her notebook and folded her hands over them both. "So, you may know that my father is sick."

I nodded but didn't say anything.

"He has cancer, and the outlook for him is not good."

"I'm so sorry."

Her face shifted from being a naïve young girl to a wizened adult. She was so changed with only one breath.

"My mother has never earned money at a job, so I have no idea what she'll do when he passes away. So I felt it was my responsibility to bring in enough money to support the family. I have cut back my schooling this semester to one class. Just the one." She held up one finger. "And I want to be home to help out at least two days a week. This means I have plenty of other hours to put towards work."

My heart squeezed as I imagined having to do this at her age. No beers with friends. No cheap food in alleys in Tokyo. No laughing and late nights out at the clubs. This was serious business, life and death.

"I can give you lots of hours at a competitive rate," I blurted out. I had meant to go into this deal as a negotiation. But I had the compulsion to 'save' her, even if I knew she was more than capable of saving herself. "If you like helping customers, you could even do that here."

She dipped her head and shifted a lock of hair over her ear. "I'm not sure I would be good at it."

"Well, I guess we'll see." I bit my lip as I thought about the other things Emi said about her. "Emi mentioned you're also an artist?"

"Oh, I wouldn't say that." She immediately started the humble sidestep. "I dabble with digital photography and scrapbooking. That's about it."

Digital photography?

"My mother is looking to publish a cookbook and needs a photographer, actually. Maybe that's something you could also do. We have a budget for a photographer and no photographer."

She flipped open her notebook and wrote it down. "That

would be a great opportunity. I take photos of food all the time. It's the way of social media."

She wasn't wrong there.

"So, what do you think? I know you're three stops away on the train, and this may be a bit of a hike for you —"

"I'd love to give it a trial run."

I blinked in surprise, impressed by her ability to make a quick decision without committing one-hundred percent.

"A trial run is a perfect idea. I have your number, so let me speak to my husband tonight about when we can have you over to our apartment for the first time. This week is already so hectic, but I want to get a schedule going before the days slip away."

Mari stirred in her car seat, her little fists reaching and stretching.

"Aw!" Nahomi's demeanor changed again, back to the starry-eyed young woman. I had a feeling she kept both personalities around depending on the circumstances. "This is your baby, right?"

"Yes," I said, getting to my feet and unstrapping Mari. She began to cry a bit, so I picked her up and held her to my chest. "This is Mari. She's three months old and quite the handful." I winked at Nahomi, and she grinned.

"I know absolutely nothing about babies," Nahomi said as she put her notebook away. "I'm an only child and never did any babysitting."

"Well, if you want to learn, I have the perfect opportunity for you."

She smiled and bowed. "I'm sure I'll pick up some pointers along the way."

I returned her bow. "I'll call you tomorrow morning."

I watched her as she browsed the tea along the wall and made her way back out to the street. Something told me I had just met an old soul stuffed into a young body, and I wondered what the coming months would bring us.

Kissing Mari on the forehead, I hoped for good things, for me, for my family, and for Nahomi too.

———

I SIPPED ON MY GLASS OF WINE WHILE BOUNCING screaming Mari on my hip and watching Yasahiro grill hamburgers on the stove. Mari let out a particularly heart-breaking wail and almost screamed herself hoarse.

"Oh my," I groaned, setting my glass down and moving her to a horizontal position along my left arm. "You are in fine form tonight." I rocked her side to side and wondered how much longer this would go on. Would she scream and cry for the next few months? The time already felt long and arduous.

Yasahiro groaned as well, threw his head back, and sighed. I glanced at him from the side of my eyes. His shoulders drooped, and even his hair had lost its vibrancy. Between all the noise at home and the craziness at work, his patience had thinned. I couldn't really blame him. I was in the same boat.

But something about seeing him suffer spurred me forward.

I approached him from behind and set my hand gently on his lower back.

"How long till dinner?" I asked, keeping my voice on an even keel.

He sighed. "About five minutes for the burgers. The fries have another ten minutes, and the salad is ready."

"Okay." I bounced Mari back and forth even though it didn't seem to help. "We'll be in the bedroom."

I closed the doors between the bedroom, the bathroom, and the main room, grabbed the vacuum cleaner, and entered the bedroom from the other side, shutting the door behind us.

I wanted to be out in the kitchen with Yasahiro, trading stories of his day at Sawayaka and my day at the funeral, but desperate times called for desperate measures.

"Okay, little one," I cooed, trying to soothe her, though I had less patience than she did. I set her on the bed, plugged in the vacuum cleaner, and turned it on. It whirred to life, and Mari turned her head to see where the noise came from.

Returning to the bed, I lifted my shirt and got her latched on for some comfort feeding. I didn't like pacifying her with my own breasts, but... desperation.

I closed my eyes and savored the steady white noise of the vacuum cleaner, a break from the screaming and crying. Mari ate like I hadn't fed her an hour ago. Maybe her growth spurt was finally peaking, and we'd get a break soon?

And we needed that break, just like we needed the house-keeper. The pile of clothes in the corner of the bedroom had grown in the last few days, and we had added three new card-board boxes to the collection next to my wardrobe. Now that I had met Nahomi, I was hesitant to welcome her into my messy home. A good deal of shame plagued my conscience as I imag-ined her in here, cleaning and organizing. Two things I could totally do, but yet... Well.

The door cracked open, and Yasahiro stuck his head in. He blinked in surprise.

"The vacuum cleaner again?" he asked with a smile. My glass of red wine was in his hand, so he lifted it up with a raise of his eyebrows. I shifted Mari so I could hold her to my chest one-armed. The glass of wine was in my hand a moment later.

"I really shouldn't drink and breastfeed, you know."

"Seems to me you both could use it right now." He leaned forward to look at Mari. Her arm was thrown over her face, and her lips twitched at my breast.

"Dinner's ready. Do you think you could detach? Will she go to sleep?"

I looked at the clock. Seven in the evening. "Hmmm. Doubt-ful, but I'm willing to try."

I shifted over so I could lay her on the bed. Once I was sure she was out, I gently pulled myself away and slid off the bed like a ninja.

Both Yasahiro and I raised our fists into the air and mouthed, "Success!" at each other. He pumped his fist. I covered back up, built a small wall of pillows around the bed for her, and kept the vacuum cleaner on.

Out in the dining area, we sat down at the table with a synchronized sigh.

I wanted to ask him, "Does it get any better?" but I'd sound like a broken record because that was pretty much all I had asked for the last week.

Instead, I ignored the parenting situation entirely and stared down at my meal.

"This looks *amazing*." My mouth watered as I contemplated the thick hamburger, the homemade bun, the leafy greens, and the condiments on the side. Lifting the top of the bun, I lathered on the ketchup and mayonnaise like it was going out of style. Yasahiro liked ketchup on his burger and vinegar with his fries. That habit came from his time in Europe.

"Thanks. It was an easy meal, and it's been a while since we cooked red meat at home. It was time. How was the funeral?" He bit into his burger, and my mouth watered. I started with my fries.

"Dramatic. Goro had to show up and take some people into custody."

He gasped. "No!"

"Yes. I think we're close to figuring out who committed the murder. I have my suspicions but no clear evidence yet."

I bit into the burger, and it tasted even better than it smelled. I closed my eyes and savored the mouthful. I should've been eating faster. Who knew when Mari would wake up again?

"Are you keeping your suspicions to yourself?"

I revealed a small smile. "Yep. But you get all the secrets."

His returning smile warmed my whole body.

"I have a feeling about the ex-husband. For a while, I thought maybe Noriko's student — her name is Erina, by the way — was the one to kill her. But something's not right about her nor the circumstances of Noriko's death. Still, it could be this other guy, Yutaka Mikami. He was involved with Noriko, and if she had contemplated going back to her ex-husband, then the new guy could've killed her out of jealousy. And this morning we found love notes in her desk and a discarded necklace out in the garden too that I think might be connected."

I shrugged and took another bite.

The main suspects were Noriko's lover, Yutaka Mikami, her husband, Takuma Kubo, and Erina Ichisé. They all had plausible reasons to kill her, too. It was a real head-scratcher of a case. I suspected them all but had my doubts about each.

"Tell me about the people you interviewed for Sawayaka," I said, changing the subject. "Are you happy with any of the new candidates?"

"Actually —"

His phone buzzed.

This was an abnormal thing to happen to us. My phone was always buzzing and pinging with messages and calls. When I sat down to eat, I had to turn it off or I'd be continuously bombarded. Yasahiro, though, kept his phone on all the time, yet he hardly ever received calls. People respected his private time. I was the only person who had permission to contact him whenever I wanted to.

That meant this was an emergency.

So I wasn't surprised when I saw the Sawayaka main number on his screen before he answered it.

"Hello? Hi, Ana. What's up?"

He listened for a long moment, removed his napkin from his lap, and set it on the table next to his half-eaten meal.

"I understand. I'll be there in ten minutes... No, it's okay. I'm glad you called. See you soon."

He set his phone down and pinched the bridge of his nose.

"Sadachi called in sick, and she's never sick." Sadachi was one of the prep chefs, someone the whole staff relied on.

"Oh no. Is she okay?"

"A double ear infection and vertigo. I'm glad she called in sick because no one with vertigo should be using a knife."

He stood up and crossed the space between us to kiss my forehead as I looked up at him.

"Sorry."

"No, no. I completely understand." I grabbed his hand and squeezed it. "Get going. Will you eat there? Or do you want to bring your dinner?"

He began to undress so he could get into his work clothes. "Put it in the fridge for me. I'll eat it tomorrow."

He hurried through getting dressed, pulling dirty clothes out of the bathroom and wearing them again. He could do this since he wore chef whites at the restaurant.

I kissed him goodbye and watched him descend the stairs two at a time, get in the car, and drive off.

Okay, then. Just me for dinner.

That's when the vacuum cleaner quit in the bedroom.

I froze in place, not believing my ears.

Oh no! Was it dead permanently? Had it blown a fuse? What happened?

Mari woke with a cough and a cry, and my heart dropped to my toes. I raised my fists to the sky and cursed all the gods that ever were.

So much for a quiet dinner tonight.

CHAPTER
TWENTY-THREE

Yasahiro gave me another morning off before I would have to return to work at Oshabe-cha, but the time would not be free. I still had plenty of other mysteries to solve.

I popped the trunk on the car, and Kumi and I looked in on the large cardboard box inside.

"Are you sure this is going to help?" She looked past the construction fence to our property, her face wide with worry. "I was thinking we should call in an expert on ghosts and paranormal creatures."

I paused and tried not to roll my eyes. "I think that's a sweet idea but unnecessary." It was a completely bonkers idea, but I knew better than to say that out loud. "There are no ghosts or paranormal creatures here. I'm sure of it. There's a logical explanation for these accidents, and we're going to find out how and why they've been happening."

"Didn't your neighbor say that she heard a baby crying in here the other day?" Kumi reached over and grabbed my shoulder. "Does anyone around here have a baby?"

I swallowed my fear. *Remember, Mei, you don't believe in ghosts.* Nope. No, I did not.

"She didn't say it was recently. Moeko is older, and her hearing is failing her. And here she comes right now..."

"Hello! Mei! Kumi!" My neighbor, Moeko, waved at us as she crossed the road to meet us. She was wearing three layers of old sweaters and coats that looked like they were leftover from World War II. But her smile was new and fresh, and it brightened her face.

What a difference from last week when she practically assaulted me while I was getting Mari out of the car.

"Hi!" Kumi smiled and waved back. "How are you? Are you well?"

"I am, thank you. Oh, I'm so glad you're here today." She stopped, and we all bowed to each other. "I wanted to say thank you for the lovely donuts. My husband and I enjoyed them with tea. It was such a treat. I must admit I've been craving them ever since."

Note to self: Moeko loved sweet pastries. Now I knew how to bribe her and keep her happy.

"I'm so glad you liked them," Kumi cooed. It was one of her favorite missions in life to find the perfect gifts for every person. You could never go wrong with pastries.

"We did. Thank you again." She bowed. "So, I was sipping my morning tea by the window this morning when I saw movement in here."

I held my breath while I waited for her to continue. Her smile dissolved away.

"Unfortunately, it was not who I suspected. A man was injured on the property, yes?"

My stomach knotted into a ball.

"I think he was the man I saw. His shoulder was wrapped, and his arm in a sling."

Ugh. No.

"He toured the property with your foreman, Mr. Imai, and a few men in suits. They took photos." She clucked her tongue a few times. "A shame. I'm afraid you might be expecting a lawsuit soon."

I cursed up a storm in my head as I turned to look at the property.

My goodness, was my new home already cursed? I kept trying to have a positive outlook on the whole business, but my confidence was wearing as thin as my patience.

"No worries, Mei," Kumi said, wrapping her arm around my shoulder and squeezing. "I'm sure it'll work out." She let go and clasped her hands together. "So, Moeko, have you heard anything strange coming from the property lately? Hmmm?"

This time my eyes rolled so hard I saw my brain.

"Heard anything? What do you mean?" Moeko wrapped a threadbare scarf around her neck and pulled down her knit hat.

"Oh, you know. Bear calls? Maybe ghosts sifting through the trash?" Kumi's eyebrows climbed, and I held back a snort of a laugh.

Moeko's smile returned. "Nothing but some quiet crying noises. Reminds me of a baby, really."

"Again?" I asked.

She shivered, and my mood changed like clouds obscuring the sun.

"Again, sorry. Just last night." She tried to warm her arms by rubbing them. "I should go back inside. It's a bit chilly out here for me. I just wanted to say hello."

"Go get warm," I said with a reassuring smile. "I'll be sure to drop by soon."

She left with a wave, and Kumi elbowed me in the ribs.

"See? A baby crying. *Ghost* babies crying, Mei."

I sighed as I looked at my box in the trunk again. "She could've heard a cat fight or cats mating and thought it was a baby crying. It *is* spring, after all. All the horny cats are out looking for mates."

Kumi snorted a laugh. "Not Mimoji."

I remembered when Mimoji, my mom's ginger cat, used to go on the prowl for females. What a noisy affair that always was. And it didn't matter that we had him fixed. He still hunted for lady cats until he got mature enough to ignore the cravings.

"Mimoji is an old soul. He has no interest in young lady cats anymore. Help me with this?"

We each grabbed a side of the cardboard box and tugged it from the trunk.

"Wow. What did you buy?"

"Lots of fun stuff. Yasahiro nearly died when I showed him the receipt, but I assured him we can reuse the cameras around the house and at Sawayaka when we're done with them here."

After much deliberation, I had purchased six battery-operated game cameras for the property, and an additional wifi security system for when electricity was hooked up on the property. Right now, the construction crews used generators to run any heavy equipment, but once the walls were up, electricity would power most everything on site.

Still, I needed to get to that point. I needed this house. I needed the space and the peace of mind from having our family home around us. Though I'd had some time and energy to clean up the apartment a little over the past week, our current space was far from perfect. We were still bursting from every cabinet and drawer. My sanity was filament-thin and seemed to break every time I tripped on a baby toy.

Kumi and I carried the box onto the property, past the fence, and into the main space.

"Have you made any more progress with finding out about the family who used to live here?" Kumi asked as she walked backwards over the gravel.

We dropped the box on a leveled area of ground near the main building structure that was half erected. I could see my constructed house in my head. I just had to get the building moving again.

"The one whose child died here? Not yet. I texted with Sakiko Yoshida —"

"The private investigator?"

"Yes, the same. And she said she'd stop by Oshabe-cha with information later this morning. I'm hoping she has details I can follow up on. We'll see."

"I hope so, too. It would be nice to put this situation to rest finally," Kumi agreed. She bent over to look into the large box and take inventory of all I had in there.

"We should get moving on this so I can return to Oshabe-cha and you can get to Kutsuro Matsu. Last night, I opened the boxes for these cameras and installed the batteries and the memory cards," I said, opening the box and looking around at the property. "Now we just need to set them up in the right spots and hope for the best."

Kumi wrapped her scarf around her neck tighter. The day had dawned with cooler temperatures and a stiff wind. Any day now it would be warm for good. Any day now was not soon enough. I needed summer... soon.

"Where do you think most of the commotion has been happening on the property?"

I looked around and tried to remember where the foreman had pointed when Akira had broken his leg. He had fallen into a hole that had appeared out of nowhere.

"Look around for a hole that was dug on the property. And then some of the workers said things had been moved inside the main structure." That was how Wada, the man who hated me and thought I was a witch, had fallen and hurt his shoulder. Something had skewed the supports inside the main building.

Kumi and I searched and found two holes dug into the wet ground. Hmmm. I didn't remember there being more than one. They were almost a meter deep, curved with scratch marks along the length of it. I squatted down and ran my fingers along the long marks. This was the part of the property where there used to be a small garden plot, but it would eventually be a stone patio. The foundation of the house was only a few meters away. Since we were sandwiching two plots together, my house would take up more than the footprint of the old house that had been here. Hmmm, why these particular spots?

Kumi gasped when she squatted down next to me. "See? Paranormal creatures. Maybe it's a shifter bear or a fox... or a family of foxes. Oh, Mei. A family of foxes is no good. They bring bad luck to properties. They'll lure away Yasahiro or even little Mari."

I stood up and lost what was left of my cool. "Will you stop, please?" I held up my hand and tried to keep the annoyance out of my voice. "There's a simple explanation for this."

Resting my hands on my hips, I took another survey of the property. Our plots edged on a forest near the boundary of town. Anything could be in those woods. Yes, Kumi was right. Maybe even bears. Not shifter bears because, come on. This was not some romance novel. But it could be anything.

Yet, I had an idea.

"I'm going to make a guess." I smiled as my betting nature came over me. I had bet on plenty of things over the last two years. I'd won some bets and lost others. This time I felt confident. "How about we make a wager?"

Kumi stood up next to me and laughed. "Remember when you bet Goro you would solve the murder case of Akiko's father?" She threw her head back and cackled. "That was so much fun. I'd never seen him so determined before." With a sigh, she folded her arms across her chest. "I think that's when he really started taking things seriously, wanting a real career." She bumped her shoulder into mine. "You may have had something to do with that."

I smiled at the memory. I was newly back in town then and feeling plucky. It was hard to believe how far I had come from there.

"So, here's my wager. You bet it's a bear or a paranormal creature?"

"Absolutely. Something strange is going on here."

"I bet it's a dog. Maybe it's a stray, or it belongs to one of the neighbors. It can't dig up its own yard, so it comes here for some digging fun."

She pinched her lips. "Your explanation sounds more reasonable than mine."

"You think?" I held out my hand to shake on it. She reached out to meet my hand and stopped.

"Wait. What are we betting?"

"A night of drinks at Izakaya Jūshi. I'm dying to see if Kayo has the hots for Hideo."

"Oh! Me too!" Her face broke into a huge smile, and she folded her hands together at her chest. "This sounds like a win-win situation to me. I'd gladly pay for drinks to see if Kayo flirts with Hideo."

"I thought so," I said, thrusting out my hand.

She met mine and gave it a firm shake.

"You're on, Mei. Now let's set up these cameras and get the heck out of here. It's freezing today!"

She shivered as she pulled her coat around her, and before we left, we had six cameras all set up and waiting to nab my mysterious trespasser.

CHAPTER
TWENTY-FOUR

I stepped into Oshabe-cha and felt like I had entered a strange place for a moment. It reminded me of being away from home and forgetting what home felt or smelled like. The moment was a disconnect, a lapse of memory that tripped over itself.

Oh right. I remembered this place.

"There's Mommy!" Yasahiro turned away from talking with Emi to wave Mari's hand at me. "I gave her some tummy time this morning, and then she hung out on the play mat for a bit while I cooked up lunch for you. There's sweet potato, wild rice, chicken and greens in the fridge upstairs."

He handed her over, and my stomach growled immediately. I rarely ate such healthy food, but all of that sounded amazing. Maybe I was changing...

"Do you make that at Sawayaka?" Emi asked. "That's just the kind of food I love to eat."

"Come by anytime..." His speech faltered. "Except for right now because we've been slammed for the last week with customers. Things will get better once I figure out how to fix the restaurant overflow."

I held Mari and bounced her to keep her happy. "We never did get a chance to talk about how we'd proceed with your ideas at dinner the other night."

"My date ran out on me," he said with a chuckle. Then he leaned in and kissed both Mari and me on the cheek. "That's okay. I still have more research to do. We'll talk more at dinner. Gotta go!"

He rushed for the door but turned around before exiting. "Oh, how did the camera setup go?"

I gave him a thumbs-up, a habit I picked up by watching episodes of *FRIENDS* online. I needed to do that again. My English fluency was slipping away. "All good! I'll check on the memory cards tomorrow."

When the door shut behind Yasahiro, I sighed and rested my creaky body at one of the unoccupied tables. Two older women I only vaguely recognized sat at a table drinking tea and chatting while my usual client, Mr. Shigimo, read the newspaper at a table near the front door.

"No Mrs. Murata today?" I asked Emi as she sat down opposite me.

"She called and said she would stay home and bake bread today. She'll bring you a loaf tomorrow."

"Ah," I said, reminiscing about last year. "She tried to teach me how to bake bread. I can make a passable loaf if I don't forget about it."

Emi smiled. "That's the trick, right? It's hard to remember to keep one's mind on every task all the time."

I looked around at my feet for the diaper bag and grabbed one of Mari's colorful squeaky toys from the mix inside. She pounded it on the table.

"Speaking of which..." I also reached into the diaper bag for my handy notebook. I set it on the table away from Mari's hands. "I'd like to have a little going away party here for you if you don't mind."

Her eyes widened. "Oh no. I couldn't. That's far too generous."

"Oh, please, stop." And then I added on a smile to let her know I wasn't offended. "You've been a vital part of my life and business for the last few months. I simply must throw a little party to bid you farewell. Not that you shouldn't ever come back!" I held up my hand. "You are always welcome here."

"Well, that's very sweet. I suppose I'll have to accept."

"Thank you." I blew out a slow breath. I appreciated her not making a big deal out of it. "I was thinking we'd do it on your last day... which is next Wednesday, right?" I looked at the calendar at the front of my notebook.

"Yes, you're right," she confirmed. "That sounds lovely. Please let me know what I can do to help."

"Nope. You don't need to do anything. I'm going to ask my mother to help. She's been working on new recipes for her cook-book, and I'm sure she'd love to test them out on an unsuspecting crowd." I winked at her, and she grinned.

"Your mother is an excellent cook. You must have been spoiled by her food growing up."

The embarrassment of my wayward culinary youth snuck up and heated my cheeks. "Well, that's a story for another day."

Emi was kind enough not to poke me for details.

"I think I've finished all the recent paperwork, and I left it in a pile on the back room table. Would you mind looking it over to make sure I didn't forget anything?" I pointed to my checklist in my notebook. "I'm taking notes on everything, so I don't screw it up once you're gone."

"Sure. I'd be happy to." Emi stood up and brushed off her apron. "What else do we have planned for today?"

I glanced at my phone. It was already five past eleven. "Well, I'm expecting someone soon. She said she'd show up between eleven and eleven-thirty."

Emi looked towards the front window and pointed. "Your

guest wouldn't happen to be that harassed looking woman chain-smoking and yelling into her phone outside, would it?"

I closed my eyes for a brief moment, knowing exactly what was happening without looking.

"I'm sure it is."

When I turned to look, Sakiko was stabbing at her phone with her index finger, a cigarette dangling from her lips. Her skin had grown darker and more leather-like since the last time I saw her, and her hair was streaked with gray, pulled up and wild around her head. She jabbed out her cigarette, took a plastic bottle from her purse, and dropped the cigarette butt into it, resealing the cap. I shuddered imagining accidentally drinking it. Gross. Thanks a lot, daydreaming brain.

Sakiko stormed in, and Emi retreated into the back room. I was going to introduce them, but I supposed not. I couldn't blame Emi for running away. Sakiko was a strong presence.

"Mei Suga, how are you?" She didn't bow, but instead, she stood in the middle of the tea shop, looked up and around, and nodded her head in approval. "So this is the place I've heard so much about?"

"You have?" I gathered up Mari and met her in the middle of the shop.

"Absolutely. You know small towns." She made a chatting motion with her right hand though it looked a lot like a crocodile. "It's nice." Her voice rolled over the compliment like a dusty gravel driveway.

She threw her arms up in the air unexpectedly, and Mari squealed with glee.

"And look at this little one! Ah, she's a peach." Sakiko reached in and tickled Mari's neck. Mari immediately fell in love.

Gotta say. Didn't see that coming. This woman was a consummate bachelorette, not a mother. She was so rough around the edges, I couldn't even picture her being a treasured aunt.

Apparently, I hadn't done enough daydreaming about the life she led outside of stalking cheating men and women.

"Thanks," I said, smiling at Mari and Sakiko. "And thank you for coming here. I've been running around like crazy lately. It's nice to stay in one place for an hour."

She swatted her hand. "No problem. I'm always out and on the run."

"Let's have a seat over here." I showed her to the table I was just sitting at.

Before sitting with her, I said goodbye to the ladies who were leaving. Shigimo had fallen asleep while leaning back in his chair. I was massively jealous of his ability to sleep anywhere. I pulled Mari's stroller closer to the table and strapped her into it. The stroller was just a glorified car seat holder at this point in her life, full of toys and a window on the world.

"So, you gave me a name and an address. I didn't think I'd find the family, but I got lucky."

She handed over two papers. On top was a broken down family tree and sequence of addresses. Sakiko had started with the couple who had lost the child on the property and then she found them, their other children, and their children.

I scanned down the paper, hoping to see something that looked familiar to me. A name, a location, anything I could use to my advantage when I called on these people.

But no, nothing here looked familiar except for the names of the parents.

Sakiko pointed her crooked and knobby finger at their names. "Here's the couple who lost the child on your property. They're in their seventies, and they have a fairly big family now. After the child's death, they stayed in the house for another year before selling and moving to Yamanashi."

She turned the page to show me photos of the husband and wife and their current house. My cheek twitched as I held back a smile. I was impressed with Sakiko's thorough investigation.

"Once they started afresh in Yamanashi, they had two more children. Both healthy. Both still alive. One son, one daughter. Both are married and have their own kids. By all accounts, they appear to be a happy family who put the tragic past behind them and moved on."

My eyes locked on the mother, now in her seventies. She still had that vitality of youth around her eyes and lips, a lucky combination of genes and staying out of the sun. It was easy to picture her as a young mother, fawning over her first son. I was relieved to hear she and her husband stayed together and tried again. A tragedy like the one they experienced could have sunk their marriage.

I sucked a deep breath in through my nose and looked up, breaking the spell of this woman's past.

"Where are my manners? Can I get you some tea?" I asked, ready to stand up and prepare a cup. I looked over at Mari, and her eyes were getting droopy. It was almost time for a meal for her and a walk to put her to sleep.

"No, thank you. I'm not really a tea person. More of a black coffee with extra shots of espresso."

"Just the thought is enough to give me a heart attack." I placed my hand over my heart.

Sakiko slipped into a lopsided grin. She sat back in her chair and folded her arms over her chest.

"You know, Mei Suga, you and I couldn't be more different."

I felt the surrounding atmosphere change and become more relaxed and personal. "I think that's possibly the understatement of the year."

Sakiko nodded slowly. "Tell me something. If someone had come to you with this little problem and needed help, and you had had time to solve the mystery, how would you have gone about it?"

"Well..." I said, stopping to chew on my bottom lip for a

minute. "I was thinking about solving this on my own, but with Mari..."

"Of course. This is a hypothetical situation."

"Well, I had the family name, so I would've searched for distant family nearby. Maybe asked former neighbors and then checked landowner records."

In Japan, we had a system of family registries, *koseki,* that record the names of everyone in the family — born into, adopted into, or married into that family. But these files are privileged and private. Only people who are listed on the koseki can access the documents though lawyers can file to see the registry if someone listed is involved in criminal proceedings.

The registry of current addresses, *jūminhyō,* was not private. Kumi and I had accessed it from the town hall to find out who had lived at my future address.

"Because you don't have access to the family registry," Sakiko prompted me.

"Yes, of course. Hmmm. I probably would've then put my internet searching skills to work and searched for someone to go talk to. Is that what you would've done?"

"That's an excellent start, Mei," she said, "and I think that would've gotten you pretty far. Do you want to know how I found them?"

I nodded and leaned forward to rest my chin on my propped hands.

"The boy who died had been four years old when he passed away, and I had guessed the parents had been active in the community until that point. I figured he had probably gone to some preschool and had play friends he hung out with. So I searched for people who lived in the area at the same time with the same aged kids. I found a woman living in a retirement community in the next town over who had known them well."

Oh, that was a good idea! I should've thought of that!

"She told me the family had moved to Yamanashi to be close to the wife's mother and father. The husband worked for a bank and got his job transferred there too. After that, it was easy to find them. I called a friend I know in Yamanashi, pulled the land records, and once I knew where they were, I followed them for a few hours and took photographs."

She shrugged like it was no big deal, but to me, it was magic.

"It was a lucky break, though. They could've moved to Hokkaido or Okinawa, someplace in Japan but far away. Or they could've moved overseas. You just never know in this business."

"It's so fascinating. I should've thought to ask an older resident. I'm practically surrounded by them here."

"We have a thriving elderly population. It's best to talk to them and use their knowledge. Most of them want to help or be involved. The internet is a great resource, but I believe in the 'boots on the ground' approach to private investigation."

I yawned and looked over at Mari. She was still awake and chewing on her fist.

"Sorry. It's not that this isn't totally thrilling and interesting because it is. It's been a hectic few days. And whatever your approach is, it works and pretty fast too. Thanks for taking on the task so quickly. I'll pay your fees straight away tonight."

"Thank you," she said with a head bow. "I should get going, but I have one other thing to mention." She tapped her fingers lightly on the table while she considered what she wanted to say. "You wouldn't, perhaps, be thinking of becoming a private investigator someday, would you?"

I must have turned white because her smile became ruthless.

"I guessed as much."

"Have you been talking to Goro Hokichi?" I asked, my chest light with surprise.

"The Chikata police officer? No. I barely know him. Why?"

She had come to this conclusion all on her own. Because I had the skills for this?

"Doesn't matter. Uh, yeah, I had been thinking I would try to train as a private investigator once Mari was a little older. My mother has offered to help with babysitting, and my husband is all for it. But I..."

"Perfect." Her voice rose and caught on the last syllable. She coughed into her elbow for a moment and then laughed. "Don't go to one of those P.I. Schools in Tokyo. They're a waste of money."

"Well..." I began. I was hedging my bets. I had said '*try to train,*' and I had been living on maybes for the last few days.

"I'm telling you, a waste. I can teach you everything you need to know to get your certification."

I couldn't believe what I was hearing.

"You? Train me?"

Sakiko clapped her hands together and rubbed them with a cackle. "You're going to do great." She reached over and pounded me on the shoulder while I sat frozen in shock. "I've been waiting for the right student to come along, someone I could hand down my business to so I can move to Bali." She lifted her eyes to the ceiling and sighed. "I plan to eat all day and swim with hot young men."

I... I had no words.

"Excellent." Sakiko slapped her knees and stood up with a broad, smoke-stained smile. "We'll get started soon. I'll send you some books on laws we need to abide by and a list of all the equipment I recommend. You get the kiddo some babysitting, and we'll get started."

She pointed to the papers she had given to me. "Let me know how this turns out."

I watched in silence as she strode out of the tea shop. She spun around at the door and thrust her finger into the air.

"Talk later, Mei!"

The door closed, and Shigimo snorted awake.

I rewound the conversation in my head. In no way, form, or fashion had I agreed to be her student.

But I guessed it didn't matter.

I had a new teacher whether I liked it or not.

CHAPTER
TWENTY-FIVE

I ate lunch in the car as I drove to Yamanashi prefecture. The food Yasahiro had made for me and left in the fridge sat there while I jammed rice balls in my mouth and chugged down iced coffee from the convenience store. Did I feel guilty? Possibly. Okay, yes, I did. But I had to run if I was going to make it to Yamanashi and be back home by dinner.

Mari fell asleep after fifteen minutes of cooing, kicking her feet, and slamming her toy against the car seat. I glanced in my rear-view mirror, and her little face was slack, and her mouth was open. I had fed her right before we left in the hopes this would happen. Lucky me!

I turned up the music a little and kept my eyes on the road. It was a long way to Yamanashi, and I needed to stay with it so I'd hit all my exits and turns. I rarely drove long distance. Not many people I knew did. Driving in Japan was expensive, both for fuel and tolls. For me, it was too much of a headache, and honestly, I had nowhere to be that was far from home. But this time, I needed to go.

When I pulled up to the suburban old-style Japanese house ninety minutes later, I sighed with relief. I'd made it, and I didn't get lost. Mari woke up as I turned off the engine, so I immediately got out of the car and strapped her into the baby carrier.

"There we go," I said to her as I sandwiched her to my chest. "Let's go meet the nice family who lives here, okay?"

My hands shook as I approached the house. I tried to practice a greeting in my head, but I kept tripping over why I was there and what I wanted. Should I open with that? Or should I start somewhere else in the conversation?

I didn't even have the chance to knock on the door. It slid open when I stepped onto the front deck.

"Hello," a woman said, and it took me a moment to realize this was the woman who had lost the child.

I glanced at her name on the piece of paper in my hand. Ayaka Nogami. I would stick to her last name.

"Hi. I'm so sorry to bother you in the middle of the day. My name is Mei Suga. Are you Mrs. Nogami?"

"I am." Her eyebrows drew together, and a voice called from behind her, "Who is it, Mom?"

"I, uh…" I waited until a younger woman joined her at the door.

"What's going on?" she asked, wiping her hands on a towel. They must have just finished with lunch.

"I'm sorry to bother you… again." I bowed, realizing I was repeating myself. "I'm actually a Chikata resident. I'm not from around here."

"Oh? Chikata?" The daughter asked. "Didn't you used to live there, Mom?"

"I did." Ayaka's jaw tightened, and her words became clipped.

"My husband and I bought the land where your old house was… and the property next door. I'm afraid to say we knocked the house down. The previous owner had abandoned it for some time."

They both tilted their head the same way and listened. I wondered if my mom and I ever did that kind of thing.

"Why don't you come in?" The daughter stepped aside to beckon me into the house, but Ayaka hesitated. Did she know why I had come?

"Thank you. That would be nice. My daughter and I just drove a long way."

"She's adorable," the daughter said, smiling at Mari. "I love babies that age. They're so fun and don't talk back." She winked, and I chuckled. "I'm Kiho, by the way."

"Nice to meet you. This one loves to be sassy, usually for about five hours every evening."

I followed them into their sitting area, took Mari out of the carrier, and held her upright on my lap.

"Anyway, so we've been building a new house on the land. We combined the two plots, and we're going to have a house and garden there. My husband is a chef, and we're both pretty good with gardening, so I'm hoping it'll be a lovely home for us."

"That sounds nice," Ayaka said, nodding her head.

I cleared my throat, well aware that I was on the verge of stepping on toes.

"It'll be nice if the house is ever built. You see, about a week ago, strange accidents started happening on the property. A few people were injured. They claimed their equipment was moved overnight or ghosts were haunting the land."

I tried to laugh but looking at Ayaka made me ill. She was white and her eyes were wide.

"I searched the property records to see if the land was stigmatized, and I found your family in the records."

"Stop!" Ayaka yelled, and she rose to her feet in a smooth, swift motion. "You should leave. Now."

Her daughter's eyes widened in alarm. "Mom! There's no need to be rude."

"Yes, there is," she hissed at her daughter. "You should go," she snapped at me.

I stood up as fast as I could, but with Mari in my lap, it was difficult to get my feet under me. Mari sensed the mood in the room had changed and began to cry.

"But I —"

"Don't say another word." Ayaka's voice was a growl, and she raised a finger at me. "Leave."

I pressed my lips together and tried to get out as quickly as I could. Mari screamed in my ear as I slipped my shoes on at the front of the house and grabbed my coat.

"Can I give you my business card?" I reached into my pocket, but Ayaka actually shoved me towards the door.

"Mom!" The daughter yelled.

My eyes filled with tears, and I tripped through the doorway. My hand snapped out, and I caught myself on the deck railing before pitching into the gravel walkway. Before I could turn around and apologize, the door banged closed, cutting me off like a katana swishing through the air.

I stood for a moment and watched the door, hoping it would open again, but instead I heard the daughter yelling at her mother.

"Mom! What's gotten into you? Why would you do that?" she yelled, and their voices faded off. I couldn't hear anything else.

"Shhh." I tried to soothe Mari and bounce her on our way to our car. But I was crying, and she was crying.

We were total messes.

I leaned against the door of the car and held Mari to my chest. I had just driven an hour and a half to be yelled at by a stranger.

Mei, this is a crappy way to spend your day!

I shushed Mari more, and as my hand cradled her bottom, I realized her diaper was full. Of course.

Circling the car, I opened the back door opposite her car seat, reached into the diaper bag on the floor, and laid out the diaper mat on the seat. I cried through changing her and cursed at the poop diaper. Great. I threw it in a plastic bag and hoped it wouldn't smell for the ride home.

"You have awesome timing today," I said to Mari, trying to put levity into my voice. She was calming down, and if I could just calm down too, we could make the ride home without any more drama. I didn't want to return to Chikata in tears.

Just as I was buttoning up her onesie and slipping her pants back on, I heard a voice from behind me.

"Excuse me!"

I sniffed up quickly and dried my eyes. It was stupid of me to get so emotional over the mother's unwillingness to talk, but she did push me. I hadn't expected that.

When I turned around, the daughter, Kiho, was running out of the house towards me, waving her hand in the air.

"My goodness! I'm so sorry. I don't know what's come over my mother." She bowed, but I stopped myself from returning it. "I can't believe she put her hands on you, especially when you're carrying a baby around." She peeked over my shoulder into the car. "Is she all right? Are you all right?"

I wiped the tears from my cheeks. "We'll be fine. You should go back inside."

I reached in to grab Mari.

"Wait," she insisted and then she sighed. "I don't know what's going on. I've never seen my mother do anything like that before. Can you tell me why you're really here?"

I hesitated and looked past her to the quiet house.

The quiet house where secrets were kept.

That's why she had cut me off so quickly. No one else knew about the dead little boy. No one but Ayaka and her husband.

I considered for a moment just blabbing and telling her everything. I was under no obligation to be kind to a woman who had roughly ejected me from her house.

But everyone had secrets, right? It wasn't my business to put my nose in where it didn't belong.

"I'm sorry I can't. It appears as if your mother would rather not talk about what happened in her past, and it's not my business to tell you."

I reached into my pocket and grabbed my business card. I handed it to her in two hands.

"Please. If she changes her mind and wants to talk to me, have her call me or come by my tea shop."

I circled the car and put Mari back in her car seat. Maybe we would go to a nearby café and have a snack before heading home. I didn't know what to do now.

Kiho stood to the side as I got in the car and started it up. She raised one hand and watched me drive away, and I didn't breathe again until she was only a speck in my rearview mirror.

CHAPTER
TWENTY-SIX

"Surprise!"

I walked into the apartment and straight into Kumi, Goro, and Taiga.

"Whoa!" I laughed as I jumped backwards and covered my beating heart. I was definitely not expecting a surprise. "What's going on?"

Yasahiro stood behind them, dressed in clothes that weren't stained or dirty. His hair was swooped up, and he looked relaxed. Huh.

"Tonight's the night!" Kumi nearly burst with happiness. "You and Yasahiro get a date night. Goro, Taiga, and I are going to watch little Mari."

She thrust out her hands to beckon Mari's car seat to her, and my brain ground to a halt.

"What?"

"Remember? I said we were going to treat you to a dinner and date night on your own." She took the car seat from my arm and set it down to get Mari out.

"Yes, but..." I stopped in the middle of my protests. But no, not today. "I thought we'd make plans. Not that it would be a surprise. Do you have any idea how tired I am?"

I was bone tired after being in the car for three hours, being yelled at, and suddenly being turned into a student. I had spent the entire car ride either angry about the way I had been treated in Yamanashi or worried I had made the wrong decision to be Sakiko's student. Not that I had any choice there. And that led me back to being angry again.

"When are you ever going to be rested enough to take the time for yourself, huh?" Kumi held Mari against her cocked hip. Her tone was motherly and exasperated. "Never. From now on, you will always be tired. Trust me. Do you see Goro? He hasn't slept more than five hours a night in a year."

Goro shrugged.

He looked fine to me.

"I'm only here for a beer, and then I'm heading back to the station. There are more notes to go over and questions to be asked. We still have Erina Ichisé and Takuma Kubo in custody."

"You let Mikami out?"

"Chief felt it was the right move." He shrugged again.

I nodded and kept this turn of events in mind. I supposed Mikami had enough evidence to excuse himself from questioning.

"Did you know about this surprise dinner?" I asked Yasahiro.

"Well, I knew they wanted to do it, but I didn't know it was today. They came here thirty minutes ago to tell me to get changed. Where have you been?"

It wasn't an accusation. I hadn't told him about my trip to Yamanashi in case he tried to talk me out of it. I kind of wish he had.

"It's a long story." I sighed as I dumped everything I was carrying — the diaper bag, my bag of trash from the car, and my purse. I moved the empty car seat to the side and rested it on a stack of cardboard boxes. Rubbing my face, I considered making a run for it. "Fine. I need to clean up a bit. I've been in the car for three hours, and I'm a wreck."

Everyone must have sensed my irritation because no one followed me. I stripped out of all my clothes and changed into something semi-clean, though I had to dig through the pile of laundry for a bra that still had some life left in it. I washed my face and brushed my teeth, then took out my sorry, neglected makeup stash and applied powder, blush, and mascara. It was all I could do.

I was staring at myself in the mirror when I spotted the dead vacuum cleaner in the corner of the bathroom.

"Oh no." I leaned forward and gripped the vanity. Strength... Where was my strength?

I marched out into the main room.

"Look, Kumi, I don't think tonight is a good night for this. The vacuum cleaner died yesterday."

Goro and Yasahiro were downing beers in the kitchen, and Kumi had a child in each arm.

"Vacuum cleaner? Mei, I won't be doing any cleaning. Sorry. Though, I'd be happy to wash dishes."

I shook my head. "The vacuum cleaner is the only thing that will keep Mari from screaming for five hours straight."

She waved her hand at me dismissively. "Don't worry about it. She'll be fine. I've never had a baby scream for five hours straight with me."

Well, tonight would be the night for her to break that winning streak.

"At least let me feed her before we leave? Otherwise, I'll be sore all evening."

She nodded and handed Mari over. "This I'll allow. But you feed her and go. You guys are going to the beer garden for the night, and I don't want you driving either. Kayo will pick you up when it's time to come home."

Man, she was bossy. But I had to hand it to her. I would've

put her off for months if she hadn't just taken control of the situation.

I fed Mari, and before we left, I gave her a big kiss and whispered in her ear, "Be nice to Aunt Kumi. And please, no screamfests."

But by the time we had made it down the stairs, I could already hear her crying in the apartment.

Great.

———

It was too cold to sit outside at the beer garden which was a shame. In another month, the sun would be out every day, and the weather would be warm, almost hot. Then the rainy season would hit us. We'd be lucky to see the sun for a few weeks before it went behind rain clouds till August. Ah, Japan.

I confessed my entire day to Yasahiro, and good man that he was, he did not get on my case about my rash decision to drive ninety minutes away to confront someone I had never met before.

"If only I could've convinced her to speak with me, maybe share photos or *something*, I don't know... Then we could've moved on with building our house. I don't think anyone will come back to work on the grounds unless I get them blessed again. No matter what I find on the cameras."

Yasahiro sipped his beer and popped a chip into his mouth. We both ordered barbecue chicken sandwiches with chips and salads. Beer for Yasahiro and wine for me because the day had messed with my stomach and I didn't think I could digest beer.

"What do you think you'll find on the cameras?"

"Kumi thinks I'll find paranormal bear shifters."

Yasahiro chuckled. "That's awfully specific. What made her think bears?"

"Oh, you know Kumi..."

My voice caught in my throat as I spotted the two men heading in our direction.

All the blood in my head traveled to my feet. I recognized these two. They were friends of Daiki Wada, the guy who hurt his shoulder on my property and accused me of (still) being a witch.

Yasahiro's back was to them. "What's wrong, Mei? Are you okay?"

"Have you heard about Daiki?" the first man asked as he approached the table. I couldn't remember his name, and at this point, I didn't want to.

Yasahiro looked up at him, his brow furrowed.

I couldn't answer. My voice was trapped in my throat.

The man lifted his eyebrows at me. "Don't care? Did you know he has to have surgery on his shoulder? He may never get back full range of motion on that side of his body."

"I... I'm sorry to hear that." I wanted to be louder and more confident, but I was too far out of my element. Tiredness pulled me down, and the beer garden was out of my comfort zone now that I had a kid.

"Are you really?" the second guy asked. "What are you going to do about it?"

Yasahiro stood up. "What does she have to do with any of this?"

The blood that had moved to my feet rushed back to my cheeks. I was so used to defending myself that I didn't expect Yasahiro to stand up for me. Besides, he was usually working while I got myself into trouble.

Yasahiro seemed to grow by five centimeters, and the guys turned to him instead.

"*She* is a witch. She's responsible for Daiki Wada's injury, and she should pay the remainder of his medical bills."

"Was she there when he hurt himself? Because I don't believe she was. And for that matter, he hurt himself on *our* property. Why have you not brought this to *my* attention? Or were you planning on bullying and harassing my wife?"

My mouth dropped open.

"If Mr. Wada needs help with his medical bills, he should contact me, and I'll speak to him about it. Until then..." He stepped forward into their space, and they edged back. He lowered his voice. "*You* should stay away from us."

The second man moved in front of his friend. "How can you sleep with a woman like her?"

The smile that slid onto Yasahiro's lips was self-satisfied. "I sleep quite well, thank you. It's women like Mei who keep their families and friends safe and cared for. I'm a lucky man."

My blush grew by ten degrees, and I noticed all the faces turned towards us. They were taking in the conversation like it was a daytime drama, their eyes sparkled and tuned in.

From across the room, two other men approached us, and my heartbeat slowed. These were men I recognized but found them strange in pairing — Ichi, the part-time Sawayaka prep cook and bartender at the beer garden, and Yutaka Mikami, the investor and a suspect in Noriko's murder.

Or 'previous murder suspect?' Goro had said they let Mikami out of custody at the behest of the chief.

"I already told you both to leave the Sugas alone last time you were here," Ichi said, stepping in between Yasahiro and the two men. "I'm going to have to ask you to leave and not come back. You're not welcome here anymore."

Mikami stood on the outskirts of the confrontation. He wasn't going to get involved, but he was waiting to see what happened.

"You know what to do," Yasahiro told the two men. "And tell Mr. Wada to contact *me*. He is to have no contact with my wife."

I thought they were going to stay and cause more trouble, but they turned and left. I let out a long-held breath, and my knees shook under the table as I let go of the tension in my body. I was worried that would end in a brawl.

"It's okay," Yasahiro said, laying his hand on my shoulder. "Now I know what you've been going through."

"That's only half of it, I think." My voice shook as much as my knees. My phone buzzed on the table, but I ignored it while I chugged down the last of my wine.

"Let me get you both another round of drinks." Ichi shook hands with Yasahiro. "And some dessert? I'll send the waitress by."

He turned away, and Mikami just stood there, his lips tightened in a straight line, before relaxing and coming forward.

"I'm sorry to bother you, especially after that," he started, and Yasahiro turned to confront him.

"Wait," I said, holding up my hand to Yasahiro. "He's not one of them."

"I'm sorry. Who are you?" Yasahiro asked, shaking himself out of the defensive posture.

Mikami gestured to the empty chair at our table. "May I?"

I pulled out the chair, and he sat. Yasahiro slowly sank to his chair, and I made the introductions and told Yasahiro about how I knew Mikami. Yasahiro was dubious, for sure. His eyes were hard as they took in Mikami.

I sighed as I tried to calculate the chances of meeting both Wada's buddies and Mikami in one night when I was supposed to be on a date with my husband. How unlucky was that?

I shouldn't have been surprised. This kind of thing happened to me all the time.

"You're Officer Hokichi's assistant, so when I saw you arrive here with your husband, I knew I had to speak to you."

"Is this about the case? About Noriko's murder?"

"Yeah. I was at the station all day until a few hours ago when they let me out. I went home to shower and change, and that's when I saw Noriko's things in my drawer." His eyes welled with tears, and Yasahiro lost his frosty glare. "She always kept a few items of clothing at my place, some of her toiletries, and her jewelry too."

He hung his head and looked at his hands folded together.

"I realized, as I was going through her things, that I didn't see the necklace I had purchased for her. It was a silver heart on a chain."

I inhaled and stopped myself from interrupting him.

"She loved that necklace. She only took it off to shower or sleep. And I don't remember seeing it among her other jewelry at the funeral. Do you remember if it was on her or brought in as evidence? I was hoping I could keep it."

My brain searched back through everything I knew of police procedure like a film on one-hundred times rewind. Could I tell him the necklace was in evidence?

Forget that. How would he react if he found out it had been in the bushes? If the necklace had been precious to her, and a gift from Mikami, then it would be an outrage for someone to break it and leave it out in the cold.

I decided to lie.

"I'm not sure. I'll have to ask Officer Hokichi and find out. Can I call you back when I know for sure?"

"Of course," he said, pulling away from the table. "You still have my contact details?"

I nodded and then an idea struck me.

"Did the police ask you about love letters?"

He was just about to get up, but he sat back down again. "Love letters?"

"Yeah, did they question you about love letters that had been sent to Noriko?"

His shoulders straightened, and his jaw worked up and down slowly for a moment, almost as if he were tasting his words before he spoke them.

"Was Noriko receiving love letters from someone?"

I swiped on my phone and ignored the text message from

Kumi. I'd get back to that in a minute. Navigating to my photos, I pulled up the picture of the first love letter. I handed my phone over to him and let him zoom in and read.

"Noriko had a stack of about fifty love letters, some opened, some not. None of them were signed. But she had been receiving them for about a year."

His eyes narrowed as he read the letter, and then he quietly swore.

"No. The police did not tell me about these letters. I thought it was strange that they asked me to write out where I had been the night Noriko was killed. They wanted a detailed accounting of the whole night in my handwriting. We had gone to dinner at Izakaya Jūshi —"

"I saw you there. Do you remember?"

He nodded. "I realized after you came to see me with Officer Hokichi that you looked familiar."

I had wondered why he hadn't recognized me.

"Anyway, after dinner, I dropped her off at home and then I took the train to Tokyo to speak with some foreigners I was doing business with. It was late on a Sunday evening, not usually my time for being out and about. But they had a flight out the next day, and it was their only open time. So I stayed at a capsule hotel that evening instead of hiring a driver to get home." He shrugged. "It was easier, and I can sleep just about anywhere."

He had an airtight alibi. The police had a handwriting sample now, and they probably let him go because he hadn't been in town during the murder and hadn't sent the love letters.

"I didn't know about the letters," he said, handing my phone back. "The police didn't mention them. Neither had Noriko, for that matter."

He rubbed his face hard, and sadness returned to his eyes.

"No wonder she always put off my advances to move past dating, to something more permanent. The most I could get her to do was take a drawer at my place. A year of dating and she barely admitted to friends that we were together." He nodded slowly as he turned to look out the window. "There had been someone else. I'm such a fool."

Mikami lost the emotion on his face and stood up straight. He had a lot of clout in this town, and he was aware of his appearance in public. He pulled on his strength like the cape of a superhero.

"It was good to meet you both." He stuck out his hand to Yasahiro, and Yasahiro shook it. "I've heard great things about your restaurant. Let me know if you ever need an investor."

Yasahiro nodded, and Mikami withdrew his hand and strode out the beer garden's door.

We were silent as two new drinks arrived at the table.

"That was strange," Yasahiro finally said.

"I'm not even sure that actually happened. Did that happen?"

"It appears it did."

I paused for a second as I assessed my husband. There was something behind his eyes I didn't know. Yet.

"Are you angry with me?" I asked, keeping my voice low.

"You?" His surprise put me at ease. "No. I'm... puzzled why people keep trying to pick fights with you."

I poked at my cold sandwich. "It's because I'm different. No one here likes different. Even in Tokyo, where I thought I'd fit in more, I didn't."

"Different is what makes you special. It's to be cherished. Change and creativity and innovation? Those don't come from thinking the same as everyone else." He said it so matter-of-factly that I believed it in an instant.

My phone buzzed again, twice in a row. He looked at it from across the table.

"Are you going to get that?"

"I don't know. Should I? It's probably more bad news."

This time my phone rang. I picked it up, and Kumi's name

was on the screen. I swiped the phone on and knew immediately what was going on.

"Hi," I said, putting fake cheer into my voice.

Mari's wails were like she would never see us again. Those wails declared this was the end of her life, now and forever. I knew it wasn't. I had heard them before.

"Okay, I give up," Kumi said, and her voice shook. "Mei, this is well beyond what you said she was like."

"No, it's not. I told you, she will cry as if her life is going to end for five, sometimes six, hours straight every night, and only the vacuum has given her peace."

Yasahiro chugged his beer while I mouthed that we should get the remainder of our meal to go.

"Are you sure there's nothing wrong with her?" Kumi asked, desperate for an explanation.

"She wakes up every morning right as rain, Kumi. The doctor tells me this is, well, not normal but also not abnormal. It's just the way some babies are."

I felt as if the roles were reversed. Usually, it was me on the verge of tears trying to care for my crying baby, and someone else was telling me these useless things.

"Well..." She paused to swear. "I'm sorry I didn't listen to you. Really sorry. Goro took Taiga home to Chiyo because there was no way Taiga could go to sleep with all this crying, and —"

"Don't worry about it," I said, interrupting her and standing up.

Yasahiro waved over our food and mouthed, "Let's not take it with us." I sighed and wished I hadn't. I did nothing but sigh lately.

"We're heading home right now. It's still early, so we'll catch a cab. You don't need to call Kayo."

"Okay... I'm sorry. Again."

"It's okay. See you soon."

I hung up and dropped the phone in my bag.

"So much for a quiet evening out." I took my coat from Yasahiro's outstretched hand.

"Well, we did manage to eat most of a meal and drink something. And you got another clue to your mystery." He shrugged as he held out his arm to lead the way. "All in all, it was a zero-sum night. Not awful but not great."

"Excellent. I've always wanted to lead a mediocre life."

He let out a tired laugh, led me through the door, and hailed a cab to bring us back home.

CHAPTER
TWENTY-SEVEN

"The chief felt it was the right move to let all the suspects out and go over all the evidence again," Goro said on the other side of the phone call.

I rubbed my eyes and tried to concentrate on the ceiling light. The three hours of sleep I got between comforting and feeding Mari were barely enough to function on, much less have a coherent conversation.

"Why would he do that?" I closed my eyes and sunk farther into the pillow. "He can hold them indefinitely if he needs to."

"Well…" Goro dragged out the word. "Sure. That happens a lot in Tokyo or Osaka, but here? We don't have the facilities or faculty for it. We're putting Takuma Kubo under house arrest and an officer on Erina Ichisé. We've confiscated their passports too."

"Hmm," I grunted. A wave of tiredness washed over me. I could use another, oh, thirty years of sleep.

"Mei?"

"Yeah."

"What does your gut tell you?"

I cleared my throat and opened my eyes again. The smell of fried eggs wafted under the door, and my stomach growled.

"What about their alibis?" I asked. "I spoke to Yutaka Mikami last night at the beer garden, and his alibi seemed pretty solid." I detailed what happened with Daiki Wada's friends, and how Mikami approached us, we spoke, and I showed him the love letter. Then I relayed the conversation that happened afterward.

"Yeah, we didn't show those letters to him. He had a strong alibi, and his handwriting was different from the letters, just like you surmised. Takuma Kubo's alibi is that he was out drinking with Erina that night. They were both spotted at an izakaya on the west side of town. He then caught a cab home with her, and she stayed the night with him. All verified. The cab driver remembers them and dropping them both off at Kubo's home address. The driver said Erina was sloppy drunk, and Kubo had to drag her inside. That was around one in the morning. I asked the cab driver if he thought there was anything amiss, and he didn't seem to think so. Erina was all over Kubo, and she was happy to go home with him."

"What was the time of death again?"

Goro hummed on the other end. "Sometime around three in the morning."

"My gut says I should question this. It couldn't have been midnight or one in the morning? I mean, I can't imagine Noriko getting out of bed and coming down into the garden to talk to someone. But I could see her coming outside if she was already in the kitchen. One in the morning is not *too* late to be up doing work or getting a snack or whatever. Did you speak to the next-door neighbor again? The one who saw someone in the garden that morning?"

"We had her into the station to give a description, and she looked at a line-up too with both of our suspects, but she didn't identify anyone. Said she was too far away and only saw a manly build."

I yawned and tried to wake up a little more.

The time of the murder didn't seem right unless someone was breaking into Noriko's house, but she would've confronted that person inside. She had to have come outside voluntarily. The necklace was broken and thrown into the bushes.

Did she struggle with someone and it came undone? Maybe she had fought with her assailant, and it had flown into the bushes then.

"I need to see the photos of Noriko again, the ones that were taken at the crime scene. Can I come by there today and take a look?"

I heard papers and shuffling around in the background. "How about I bring them by your place? I don't suspect you got a lot of sleep last night. Kumi came home looking like she fought in a cage match. Your little girl has some lungs on her."

"Yes, she does." My voice was emotionless. "I'm buying a vacuum cleaner first thing today."

"I'll be there in twenty minutes."

He hung up, and I let my arm relax to the side. Could I get a nap in in twenty minutes? I smelled bacon this time, and my stomach growled even louder.

Okay. Gotta get up.

I pulled on some semi-decent clothes, and Yasahiro met me at the door with a giant cup of coffee.

"I'm going to have to buy stock in coffee." Yasahiro's voice was raspy.

"I think that's an excellent idea."

I smiled as I crossed the kitchen to Mari. Yasahiro had set her up on her play mat, far from the stove but still within eyesight. She was as happy as a lamb, smiling, gurgling, and batting at the toys hanging above her. All like last night had never happened. I set the coffee aside and leaned over to kiss her face and neck.

"Look at you, all smiles. Are you ever going to confess about why you hate nighttime so much?"

She giggled and squirmed, and I sat back on my heels to stare at her. I should've been bitter or angry about all the suffering she'd put us through last night, but I just couldn't be. I could forgive this little human. She didn't know any better, and she couldn't help it. But I could help and control my own emotions.

Yasahiro stood over us both.

"I think that was the worst it's ever been. Maybe we've turned a corner?"

"Maybe," I said, squeezing Mari's foot. "Goro's going to come by in about fifteen minutes. Can you make more coffee?"

"Sure. Is he staying to eat?"

"Probably. You should make rice too."

Of course, Goro's eyes lit up as he walked in the door and smelled the food. It was a good thing Yasahiro had made extras.

"I can't stay long, but thanks, yeah, I'll have a bite to eat." He took off his shoes and coat then pulled a folder from his bag. "Here, Mei. You should look at these before you eat. Not after."

I steeled myself and moved to the couch before I looked at the photos again. When I opened the folder, though, I wasn't as affected as I had been last time. Kayo was right. You could become immune to blood and death.

It didn't take long to know what I was looking at. Goro had brought both the crime scene photos and the ones taken by the coroner. I examined them, and one detail jumped out at me.

"Goro, come here," I said, beckoning him to me.

He already had a cup of coffee in his hand as he approached.

I showed him the two photos of Noriko's head wound. They were ghastly; she had been struck hard and bled heavily. I pointed to the location of the head wound.

"See? From the top. It couldn't have been Erina. It had to be someone taller than Noriko."

"Yes, you're right. I thought that too, and the coroner did mention it. We kept at Erina because of the bad blood between her and Noriko, because of their argument. But Erina and Takuma Kubo are using each other as an alibi, so..."

I nodded as I put the photos away. "What was her story, anyway? Sure, she's dating Takuma, but how?"

"She had taken one of Noriko's classes, and Takuma Kubo was there to observe. She introduced herself to him, and the two hit it off. He offered to help her with her businesses, and that was pretty much all we got out of her. She was tight-lipped and thought it was rude we were asking about her personal life." He rolled his eyes. "As if hiding stuff from the police is a good idea."

I remembered how Yasahiro had hidden his personal life from the police too. During the investigation into Amanda's death, he'd withheld that he'd purchased an engagement ring for me. I glanced down at my ring, and a twinge of regret pulsed through me. I could understand this desire to cling to privacy even if it was at one's own detriment.

We joined Yasahiro at the table, and I grabbed Mari from her play mat so she could sit on my lap. Goro stared at her.

"She's a completely different baby now. Like night and day."

"Exactly," I said, picking up a piece of bacon and pointing it at him before sinking my teeth into it. It was delicious.

"So anyway, despite the public fight that several people witnessed, the entire time Erina was in custody she stressed there was no problem between her and Noriko. They had a difference of opinion about some business matter, and that was it." He dug into his eggs and toast with gusto, and Yasahiro smiled as he watched him eat.

"There seems to be a lot of lies between these people, don't you think?" Yasahiro asked, and I was surprised he had an opinion. He had been paying attention. "Reminds me of a love triangle." He paused. "Well, more like a love rectangle."

A love rectangle.

I set my chopsticks down, and Mari grabbed them. Stunned

by how fast she was, I wrestled them from her grip. Wow. She was strong.

"A love rectangle," I whispered, certainty settling into my thoughts. "Or maybe a triangle and someone left out."

As I thought this through, I lowered my lips to Mari's head and rested them there. This was the last piece to the puzzle.

"Yes," I said, lifting my head. "Yes! It was a crime of passion, but I wasn't sure who. It could've been Erina who was passionate about whatever business problem had been between her and Noriko. Or it could've been Yutaka Mikami who was Noriko's current lover; he had been spurned and kept hidden. But no. It was Takuma Kubo, her ex-husband. He wanted her back, *he* wrote her the love letters, and she refused him."

Goro's expression was dubious.

"Mei, that's quite the leap. He was home at the time Noriko was killed, and Erina vouched for him."

Hmmm. "Nope. My gut says it's him."

Goro paused, his chopsticks holding a large piece of egg, but after a moment, he stuffed the food into his mouth and picked up his bowl of rice. There was never a meal without rice, even with eggs, bacon, and toast.

"I'll take it under advisement."

I supposed that was the best response my gut would get until more evidence presented itself. And with Takuma Kubo under house arrest, that only left Erina to talk to.

I sipped my coffee and resolved to go find her later in the afternoon.

But there was more work to be done, and I had a theory to prove...

"Goro, any chance we could return to the scene of the crime this morning before I go check the cameras on our property?"

Goro stuffed more rice into his mouth.

"You want to go search Noriko's house again?"

I cringed at his mouth full of food.

"What?" he asked, downing the food with a cup of orange juice. Yasahiro just smiled.

"Yes. I want to search the house again. There are things I want to see that I only glanced at last time. Unless you've taken the whole place into evidence?"

"No. No, we have no room for that," he said, shaking his head. "We took photos of everything and bagged the major stuff. Her belongings will be packed up and kept in a storage unit we have set aside. Probably in a few weeks. Her landlord wants to rent the place out again."

"Perfect. Let's eat and go. I'm going to prove that my gut is right."

"And what if it's wrong? What if I told you I'm sure it was Yutaka Mikami?"

I raised my eyebrows at him.

"Capsule hotel records can be falsified, and he was in love with Noriko and didn't want to lose her. Not to mention all the other times people have accused him of threatening them."

I shrugged. "We'll see who's right, now, won't we?"

"Okay. Why not? Let's finish up."

We both ate in silence, and Yasahiro just smirked and watched us.

I wanted answers, and we were going to get them.

CHAPTER
TWENTY-EIGHT

shivered when we entered Noriko's home. Not only did it feel creepy to be there when I knew she was dead, but it was also cold. The heat had been off for several days by this point. Most of the space heaters sat tucked away and unused. If the place had central heating, like our apartment did, it was off.

"I'm going to leave my jacket on," I said, taking off my shoes at the door and slipping on the disposable booties Goro handed me. Next came the purple nitrile gloves, like the last time.

"I don't know what you're looking for, so I'm just going to wander around." Goro left me to go snoop in the kitchen while I inspected Noriko's desk again.

Last time I was here, I hadn't taken in the details, but now I wanted to dive deeper on a few items.

First, the photos on Noriko's desk. They were still faced down or tucked away in nooks. I looked much harder at them this time. Noriko and Takuma Kubo smiled out from faraway destinations in each of the photos. They seemed happy and in love. I recognized the waterways and buildings of Venice in one picture, and I was pretty sure another had been taken in Amsterdam. A third framed photo in a drawer was of the two on a white sandy beach. It could have been anywhere tropical but felt like a honey-moon photo.

I only had my own experiences to go on, but if I were divorced and ready to move on, these photos wouldn't have existed in my house. I would've either stored them away in boxes or gotten rid of them all together. Noriko had kept them, though she had put them temporarily out of sight. She hadn't destroyed them but had turned them over or stuffed them in a drawer. These actions told me she had recently displayed the photos as if she were still in love with Takuma, but she had changed her mind and wasn't sure if it was a permanent situation.

Filing away that bit of information, I moved on to a bookcase nearby. A small photo album bookended a shelf of personal items, right next to a high school yearbook. When I pulled the photo album off the shelf, a cloud of dust puffed into the air and made me cough. I waved away the dust and swiped the rest off the leather cover. Not many people kept photo albums anymore, what with everything being digital now, but for older photographs, I could see the appeal. Noriko had packed this photo album with family and school photos. I absently flipped through it since I didn't know anyone, but after a moment, a pattern of rural life emerged.

Snow and a farm filled most of the photos. A mother, old and bent over. Daikon radishes hung in a smokehouse. A sparse home, but a childhood room crowded with posters and plush toys. Later in the photos, Noriko as a teenager stood with friends in a school uniform. Then Takuma Kubo appeared in group photos.

I held the photo album to my chest as I pulled the high school yearbook out. It was just as dusty as the photo album. I found Noriko's senior year photo, then looking closer, I found Takuma's as well. My skin prickled as I remembered he had known her his whole life. The school was located in a isolated area of Hokkaido, our snowy northern island, one of the most remote regions of

Japan to the north. Growing up in Hokkaido was tough on anyone, not just kids trying to make something of themselves.

Scanning the room, I saw other things that reminded me of Hokkaido now that I was looking for them. Memorabilia from Sapporo restaurants and businesses. A snowy landscape photo framed on the wall.

I opened the yearbook again, and this time I looked for the handwritten messages in the back. It was a tradition to sign each other's yearbooks or leave a personal note. Takuma's jumped right out at me. He signed it with love and 'Yours forever.'

Hmmm.

I took out my phone and swiped to the photos of the love letters. A chill climbed up my scalp as I compared the two. Same handwriting, same salutation.

Yours forever.

Forever.

Well, when I was in high school, I certainly thought my friendships would last forever. It wasn't out of line to think others thought that as well. Still, this level of an outright declaration felt wrong unless they were already talking about marriage at a young age. They may have been.

"Hey, Goro?" I called out. "Do you remember when Noriko and Takuma got married? How old was she?"

There was a pause, and I imagined him looking through his notebook. "Twenty-three," he said, poking his head back in the room.

"Wow. That's pretty young."

He nodded. "Most of us down at the station thought so too."

"And they didn't have kids?"

"Nope. Both of them were workaholics, according to someone they used to work with in Tokyo." He flipped around in his notebook. "You'll love this one. One woman I questioned said Takuma openly told people he didn't want Noriko to get pregnant because it would 'ruin her figure.' Can you believe that?"

I slid the album and the yearbook onto the couch, saving them for Goro to bag up.

"Yes, I can."

I wandered around the living room, past the flat screen TV, the bookcases, and the couch. Then I sat down and really looked at her space. This was *her* home. Everything within eyesight was about Noriko and her life. Nothing was about Takuma. She had those tucked-away photos, but this apartment belonged to her.

"What are you thinking, Mei?" Goro came over and stood next to the TV, his arms crossed and leaning on the bookcase.

"I'm thinking Noriko grew up poor and alone, somewhere in the backwoods of Hokkaido, and she met her future husband in high school. They got married young, moved to Tokyo, and got involved in the same company together. And then I get a little lost in the story."

Pressing my back into the couch, I heaved a sigh. "The man who told Noriko not to get pregnant because it would ruin her figure is the same man who cheated on her with someone else, right?"

"Apparently."

"Does he strike you as a narcissist? Someone controlling enough to freak out if the person he controlled left him? Narcissists will say anything, do anything, to keep their power over others." I couldn't even bring myself to say 'loved ones' because narcissists didn't love anyone but themselves. I saw that in my old boyfriend, Tama, and he went to jail for murder.

Would Takuma kill Noriko if he didn't get her back?

Did he want her back? Yes, I believe he did. Those love letters started right around the time Noriko and Yutaka Mikami began dating. Takuma probably saw them together or heard of them dating, maybe even spied on them, and it sent him over the edge.

Goro shrugged. "He divorced *her*."

"He did. But he never expected her to move on. And when

things didn't work out with the new woman?" I shrugged. "A narcissist would want her back."

"Maybe he *is* a narcissist. That's possible. But if he is, he's hiding it. He proclaimed his love for Erina Ichisé during questioning, and he insisted he was with her that evening. She corroborated it."

I rubbed my arms.

"He must be lying."

Goro laughed. "You and I know that, but we have to prove it somehow. After all, the coroner's report puts the time of death around three in the morning, a good hour past when Takuma and Erina were at home, and before that, they were out together drinking."

I ran through the whole scenario of the murder in my head. It was late at night, midnight or later, and Noriko had come outside to talk to whoever was there. She was killed and then laid there all night? But a neighbor saw someone leaving the property in the morning, assumed to be the killer. Had he stayed here after he killed her? Or did he return in the morning? If so, for what?

Nothing about the time of death made sense to me. It *had* to be wrong.

"What's one way to change the time of death?" I asked, standing up from the couch.

Goro inhaled deeply while he thought. "Change the temperature of the body. Either move the body into cold storage or heat it up somehow. Sometimes coroners will estimate the time of death based on a broken watch or rigor, but that wasn't the case here. She estimated it based on ambient temperature."

"So, what if the killer placed a blanket or something similar over the body, to keep it warmer, or protect it from the cold night air?"

He pulled himself away from the wall. "We didn't find a blanket. But we weren't looking for one either."

I strode past him and out the back door. "Let's start looking."

Goro checked behind the shrubberies that lined the rear of the property right up to the picket fence, but my eye immediately caught the gardener's chest at the edge of the stone patio.

"What about this?" I asked, approaching the chest. The thing could hold plenty of gardening tools or cushions for outdoor furniture. Or even a body though I was sure there wasn't one in there.

Goro turned to peek out of the bush he was searching.

"That? We never opened it. The murder weapon was right next to her body, and the lock was shut."

I held the combination lock in my hand and flipped it up to look at the back. Damn. She didn't write the combination on the back like so many people did who forgot their codes. That would've been too easy. What if the lock hadn't been engaged when the murderer was here?

"Any chance you have something that can open it?" I asked Goro. The only thing big enough to do any damage to a lock had been the murder weapon and its partner gnome on the other side of the garden. I considered grabbing it when Goro interrupted my thoughts.

"Yeah, actually I do. I have bolt cutters in the car. We sometimes have to cut bike chains or locks for people." He extracted himself from the bushes. "Be right back."

My foot bounced as I waited for him to return. Had I found the last bit of evidence we needed?

Goro returned and made swift work of the lock. He swung the lock free and opened the chest. And there it was.

Hidden under a collection of gardening tools was a thick, quilted stable blanket, the kind we had kept at home for when we had to kneel or do a lot of planting in one area. Mom usually bought hers from a stable supply store for large animals, like horses. Dried blood had stained this one dark red.

"Don't touch it," Goro said, stopping me from reaching in. "I need to take photos and call Kayo and the chief first."

Goro stepped away from me to make his call, so I turned on my phone and engaged the flashlight so I could see inside better without touching.

My hand shook as I swept the light over and around the blanket. Blood covered a good deal of one side. If he had tried to remove this from the property, someone would've seen it. He had to leave it here.

Now, I was certain who the killer was. Still, we needed to put together all the evidence to support my suspicions, and I couldn't do that without hearing from Erina.

Goro had said it was usually the ex-husband.

This time I knew he was correct.

CHAPTER
TWENTY-NINE

Putting the crime scene at the back of my mind, I motivated myself to continue with my day. The turn of the weather made me happy. Despite the doom and gloom of the previous evening's date night, my attitude brightened the moment the sun came out. I pulled the car into the new house's property this time, not parking on the street. This way I could leave Mari in the car for the ten minutes I needed to get this task done. I smiled as I rolled down a window on the car and let the fresh air in. I didn't even need a heavy jacket as I trudged along my property and gathered the memory cards from all of my cameras.

Paranormal bears, my foot. I was sure I'd get an answer to this mystery *today*. I grinned as I snapped one of the game cameras shut and locked it against the elements. There was a logical explanation for all the chaos on my property, and I was going to find it.

I slipped each card into a labeled envelope, so I'd know which card was for which camera, then tucked them all away in my back jeans pocket. That was when I saw the pile of dirt next to a new hole dug on the property.

Huh.

Okay, now I was sure there was an animal causing havoc.

I approached the hole carefully in case something was inside of it or the edge was unstable. The hole was dug down a good half a meter, and this time I could see what the animal had been rooting around for. Potatoes!

There were potatoes in the ground.

I stood up and took a visual survey of the area. Yes, if my memory was correct, this area of the property used to have a garden on it, and it had been pretty large too. The area was almost ten meters square, and all the holes had been dug in this section of the land.

Getting down on all fours and lowering myself into the hole, I scraped four potatoes out of the dirt. My keys were the only thing I had on me that were sharp, so I used them to cut into the sides of the potatoes. They were just okay, maybe a bit spoiled but not black or rotten yet. Not poisonous. Huh.

I had seen this happen on our own farm. It wasn't the best idea to store potatoes in the ground through winter, but it happened by accident. My mom had found a few good ones in the spring every year. They were happy accidents, an unexpected harvest. Depending on how cold it got in the winter, you could also plant potatoes in the fall and harvest them in the spring, and this could happen in an old garden too without planning it.

I scuffed my foot against the bottom of the hole a few times until I saw something new. Straw. It was old and decaying, but the lighter brown stalks that stood out against the dirt were definitely straw. This could've been a potato pit for the previous owners, a way to store potatoes in the ground and keep them fresh instead of storing them inside in a pantry where they may spoil. This part of the land had been abandoned only two years ago. It was a stretch, but I could believe potatoes would last that long.

I climbed out of the pit and looked across the property again.

If I were an animal, where would I go to hide from people? Into the woods.

And if I hadn't been a mother of a small child, I might have tromped right on off into the woods to see what was there. I had done as much when I tried to track down Amanda Cheung's killer. I learned my lesson on that trip. Bears and pepper spray — a lethal mix.

The envelopes in my back pocket scraped against my waistband as I climbed out of the hole, reminding me I had data on my side.

No, I wouldn't be rash about this. This time I would be cautious and consult the videos first.

———

BACK AT HOME, I KISSED YASAHIRO GOODBYE FOR THE DAY, set up Mari on her play mat, and then sat on the floor next to her with my laptop. Which memory card to choose first?

I chose the game camera closest to the hole. Once it loaded onto my computer, a giant list of videos showed up. Leaning in to look at the time stamps, the game camera had been triggered mostly in the dusk and dawn hours. I double clicked a video and gasped.

In the video, dirt flew out of the hole at a rapid pace as a dog made short work of her job digging up potatoes.

I knew it!

I watched as she lunged for something in the bottom of her hole, secured it in her mouth, and jumped out. The video ended at the thirty-second mark, and I immediately clicked onto the next one. The footage just caught her tail-end leaving the area. I zoomed in and noticed her underbelly was sagging. Oh boy. She was nursing puppies, and new ones by the look of it. She trotted off into the woods and veered to the right.

I made quick work of the rest of the videos. Between the two cameras pointed at this area and over by the house's foundation, I could see the mama dog return three times and work in both the new hole she had dug and the old one where Akira had stepped and broken his leg. She was trying to eat so she could, in turn, feed her family.

Mari kicked her legs and started to fuss, so I set the computer aside and nursed her while I thought of what to do. Chikata had an animal rescue organization, but I knew they struggled to find adopters for all the cats and dogs there.

What could I do? My heart told me to go find the mama dog and her puppies and bring them home. But I wasn't sure if that was the right thing to do. We had a small apartment and a baby, and I couldn't do this without Yasahiro.

While I was burping Mari, I grabbed my phone and texted him.

"I figured out what's been causing all the havoc on the property. A mother dog is digging up old potatoes and bringing them into the woods. I think she has puppies. What should I do?"

I waited and hoped he would have an answer.

My phone buzzed a moment later. *"Should we go investigate now while it's still light out? Do you think she's dangerous?"*

Hmmm, I wasn't sure. I opened a few more videos on my computer, and each time the mama dog came back to the property, she dug up potatoes and returned to the woods.

"I don't think so. But I've never had a dog. My mom is a cat person."

"We had dogs growing up. Several. I'll get some meat to lure her out. Call your mom and ask her to come over to babysit, then we'll go. The staff here can handle lunch without me."

"Are you sure we shouldn't call a professional?"

"We can handle it as long as she doesn't seem rabid or try to attack us. We'll figure it out. I'll be home in an hour."

Well, that settled that. Yasahiro was determined to handle it himself.

My phone rang in my hand, and it was a number I didn't recognize.

"Hello?" Who was ringing me? I got several spam calls every day, but I always answered to see who it was.

"Hi. Is this Mei Suga?"

"It is. Who is this?"

"Hi again, it's Kiho Nogami, Ayaka Nogami's daughter. I'm, uh, I'm standing in front of your tea shop. It appears to be closed, so I'm not sure if you're around."

I struggled to get off the floor and jump to the window. Throwing up the blinds, I leaned forward and looked down to the sidewalk. Yep, a woman was standing down there with her phone to her ear.

"I actually live above the tea shop. Look up."

She did, and I waved to her.

"Come to the green door, and I'll buzz you in."

I hung up the phone as I ran to the door. When I got around all of our stuff stacked in the entryway, I opened the door, and she came in.

"Hello again," I said, greeting her with a bow. "I'm surprised to see you."

She bowed and smiled. "My mother is out with friends this morning, so I decided to drive here and talk to you face to face."

"Please come in and sit down," I said, gesturing to the couch. "Sorry about the mess. With the baby, I don't have much time for cleaning." She removed her shoes and followed me over, smiling down at Mari.

"What a beautiful baby. I meant to say so yesterday but, yeah. How old is she?"

"Around three months and already a handful. We had quite the evening last night."

"Probably a growth spurt." She smiled again, and I got the feeling she was trying to put me at ease, what with the way her mother treated me the previous day and showing up here out of the blue.

"So, how can I help you?" I asked, getting right to business. "Is there a reason you came here today? I know Chikata is a long drive from Yamanashi."

She opened her bag and pulled out a few pieces of paper and... Photographs.

"Turns out I had a brother I never knew about," she said, handing the photos to me.

I held the photos lightly, not wishing to damage them. The little boy in the faded and blurry picture smiled at the camera. He had been quite the pudgy baby, with a belly and rounded cheeks. But his smile was full of life and happiness.

"Mom was upset with you because it was something she and Dad had left behind ages ago. My grandparents on both sides kept the secret for them which is almost as stunning as the revelation that I had a brother."

She rolled her eyes, and I covered my mouth with my hand to stop a short laugh.

"You have no idea what gossips my grandparents were, so this was more of a surprise than anything else." She sighed. "Anyway, I've convinced my mother I'm not upset or embarrassed. Accidents happen, and life was a lot more precarious back then. What can you do?" She shrugged.

"Yes, you're right."

"I'm sorry I don't have copies of those photos, but I thought you would want to see them. Supposedly, he was a good boy but had no fear of anything. Mom had to stop him from throwing himself into rivers or ditches. They joked he had a death wish only a week before he did actually die. Such a shame." She clasped her hands together and stared at her knuckles. "I can tell that my parents still feel his loss. I knew they wouldn't approach you and open that wound again, but I felt you should know."

The photos in my hand gave off a palpable energy. Even if I

didn't believe in ghosts or stigmatized properties, this young boy had a presence on the property. I was sure of it.

"Would you mind if I scanned the photos? I have a printer that allows me to scan."

She perked up. "Oh yes. Sure. Great idea."

She stood by me over at the desk, which was overflowing with papers and boxes, while I scanned in the two photos to Yasahiro's computer.

"Chikata is a charming town," she said, leaning in and making conversation. "I can see why my parents lived here for a while. Supposedly my father worked for a local branch of his bank at the time. I don't think the office is open anymore."

I nodded as I handed the photos back to her. "Yamanashi has fared a lot better than we have over the last two decades. We lost a lot of local businesses to the city. The houses we purchased, one of them being the house and property your parents owned, had both been abandoned. One had been vacant for almost ten years. My husband and I are hoping more people will move here if we set a good example with our house and businesses."

She bowed. "That sounds like a lovely idea. I hope your plans work out for you both."

Happiness warmed my heart. "Thank you. Now, if only I can get the house built! I'm sure these photos will come in handy. I'll have a new *jichinsai* ceremony performed, and this time we'll include these photos. Hopefully, that will put everyone's fears to rest."

I looked at the clock and realized Yasahiro would be home soon, and I needed to get on with the day. Kiho caught my nervous glance and checked her watch.

"Oh, look at the time. I really need to be going. I have a long drive back."

"Thank you so much for coming. I really appreciate it. It was very unexpected." I bowed to her as she slipped her shoes back on.

"Not a problem. I'm sorry again for the way my mother treated you. I hope the new house brings you joy."

I watched her leave the building, close the outer door behind her, and head to a car parked on the street.

This was one of those instances where I felt lucky, and it caused me to contemplate the ebb and flow of luck in my life. There were times when I made my own luck by working hard, but that wasn't always the case. The universe had plans for me, and I couldn't always see the blueprints. Luck was one of those forces that pushed me to places or extremes I didn't always want to go, or it rewarded me for sticking to the path. I needed to learn to accept that it would come and go, be bad or good. Life was a series of challenges, right?

I returned to Mari who was now chewing on her fist and looking out the window from her play mat. I lifted her up, gave her a big kiss, and set her on my lap as I reached for my phone. My laptop sat next to me on the couch, playing the videos of the mama dog on an infinite loop.

I called my mom, and she picked up right away.

"Mom, you're never going to guess what we found..."

CHAPTER
THIRTY

Yasahiro was well prepared to go on a dog hunt. He wore his dirty jeans and ratty sweater despite the warmer temperatures, plus his work boots. I smiled and admired his backside as he walked away from me. Hello.

In his hand, he carried tempting treats any dog would love. Or so he told me.

"Which way did she go?"

I thought about it as he stomped out in front, heading into the woods. He had glanced at the videos before we left the apartment, but I had watched more from several angles.

"In and to the right." Something high pitched reached my ears, and I stopped. "Wait. Do you hear that?"

It... It sounded like a baby crying. Then the sound turned and became soft growls and yelps. Moeko, my new neighbor, had said she heard a baby crying. Maybe this had been it!

"Yeah, I hear that." Yasahiro's head whipped around, trying to find the source of the noise. "This way."

When we bought the property, I was certain I'd never go into these woods. Sure, we owned them now, but I hadn't planned on spending time in here. I was more of a grass and city girl. No camping. No hikes in the forest. It just wasn't my thing.

The trees thickened, and we tripped over and through some rough areas filled with the leaves of last year's autumn before we came upon a small ravine, only about a meter deep. Yasahiro held his arm out to keep me from falling into the depression.

"Look," he whispered.

We were both transfixed with the scene below us. Mama Dog laid on her side while one puppy nursed at her belly, and two of her other pups wrestled on the ground near her. They were awfully loud with their little growls and yelps, but they were having a great time. They tumbled in the crunching leaves and dove for each other's necks.

"Oh!" The exclamation left my mouth before I could help it. I slapped my hands over my lips so I wouldn't scare them, but Mama Dog had heard me. Her eyes locked on mine, and I immediately feared the worst. She had been out here taking care of her puppies away from people like us. Was she a long-time stray without an owner?

Her ears pricked... and her tail wagged, beating the ground.

Yasahiro's hand rested on my waist, a silent agreement that we were okay and so were the dogs. They looked healthy, not 'mad' with fever or sickness. A little skinny, sure. But overall, in good shape. I was concerned that she only had three puppies because I thought dogs usually had large litters. Maybe that wasn't always the case.

The mother kept her eyes on us as we traversed the gully and approached. I squatted down and let the puppies see me. They were scared, though, and fled to their mother, scaring their sibling away from her belly. Yasahiro got close enough, within a meter, and set a serving of cooked pork on the ground near the little family. Not wanting to miss a moment, I slid my phone out of my pocket and recorded the greeting. My hand shook, and the video bounced, but I got them all in frame.

Mama Dog took a long moment to assess Yasahiro. Her brown eyes were big in her head making her almost look like a manga version of herself. Her fur was matted along her back, and her feet were darkened from all the digging she had been doing. She was alert but docile.

"She's wearing a collar, Mei," Yasahiro whispered as he backed away from the meal he left for them.

Once he had retreated, the puppies came forward. They couldn't resist the smell of the food, and I couldn't blame them. I was sure that was some tasty and pricey pork.

I put my phone away, and we sat or squatted on the leaves until everyone was fed and comfortable with us. The puppies came over and climbed on my legs, trying to jump up and lick my face. I had seen videos online of people playing with puppies, and this was even cuter than I could imagine. They smelled something fierce, but they were sweet. Mama trotted over and let Yasahiro pet her and talk to her.

"I think she's some kind of terrier," he said checking her collar. "But there's no tag. She may belong to someone though, so we should bring them all home and put out the word."

Panic nearly blinded me it hit me so fast.

"Bring them home? Are you mad? Have you seen our place?"

He waved away my concern. "We need to clean, anyway."

I broke into a hysterical laugh. How were we going to handle a dog, three puppies, and a baby in our disaster of an apartment? I was already going insane from all the chaos of our space, and my wonderfully nuts husband wanted to add more to our lives?

"What if they have fleas? Or mites? Or whatever?"

"I'll take them to the vet right away, before we go home." He held out his hand to the puppies, and one of them came over to gnaw on his fingers. "I'll make sure they're safe to bring into the house."

"Where will we keep them? We live in an apartment, remember?"

He rolled his eyes. "Mei, I literally cannot forget we live in an apartment." He lowered his voice. "I cannot wait until this house is built." He cleared his throat. "We'll pull the couch away from the wall and make them a little nest there. Don't worry." Yasahiro's eyes shone with excitement just like they did when Mari was born. "It'll be great!"

He stood up, patted his leg, and the mama and her puppies fell into line next to him. They looked up at him, instantly in love. He was the dog whisperer, a talent I didn't know he had. Wow.

But... All those puppy noises and smells?

It'll be great?

Famous last words.

CHAPTER
THIRTY-ONE

I didn't think my life could get any more hectic or out of sorts.

And then we added a dog and three puppies to the mix.

What were we thinking?

"Awwwww!" Kumi turned to a pile of mush as she watched two of the puppies tumble and play with each other in a caged off area in our living room.

"They're so cute," Kayo said, and I stopped a huff of a laugh. I had finally found something that made Kayo turn sweet and soft. Puppies.

The little balls of fluff looked better than they had the previous day. Yasahiro had taken Mama Dog and her puppies straight to a vet and a groomer to get them all cleaned up. I had returned home to find Mari asleep with Mom, so I spent the afternoon at Oshabe-cha finishing up tasks there and ran to the local electronics store for a new vacuum. Miracle of miracles, Mari only cried for two hours before bed. She watched the puppies playing, cried, and passed out.

"We are so taking one." Kumi reached into the caged area and scooped up a puppy. "I'm thinking this little guy."

"What if I wanted that one?" Kayo asked, a slight whine to her voice. Kumi smirked and handed over the puppy.

"I'll tell you what. You can have first choice." Kumi scratched the puppy's head before sitting down on the couch.

A warm spring breeze drifted through the apartment while I sipped on my coffee. I kept Mari in the baby carrier so she'd be far from the puppies, but Mama Dog was stuck to me like glue. She kept her babies in sight at all times, but if I was close by, she was my shadow. It was funny to look down and see her brown eyes looking up at me. I wasn't sure what to call her yet, or even if I should name her. She'd obviously had an owner at some point, but she didn't match the descriptions of any missing dogs, and she didn't have a microchip either.

I was already falling in love with her mocha brown fur, skinny body, and calm, agreeable manner. I couldn't believe I was entertaining the notion of adding a dog to the house.

I sat down on the couch next to Kumi and let my fingers rest between the dog's ears. She sighed and leaned against me.

"Well, I guess it wasn't paranormal bears." Kumi dropped her head in mock sadness. "I'm just never going to be a proper ghost hunter, am I?"

Kayo burst into a laugh as she held the puppy to her chest. "You thought all the problems on Mei's property were from ghost bears?"

"Yes. Don't judge." Kumi huffed and turned to me. "So I guess those drinks are on me."

"What drinks?" Kayo asked, kneeling down next to the gated area to swap one puppy for another.

"Oh, Mei and I had a little bet about what we'd find on the property. Nothing too risky. Just drinks at Izakaya Jūshi. You should come!"

I hid my smile behind my mug.

Kayo's face flashed a grin before she became serious again.

My heartbeat picked up a fast pace. She was in love; I was sure of it.

"Okay! Though, if I'm taking home a puppy, I may never leave my house again." She kissed one of the puppies on the head and set it back down with the others.

The door to the apartment building opened and shut, and footsteps thundered up the stairs. Yasahiro was home.

"Good news!" he exclaimed, shouldering the door open and bringing in several grocery bags. Mama Dog left my side to trot over and see what he had brought. Though the puppies whined and barked at Yasahiro, Mama Dog kept her voice to herself.

"I got a great deal on dog food, plus extras for a well-balanced diet. I also bought collars and leashes. And I heard from the foreman! He'll be here in, oh —"

The doorbell chimed, and I held back the wave of panic rising in my chest.

"Now. He's here now. I just beat him." Yasahiro ran to the doorbell and buzzed him in.

Four adults, one baby, one dog, and three puppies, and we were adding another adult to this cramped space? My neck broke out in a sweat, and I hefted myself from the couch to open another window. Only fresh air would save me now.

Imai entered the apartment and greeted everyone. Bowing and smiling, he took off his shoes and petted Mama Dog's head when she came over to sniff him.

"I don't remember you guys having a dog... Oh!" His eyes lit up as he spotted the puppies across the room.

"Come." I beckoned him over to the pen. "We found our property ghost."

"What?" He barely registered my statement. He only had eyes for the puppies. He picked up two of them, one in each hand and held them to his chest.

"Our property ghost," I said, waving to Mama Dog. "She's

been digging up old potatoes and eating them so she could feed her puppies. Nursing babies is hard, hungry work, as I should know." I chuckled. "She's probably been there for a few weeks, right, Yasahiro?"

"Yep!" He called out from inside the fridge. "The vet thinks the puppies are about four weeks old."

"And when I did the math," I said, patting Mari's bottom as I swayed side to side, "the neighbor across the street heard wailing one night about a month ago. I'm pretty sure that's the night she gave birth. Your men fell into holes created by a hungry dog trying to feed her babies, not by ghosts. Not by *witches*," I stressed.

"Well, that's a relief!" He perked up. "And the property's not stigmatized?"

I paused, and he noticed.

"So it is?"

"Kind of. About forty years ago, the owners of the property had a young boy who died. He fell and hit his head, then passed away at the hospital. I spoke with the family about him, and I have photos of him too. We're going to have another blessing cere-mony with the monks, and we'll cleanse the site properly. I hope that will be enough to have your men back to work? Especially now that this stray dog is not digging holes anymore?"

"Oh, yes, of course." He bowed with the two puppies clutched to his chest. "I'm sure we can return to work once we have performed the ceremony. I'll speak with the workers and make sure everyone is available."

"Great!" Relief swept over me. I looked over at Yasahiro, and he was chopping and prepping a meal. For us or the dogs? I wasn't certain. Still, he looked up and gave us all a thumbs up.

"So, uhhhh..." Imai glanced at me then at Kumi and Kayo. "The puppies. Are they spoken for?"

Kayo held up her hands. "Saved! I love puppies, but I don't think my job would be puppy friendly."

"Kumi has said she wants one. You want..." I saw the way he clutched the two puppies to his chest. "Two?"

He broke into a wide smile. "You won't believe this, but my wife and I were just talking last night about adopting two dogs. Our dog passed away six months ago, and we thought having litter mates would be ideal, and..."

"Say no more. But you'll have to wait a few weeks because the vet said they're not ready to leave their mother yet."

"Got it. No problem. We'd be happy to help pay for vet visits or food or whatever." He held up one of the puppies and kissed his head.

I had found this man's sweet spot, and it was dogs... or puppies to be exact. But something told me he loved all dogs.

"Look at that," Kumi said, sitting down with her puppy. "You found homes for all the puppies within a day of rescuing them. That must be some kind of record. What about the mama here?"

Mama Dog rested her head on Kumi's lap and nuzzled her puppy.

My heart grew by ten sizes that very moment, and I knew I had to keep her.

"I think we'll have to keep her. She loves Yasahiro and Mari."

Yasahiro appeared at the back of the couch. "You're acting like she hasn't been following you around all day. She's right up against your legs every time you stand up."

I smiled at the dog, and her quiet brown eyes seemed to smile back.

"Assuming we don't find her owner, of course," he said, breaking the spell. "But something tells me we won't. I think she had been outside for quite some time. What should we name her?"

I thought about it for a few moments. First, a few names associated with spirits came to mind, but I brushed those aside. Surely, I should step away from the spirit world for a little while.

An image of the woods popped into my head. "Sugi, after the

Japanese cedar trees we found her in. Which reminds me that springtime will be tough in that house. So many allergies. Sugi?" I lifted my voice and said her name several times while making eye contact with Mama Dog.

"I approve," Yasahiro said. "Sugi it is."

Imai reluctantly set the puppies down in their caged-off area. "I'll go get started on gathering up the men to work again. Please let me know if you need me for anything else."

He bowed, and Yasahiro saw him out to the street.

I sighed as I looked around the apartment. With dogs and a baby, I needed to get this place under control. I took out my phone and dialed up Nahomi Shimizu, my possible new house-keeper. She answered cheerfully.

"Nahomi, I was wondering if you had some free hours tomorrow to come over and get started on our apartment? We've, uh, added a few dogs to our family and now the place really needs help."

"I'd be delighted to! I have ten to two free tomorrow and then class at three. Would that work for you?"

"Perfect," I said and smiled at Kumi who was listening into the conversation. "See you then."

"See, Mei? That wasn't so hard." Kayo leaned back into the couch. "Getting help around here is a good idea."

"I agree." I stood up and pulled Mari from the carrier. "Now, I have another good idea. I'm going to feed Mari and put her down for a nap. Then we three? We're going to go talk to Erina Ichisé, woman to woman."

Kumi jumped to her feet. "We are?" She clapped her hands. "Goro said she stayed quiet through most of the questioning. Do you think she'll talk to us?"

Kayo nodded. "Yes. We should definitely go visit her."

Over in the kitchen, Yasahiro was chopping and cooking, and I knew he'd be here for a few hours. It was the right moment to make my exit.

And this time, I would persuade Erina to talk to me. No more running. We would confront her in her own home where she couldn't get away from us.

CHAPTER
THIRTY-TWO

Erina lived in a small apartment building in the outer reaches of Kawagoé, not far from Chikata. It was only a ten-minute ride to get there, but the place felt like another world entirely. Chikata suffered from neglect in many places, but this area was much closer to Tokyo and was served by three train lines. Streets bustled with foot traffic, and almost all the stores were open and in business.

My heart ached as I thought about how Chikata used to be this way...

And it would be this way again. I hardened my heart because I knew my quest to bring my hometown back from the brink of destruction would take a lot of fortitude. We were already making progress, yet we still had a long way to go.

"Here we are," Kayo said, pulling up to a vacant parking space outside of Erina's building.

We got out of Kayo's police cruiser, and she waved to an officer in a black car at the other end of the parking lot. The Chikata Police were here and watching under the cloak of surveillance.

"Erina is at home and been here most of the morning. The

officer in charge says that, for the last few days, she's been in and out to get groceries or takeout and that's it." Kayo led the way through to the rear of the building. "Which is concerning. She has a part-time job she goes to, an admin position, so I wonder if she's been calling in sick. Otherwise, she runs a few online stores which is where she makes the bulk of her money."

I thought of Noriko's notebook and wondered which of the websites she had taken care of for Erina. If Erina needed these businesses to live and make money, and if something had gone wrong, I could see why she was freaking out on Noriko.

We climbed the exterior stairs and knocked on Erina's apartment door. She had a little balcony with a chair and a clothes-drying line hung with freshly washed socks.

The door opened, and Erina winced at the bright light flooding down upon her. The day had grown sunnier and warmer, a good thing as far as I was concerned. But it looked like Erina had been living in darkened conditions, maybe for a few days. She had drawn her blinds, and one dim lamp glowed in the corner of her living room right inside the door.

"Erina?" Kayo asked, leaning down to look her in the eyes. "Remember me? Kayo Mitsuwara. I'm an officer with the Chikata police department."

Erina blinked a few times. "Yes, yes. I remember you." She looked at each of us. "I remember all of you."

"Can we come in? We'd like to talk."

The tone of Kayo's voice impressed me. She conveyed that she cared but also that 'no' would not be a permissible answer. Erina stepped aside and let us in.

"Oh my. It's so dark in here." Kumi headed straight for the blinds. "Let's open your windows and let in some light."

Erina didn't protest. She just sat on the couch and folded forward over her legs.

"Are you okay?" I asked, sitting next to her on the couch. I hesitated to touch her, but I rested my hand on her back. She didn't move.

"No. Not okay," she whispered.

I made eye contact with Kumi and Kayo. Kumi sat on the other side of Erina, and Kayo stood across from us.

"What's going on?" I paused, and then I thought she would need more encouragement to open up to a bunch of strangers. "We're here to help. Right, ladies?"

Both Kayo and Kumi agreed.

"We know you're a budding entrepreneur, just like us. You were Noriko's student like we were. I think... I think we have a lot in common." I gently patted her back before disengaging. "You can talk to us. Maybe we can help."

She was quiet for a few moments, and her shoulders shook. When she sat up, tears filled her eyes.

"Everything is a disaster. Everything I've worked *so hard* for is ruined now. That man took it all." She swore up and down so vehemently, I was scandalized. Kayo grinned and nodded. She heard that kind of language daily at the police station. Kumi covered her mouth with her fingers.

"That man? Who?" Though I had a pretty good idea.

"Takuma." Her hands balled into fists.

Yep, Takuma Kubo. I had a feeling he was at the center of this mess.

"I've spent the last three days trying to get back control of all of my businesses, but he's stolen them, right out from under me."

Kayo pulled up a chair and sat down, taking her notebook out of her pocket. "What happened? Tell me everything."

Erina's face screwed up. "Why? So you can take it all too? That's what the police do, right? They confiscate things from people."

Kayo tipped her head to the side. "Did that happen to you?"

She wiped the tears from her face. "My father. I don't want to talk about it."

Yikes. Police corruption happened in Japan, and it looked like it had touched Erina's family.

"How did Takuma Kubo steal your businesses?"

She groaned and folded over her knees again. "My stomach is killing me. Ninety percent of my income comes from the business I do online. I met Takuma about eight months ago when I was looking for someone to help me redesign my websites. Noriko introduced us after one of her classes. I should've known he was trouble the way she seemed to pawn him off on me."

I closed my eyes. I saw where this was going, and I didn't want to witness the hurt on Erina's face.

"Looking back on it now, I was so naïve... Oh yeah, I was totally conned. From the very beginning. He took control of all of my websites. I stupidly handed over the credentials from Noriko to him because he was such a sweet talker. Granted, I gave him access to everything because I had hired him to do the work, but this was..." She laughed bitterly. "Beyond stupid. He's been siphoning money off of my accounts, buying his ex-wife fancy jewelry, and using me whenever she turned him down. Ugh. I can't believe I slept with him."

Now that the floodgates had opened, Erina was on a roll.

She laid out a complex system of derogatory names for Takuma that ran the gamut from dirty animals to excrement. Kayo actually laughed.

"Wait wait. So, do you know anything about what happened the night of Noriko's murder?" I urged her back to the subject we came to talk about. "The cab driver who drove you to Takuma's apartment said you were sloppy drunk."

This caused her to groan and fold over again.

"I've never been that drunk or hungover in all my life. And I only had two beers." She lifted her eyes to Kayo while Kumi patted Erina's hand.

"I think it's possible you were drugged. Do you remember Takuma being home the whole night?"

Erina shook her head slowly. "I barely remember anything. There are flashes of memories. We were at the izakaya. Then, hailing a taxi. He dumped me on his bed, and then I woke up once in the middle of the night and he wasn't there. Then I woke up the next day." She burst into tears. "I checked, and I don't think I was raped. But... why?"

"I think you know why," Kumi said. She stood up from the couch and paced to the door and back. "Didn't it occur to you that you were drugged so he could go kill Noriko?"

Erina buried her face in her hands.

"You even covered for him!"

Erina jumped up to meet Kumi's aggressive stance.

"I had to! He's blackmailing me! He told me that if I said anything about that night, he would erase everything I had ever built. That's over a million yen in income per year! Plus, that's not all. He conjured up these fake sex photos of me." She bent over at the waist again. "Ah! It's like someone is stabbing me in the stomach!"

"You probably have an ulcer," I cautioned her. I stood up and faced her, squeezing her upper arms.

"He's set to ruin my life... and he will now that I've told you this. I'm so screwed."

"Wait. It's okay," I said, trying to soothe her. "You don't have to handle this alone."

I looked at both Kumi and Kayo.

"We'll help you."

"Mei, can I talk to you outside for a moment?" Kayo pointed to the door.

Uh oh. I knew that tone of voice. I was in trouble. I had over-stepped. I had screwed up in one tiny sentence.

I left Erina's side and joined Kayo outside on the balcony.

"Mei, I love that you have a big heart, but we don't know enough about this woman to say we can help her. *If* she's telling the truth, and that's a huge if, she may still go to jail because she lied to the police. She told us she had been with Takuma the whole night."

"I think it's obvious she lied to protect herself, don't you?"

Kayo folded her arms over her chest. "Yes, and I do think that will buy her some sympathy from the chief and the prosecutor, *but* I don't expect the process of coming forward to be easy for her at all."

I bit my lip as I looked out over the roofs that stretched along the roadway. Regardless of what happened to Erina after today, I had to be the bigger and better person, the person I strived to be.

I sighed and turned away from Kayo.

Back inside, Kumi and Erina were sitting on the couch, silent and waiting for us. I sat in the chair opposite Erina.

"Erina, it's important that you go to the police and explain what happened."

She shook her head, but I kept going.

"Listen." My voice sharpened into a hard and mighty blade, and her eyes popped. "This is murder. Not some petty theft. Takuma is under house arrest right now. If you speak to the chief about what happened, then we can seize his computers and phones and keep him from doing you any more harm. That's what you want, right?"

She didn't answer.

"Think of Noriko's family. She didn't have much, and it's obvious her ex-husband wanted to keep her so he could control her, just like he's trying to control you."

Takuma Kubo was a liar and a murderer. He probably had blackmail material on Noriko too.

"Don't let him win," I stressed while looking her straight in the eyes.

"What will happen to me if I come forward?" Erina's bottom lip trembled.

"I don't know. But it's the right thing to do. And when you're done with all of this, you come to me, and I'll help you get back on your feet. Whether it's finding a job or starting a new business, I can help." I held my hand over my heart. "I promise."

Kayo's glare was dubious, but Kumi nodded.

"Me too. I hate that you've been taken advantage of."

"We can't correct what's already happened. You must face the lies you told," I said to her, being as honest as possible. "And I don't know what that means for you. But maybe after, you can get your life back."

Erina was silent for a long moment. She chewed on her lip and twisted her hands while staring into space. Then she took a big breath.

"Okay," she said, standing up. "Okay. I don't want him to get away with murder."

Kayo's shoulders sank, and she drew on a pleasant smile.

"Come with us," Kayo said, holding out her arm to usher us out of the apartment. "And we'll straighten this out."

"And then, we confront Takuma," I added.

He was about to see why I was more than Goro's assistant.

I had a penchant for investigation, a gut for seeking out the truth, and an imagination that let me understand the how and why of a crime.

I had found my calling, and now I would put it to good use.

CHAPTER
THIRTY-THREE

"Thank you all for having me here today," I said, bowing to the room.

Arranged around the conference room table were the witnesses to my first case closing arguments — Naito Ohashi, the police chief, Goro, Kayo, Kumi, Takuma Kubo, Yutaka Mikami, and even Yasahiro had shown up to listen in. Many other officers had also come to hear the evidence stacked against Takuma Kubo, to understand the events as I imagined them. They stood in the back and spilled out the door. My mother waited out in the bull pit with Mari, feeding her a bottle. Her eyes were turned toward the conference room window. Erina was sitting tight in the chief's office.

"This has been a strange case from the beginning. As we all know, Noriko Kubo was a well-liked and active member of the Chikata community. She hadn't been with us long, but while she was here, she had made her mark on the businesses and education sections of our town."

Takuma crossed his arms and pouted.

"But it turns out that Noriko had not been the carefree and easy teacher she appeared to be on the surface. She had led a frugal and hard life, growing up in the snowy rural lands of Hokkaido, and it was there, in high school, she had met a man and fell in love. Make no mistake, she was in love with Takuma Kubo, even as they climbed the corporate ladder together in Tokyo, even as he cheated on her. She even loved him through their divorce, which he initiated, and she had almost no say in."

I cleared my throat, knowing most people in the room understood this statement. Divorce in Japan was an easy affair if you didn't protect yourself against it ahead of time. You could even be divorced and not know it. Women and men across the country often found themselves divorced, their signatures on documents forged, and no recourse at hand.

"Heartbroken and sad, she moved to Chikata to start over only to find that her ex-husband couldn't let her go. Why? Maybe he had realized belatedly how good he'd had it? Or maybe the woman he had cheated on Noriko with had dumped him? I'm not sure of the circumstances..."

I looked at Takuma, but he kept his eyes down.

"Regardless, Noriko found herself at the center of a narcissist's delusions. He wanted her again, despite the divorce, and he would do anything to keep her. He pulled her along with love notes, jewelry, and promises of renewal."

I bent down to the box of evidence at my feet and took out the bag of love notes and jewelry I found in Noriko's house. Yutaka Mikami stared at Takuma, and if looks could kill, Takuma would've been dead and buried by then.

"And she believed him for a time. I'm certain she would've gone back to him, if it hadn't been for Yutaka Mikami."

I gestured to Yutaka and gave him a sympathetic nod. His stare was ice cold.

"Mr. Mikami had given Noriko doubts about her relationship with Takuma. He had shown her a different, unconditional love. And the spell Takuma had cast over Noriko had weakened. So, Takuma did what he thought would bring Noriko back, he got another lover and tried to make Noriko jealous. It didn't work. And unfortunately, Takuma put his new girlfriend, Erina Ichisé, through the wringer. To stop her from interfering in his plans, he stole her businesses and held them hostage, then he blackmailed her to keep her quiet about his actual love for Noriko."

Across the room, Yasahiro rubbed his cheek as he listened. I believed he was just as surprised as I was that I could hold the details of this murder in my head. The chief glanced at Takuma, but Takuma kept his eyes low.

"I'm not sure what it was that finally spurred Takuma to kill Noriko —"

Takuma huffed a short laugh, and everyone turned to look at him. With so many eyes on him, his narcissistic personality couldn't say no. He lifted his gaze and smirked.

"It was the newspaper announcement, that the town council had asked Noriko to head up the committee to start a brand new farmers' market." He rolled his eyes. "Like *she* could handle something *that* large?" He poked himself in the chest. "I was the one who managed all her projects. I was the one who kept her businesses afloat. Then *she* thought she could go out and do it on her own?"

"She did handle it on her own," I pointed out. "She had several successful businesses that had nothing to do with you." I bent over to go through the folder of paperwork, but Goro held up his hand.

"Don't bother. We know she did it without him. He's the only one incapable of realizing it."

An awkward silence settled on the room.

I closed the folder and pushed it to the side.

"Takuma saw his opening on the night of the murder. He took Erina out for drinks to establish his alibi. He drugged her and took her home, making sure the taxi driver saw the two of them together. At home, he left her in bed and made his way to Noriko's house. I believe she had been awake that late at night.

She was probably up and getting ready for the breakout session she was supposed to give at my tea shop the next day. He knocked on her back door, and she came out to face him."

I backed away from the table and turned to one side.

"Takuma accused her of leaving him for Mikami."

I turned to the other side, miming Noriko's position.

"Noriko defended her choice. She was in love with Mikami, and there was nothing to be done. She would not get back together with him."

I made eye contact with Takuma who watched my performance with a touch of awe.

"He became enraged when he saw her wearing a necklace Mikami had given her. She wasn't wearing *his* jewelry which was a hundred times more expensive and lavish. He snatched it from her neck and threw it away. They fought. She turned to run back inside, maybe to call the police, when he picked up a stone statue from the back garden and smashed her over the head with it."

I brought the imaginary statue down in a swift swing, and Kumi jumped. Her hand was over her mouth, and her eyes filled with tears. Pausing for a brief moment, I saw the scene in my head, and it was so vivid it was like I was there standing over her body.

"Except this didn't turn out how he had planned. He had hoped to kill her inside where the body could sit for a while and not be found. Instead, she had left a huge pool of blood on the ground, and there was no way he could clean it up. So he covered up Noriko for the night in an effort to throw off the time of death, and he returned the next morning to remove the blanket before anyone found Noriko. We uncovered the blanket a few days later, in with the gardening supplies."

"Cold. Blooded. Killer," Kayo said, emphasizing each word. "Pre-meditated."

"You couldn't let her live, just let her be?" Mikami asked,

turning his watery eyes on Takuma. "All she wanted was to move on from you."

Takuma's arms relaxed. And then he exploded across the table, his hands reaching for Mikami's neck.

Goro was quick on his feet. He lunged for Takuma Kubo's waistband, snagged it, and pulled him back to his chair. Kumi squeaked and retreated to the door. Kayo pulled a pair of hand-cuffs out.

"I'll get my day in court!" Takuma yelled as Kayo cuffed him and hauled him to his feet. "This is all nothing but lies!"

He screamed all the way out through the main office and into the lockup.

"You certainly do paint a very believable story, Mei Suga," Chief Ohashi said, approaching me as everyone else muttered to each other. "I'm not sure if it'll hold up in court or anything. But your story fits the evidence, and I'm sure the prosecutor will agree that this is the most likely scenario. I'll be sure to show him the video later today." He nodded to the video camera propped in the corner of the room. It's a good thing I hadn't paid attention to it during my speech or I would've stammered and looked like an idiot.

I shrugged. "You might be able to find more evidence in the coming weeks. Street or video surveillance, or canvas and talk to more neighbors. Send the blanket to the high-tech labs in Tokyo? I don't know. I hope it's enough."

"I think it is." The chief smiled. "You know, I got a call from Sakiko Yoshida, the other day."

Blood drained from my face.

"She's determined to make you her student. Did you know that I've known her since high school?"

I shook my head, my voice unable to carry words.

"She asked me if I'd recommend you, knowing you helped out with the last few murder cases here. It was her belief in you that convinced me to let you participate more here with the police department. I did recommend you to her, and I told her you were welcome here at any time."

He backed away and bowed. Flustered, I paused before bowing back, but I made sure my bow was deeper than his.

What an honor!

As I returned upright, the chief stepped forward with his hand out to Yasahiro, who had been behind me the whole time and I didn't know it.

"I haven't been able to congratulate you on both your new baby and the success of your restaurant. We here in Chikata are lucky to have you." He leaned in. "Have you both."

I watched him go, my chest light with pride.

"That was amazing," Yasahiro whispered. "I had no idea you could command a room like that. And all those details? Mei, you were brilliant."

"Oh, stop," I said, pushing him lightly on his chest. I pressed my hands to my cheeks. "I can't believe I did that."

"You did, and I'm proud of you." He stretched his arm over my shoulder and turned me to the conference room window. Mom made Mari wave at us and both of them wore huge grins. "Your fan club awaits."

"Let's go out and celebrate," I said, suddenly aware of how excited and hungry I was.

Yasahiro kissed my temple. "Whatever you want."

CHAPTER
THIRTY-FOUR

The last box disappeared out the door, and I breathed a sigh of relief.

"There we go," Nahomi said, shutting the door and wiping up the floor behind the workers. They were making their way downstairs to load our extra belongings into a truck. "That's much better, right?"

Indeed, our apartment had transformed over the last week. Our two bookcases were gone, and all the books had gone with them. Not for good, of course. Both Yasahiro and I were readers, and we loved our books. But there was only so much space in here, so we made a few compromises.

Over the last week, we had moved three chairs, two bookcases and all the books, and Yasahiro's desk to a storage unit in the next town over. We also moved a lot of the baby toys and clothing which Mari wouldn't use for a few months to the storage unit. Our boxes of extra clothing that we had stored in the crawlspace above our bedroom were gone too, and we now kept extra diapers and blankets in that space. And finally, Yasahiro decided to store his lesser used pots and pans to make room for bottles and other baby feeding items.

Nahomi was the main reason we could do any of this. She packaged everything up carefully, as if the items were prized possessions, labeled and inventoried the boxes, and hired the movers. As boxes left the apartment, she cleaned up behind them. She washed dishes. She dusted. She organized like a champ. I had no idea I could fold my underwear and how much extra room that would give me. She showed me my dresser drawers, and it was as if my whole life had been a lie up to that point. And I wasn't even exaggerating.

"So much better," I said, clasping my hands at my heart and twirling in a circle. "It's like a whole new apartment. You have a knack for all of this cleaning and organizing." I sat down at the dining room table. "You know, about two years ago, I had been fired from my job, and I needed to make a little money to get by, so I helped my elderly clients clean their houses and run errands."

Nahomi nodded as she opened the cubby over the coat closet and put away the cleaning supplies.

"Now, you're helping me. It almost feels like I've passed the torch onto a new generation."

"I'm glad to be of help. And I'm thankful for the work too. It's been hard on my mom with my dad out of work and sick. I have a feeling she'll try to get a job if... well..." She pressed her lips together and looked around the apartment. "Anyway, I think we got everything taken care of here today. Would you like me to start on Oshabe-cha tomorrow?"

My heart ached for her. I knew she was struggling with her father's illness, but hopefully, he had more time left with her family. And in the meantime, I planned to keep her around and help her as much as possible.

The puppies whined in their crate, and Sugi left her spot in the sun to come over and nuzzle my hand. She lifted her front paws and rested them on my lap, leaning in for a kiss. I held her head in my hands and gave her lots of kisses.

"Who's a good girl?" I asked her. She tilted her head to look at me sideways. "You are. I'll get your babies out in a bit."

The shower in the bathroom turned off, and both Nahomi and I turned to look at the bathroom door.

"Ah, good. Right on time."

I crossed the room to my bag and pulled out my wallet. "Here's what we agreed upon for today, plus a little extra for coming so early in the morning. I really appreciate it."

"Oh, thank you, Mei. That's very kind." She took the cash I offered her and bowed, and I smiled back. She grabbed her coat from next to the door while slipping into her shoes. "So, the ceremony is at ten?"

"Yes," I said, glancing at the clock. It was still early, around eight-thirty. Mari had gone back to sleep after a six o'clock feeding. "Once Yasahiro is dressed, he'll make breakfast, and I'll get ready. Then we'll take the dogs out for a quick walk and then into the crates while we go do the *jichinsai* ceremony... again."

"Well, I wish you luck and many blessings today. I'm looking forward to watching your house being built and helping you with that place as well."

"I'm looking forward to the help. I'm afraid I won't know what to do with that amount of space!"

Nahomi zipped up her coat and grabbed her bag. "I'm sure we'll figure it out. See you tomorrow."

She waved from the top of the stairs, and I sighed as I closed the door and pressed my back to it.

The apartment looked amazing. Stunning even. I remembered what it had looked like when I first started dating Yasahiro, and it was back to that state, if not better. Now, every time I looked at the place or arrived home after a long day out and about, I smiled instead of cringed.

The puppies whined a little more and clawed at the crate.

"Okay, okay," I said, with a slight laugh. "I'm coming."

I had developed a routine for the puppies. In the morning,

they came out and got a chance to run around the apartment for a moment before I put them in their 'puppy jail' which was really three flexible baby gates tied together and lined with pee pads and newspapers. One puppy, the biggest of the three, had already gotten the hang of peeing outside, though only when treats were involved. I strongly suspected *he* was training me! The other two needed much more training. I was taking them out every two hours, but it wasn't enough. I had read that this was normal, and they wouldn't have bladder control for a few more months. Oh well. I was already changing diapers, so why not newspapers and pee pads?

I let them loose, and they clamored around my feet, hopping about and asking for scratches. I picked one up and gave him a kiss on the muzzle before heading to the kitchen. They jumped and tumbled with each other, barking and yipping like mad. Mari let out a wail in the bedroom right on cue.

"I've got her!" Yasahiro yelled from the bedroom.

He emerged a few minutes later, freshly showered and dressed, Mari in his arms. His eyes zeroed in on the area next to the front door.

"Wow. All those boxes are finally gone! The place looks great." He kissed me on the temple. "Is Nahomi still here?"

"Nope. She left right after the movers. I'll meet the movers at the storage facility after the party and have them unload everything there."

Yasahiro unloaded eggs and bacon from the refrigerator with one hand, held Mari with the other, and stepped over the puppies who were underfoot.

"And then?" he asked.

I shrugged. I hadn't any plans, for once. "Maybe get back to that painting? Spend some time with Mrs. Murata? It's nice not to have a murder mystery hanging over my head."

"Maybe you could contact Sakiko Yoshida and get to working on learning more about private investigation?"

I grabbed my cold cup of coffee. "Maybe I could. But now, I need to get ready."

"Don't put it off, Mei! You've found your calling! This is what you were meant to do!" he shouted after me as I slipped into the bedroom.

I huffed a quiet laugh as I leaned against the door and listened to him herding the puppies back to their caged in area.

Once we were dressed and the dogs had been walked, we met our family, friends, and the contractors at the construction site that would eventually be our house.

I showed Mom and Chiyo where Sugi had dug up potatoes to feed her puppies, and Yasahiro collected the game cameras. A small *himorogi,* a temporary shrine, had been set up earlier by a few guys from Sawayaka we asked to help. It was a beautiful spot under a tent, adorned with red and white banners, wooden tables, and other Shinto adornments. On a table under the canopy, we had erected a little shrine with gifts of fruit and food offered. A Shinto priest dressed in his best finery waited for us to gather and sit in the chairs provided for everyone in front of the shrine.

Once Kayo, Kumi and Taiga, and other friends and neighbors, including many of the site workers arrived, we all took our seats for the ceremony. I kept my eyes on the photo of the young boy who had died and said prayers for him and his family. I hoped that, someday, they would *all* remember him. That they would speak of him openly and with love.

The priest chanted over the shrine and our property while waving an *ōnusa,* a wooden wand with white paper streamers on it, back and forth. I was pleased to see him concentrate on the photo of the boy as well, and I hoped that this extra attention was enough to put his spirit to rest.

Since we had already broken ground on this property, and this was our second jichinsai, Yasahiro and I, while holding Mari between us, anointed the ground with saké and prayed for the local spirits to give us peace during the construction.

I breathed a sigh of relief after it was all over. Between the ceremony and my house finally being in order, a huge weight had been lifted off my heart.

Mom held Mari and chatted with my new neighbor from across the street, Moeko Asahara. I still had not met her husband. I bet I would soon enough.

"I heard a rumor that you helped solve the murder case of Noriko Kubo," Moeko said, reaching over and squeezing my arm. She was in better clothes today, but still, she had at least three layers on her upper body.

"It's true," Mom gushed, and I shushed her. "Oh Mei, stop being so modest. You should be proud of what you did."

"Mom..." I warned, but I laughed. "Yes, I guess I did help out a little. But of course, the Chikata police force did the majority of the work."

"Are you bragging about us?" Goro asked, joining the conversation. We widened the circle to bring in Kumi and Taiga, Chiyo, and Kayo too.

"I always brag about you guys. You do excellent work."

Yasahiro approached with Masaru Imai by his side. "I have good news too. I've worked things out with Daiki Wada, and we've split his medical bills, so he won't be bothering us again. Mr. Imai also assures me that he will not be working with Mr. Wada in the future."

"Nor any of his friends," Imai insisted. "They're all too unreliable and full of drama. So, no need to worry, Mrs. Suga. We have the right people on this job from here on out."

Good. I hoped that would be the end of the witch drama and the bullying from that group.

Movement at the front gate caught my attention and Chief Ohashi walked onto the lot.

"I'm sorry to have missed the ceremony, but I wanted to drop by and wish you luck with your construction project." He handed a wrapped bottle of saké to Yasahiro and bowed to us. We returned the bow, chagrined. "If you ever need any help, please let me know. We owe you for all your hard work with the community."

My grin widened. "Thank you so much."

I remembered my conversation with Mom about wanting to repair my reputation with people in town. I was finally on the right path.

He leaned in, a conspiratorial gleam to his eye. "I had a call from Sakiko Yoshida again last night. She wanted to check on the case and see how you fared with the investigation. She can't wait to start training you. Gotta say, with more sleuthing skills under your belt, you'll be a force to contend with. I'll be happy to invite you to help on the next case we get... hopefully, quite a long time from now."

Mom's and Chiyo's mouths opened with awe, Kumi elbowed Goro, and Kayo nodded.

"Well, I'm honored. Thank you." I lowered to a deep, respectful bow.

A cool breeze whipped across the construction site, and a cloud moved in front of the sun. It was time to go in.

"Everyone is invited back to Oshabe-cha for tea and snacks," I said, raising my voice for the whole group to hear. "It's also Emi's last day, and we're going to give her a goodbye party as well. Meet there in ten minutes."

As I walked off the lot with my baby girl in my arms and my husband by my side, I finally felt like life was moving in the right direction. The house would be built. Sawayaka would grow and prosper. My family would thrive with a happy husband, a healthy baby, and now a new dog, too.

And my life as an investigator was just beginning.

THANK YOU!

Thank you so much for reading *The Daydreamer Finds Her Calling*. This book was very special to me. It was a chance to see Mei get the recognition she deserves. I hope you enjoyed it!

Please leave a review of *The Daydreamer Detective Finds Her Calling* wherever you purchased it. I welcome all reviews positive or negative. Reviews are so important to both authors and readers.

Want news of upcoming books, events, or free stuff? Subscribe to Steph's mailing list at https://www.stephgennaro.com/subscribe/

If you want more books like this one, you can check for more books on my website at http://www.stephgennaro.com/books/

FROM STEPH

HELLO, READERS!

Another episode of Mei's adventures is behind us! I love spending time in this universe. It's the longest I've ever spent in one world, and I still really love these characters.

Once again, this story was inspired by another news story I saw on NHK World about women in Japan learning how to run businesses online. The story itself was sweet and focused on women who were mothers. I thought it would be a great idea for Mei and her friends, and the idea took off from there! So many of my own friends are crafty and sell handmade goods online. The story is almost universal and made a great base for the rest of the novel.

This book also shows how Mei will move forward with murder cases into the future. She finally has the confidence of the Chikata Police, and she's going to learn more about being a private investigator.

Thanks again for reading!

A NOTE ABOUT CHANGES TO THIS BOOK

In case you missed it in the Foreword...

In Japanese, the most common way of showing respect to another person's social standing is with the use of honorific suffixes that are appended on the end of either first or last names. The most common, -san, means either Mr., Ms., or Mrs.

In earlier versions of this series, I did use these honorific suffixes. But for 2019 and onward, I have switched to the English way in order to make this series more accessible to English speakers. I hope you enjoy this version!

The town in this novel, Chikata, is completely fictional, though the area I put it in is not. Saitama prefecture is located to the west of Tokyo, and many of the eastern areas are considered to be suburbs of the city. Chikata is located farther out west, nearer to the prefectures of Nagano and Gunma.

ACKNOWLEDGMENTS

Big thanks goes out to all the people who helped or inspired me with this book including...

- Tracy Krimmer.
- Charity Vandehey.
- Germaine Fletcher.
- Lola Verroen.
- All those in my favorite FB author groups.
- My sibling, B.
- My mom, Claire.
- My husband, Keith.
- And my two girls, C and D.

ABOUT THE AUTHOR

Steph Gennaro is a long-time Japanophile, and she's been studying Japanese culture and language for over 20 years. She loves dreaming of far-off places, going for walks with her dog, Lulu Ninja Assassin, hanging out with her family, and reading outside in the summertime. There is no better season than summer. She's a Capricorn, mother, knitter, and web developer, and pasta is her favorite meal. Steph Gennaro is her pen name for cozy mysteries, but she also writes science fiction romance and many other genres.

Find her online at...
www.stephgennaro.com

facebook.com/StephGennaroAuthor
bookbub.com/authors/steph-gennaro